ENTRUSTED

SHERRY RUMMLER

ENTRUSTED

A NOVEL

TATE PUBLISHING
AND ENTERPRISES, LLC

Published by Tate Publishing & Enterprises, LLC
127 E. Trade Center Terrace | Mustang, Oklahoma 73064 USA
1.888.361.9473 | www.tatepublishing.com

Tate Publishing is committed to excellence in the publishing industry. The company reflects the philosophy established by the founders, based on Psalm 68:11,
"The Lord gave the word and great was the company of those who published it."

Book design copyright © 2012 by Tate Publishing, LLC. All rights reserved.
Cover design by Lucia Kroeger Renz
Interior design by Nathan Harmony

Published in the United States of America

ISBN: 978-1-62024-671-9
1. Fiction / Family Life
2. Fiction / Christian / General
12.11.27

DEDICATION

Jared and Jesse, my love for you is eternal.
Mark, God blessed the broken road that led me straight to you.

ACKNOWLEDGMENTS

This book would not be possible without many hands' and hearts' support. Mom, thank you for your hours of work in the first edit of the manuscript and pushing me to continue. Dad, yes, your royalties are coming. Heather, your tears in reading the first draft made me believe the words on the page were worth continuing. Artie, thank you for your nautical expertise. Conor, the next writer in the family, I hand you the baton. Dori B, just because… And my rutabaga, (aka Aunt J.) I love you all. James Bare and the rest of the team at Tate, your insight has been valuable beyond measure. But most of all, my husband, Mark, without your love and support this book would still be words on my laptop waiting to be read. Heavenly Father, by your grace, *this one's for you.*

PROLOGUE

It could be Justin. "He'd be Justin's age," Anna contemplated while perched on a jagged rock on the coast of Maine, her face turned to avoid the sun. Her eyes followed a young man in a baseball cap playing with his dog. She watched as he tossed the stick out to sea and knelt down in anticipation for the black Labrador to come and drop it at her feet. She shook her head to ignore the thought.

Anna breathed the salty air and let it fully fill her lungs. The gentle misty breeze tickled her cheeks and wrapped her golden curls about her face. Since Anna had been a child, this was her escape place, the place that would summon peace and surround like a warm hug. It was the only place she could live in the exact minute; take everything around her in, the closest thing to heaven on earth. Anna was glad she had made the trip to experience this moment. She could almost hear her own childlike giggle as pictures formed in her mind. She remembered her older sister, Holly, jumping the rocks, the wind whipping her dark mass of curls, being careful not to fall in the tide pools that lingered between the sharp rocks. Holly's tender olive eyes had twinkled as she reached out her hand for Anna's grasp. Anna smiled as she reflected on the moment. She could almost feel Holly with her again. The memory quickly faded as the tide receded from shore and pulled the stones along with it.

Anna watched as a large wave pounced and sprayed the children playing in the rocks below and heard their squeals of delight. She saw him again. "It really could be Justin." Every young man who looked like a recent high school graduate could be her son. His absence from her life was an endless ache within her. She tried to make sense of it. Why he hadn't contacted her. They had been so close. Pregnant at nineteen, Anna was proud to have raised such a fine young man. Strangely, he had walked out of her life as easily as he'd come into it. It was as if he came to her, altered her inside out, then left her dazed and confused. Their last conversation replayed over and over as she searched for clues to why he wanted out of her life. She had given so much of herself to him, that when he walked away he took a part of her.

CHAPTER 1

Nineteen-year-old Anna sat on the bathroom counter, her girl-friend, Jessica, beside her. They peered wide-eyed as they studied the pregnancy test.

"I thought you said you were only a week late?" Jessica questioned as she chewed a ragged fingernail.

"I am. I know it must be right around the corner."

Jessica put the pregnancy test on the counter beside Anna. "I don't think so…"

Anna's eyes darted from the faded pink plus sign on the test to her friend. "This can't be accurate. Are you serious?"

Jessica grabbed the box and read the instructions… "Ninety-nine percent accurate," she whispered as she tucked her straight red hair behind her ear.

The girls looked at each other, horrified.

"Oh!" Anna placed her hand on her flat belly as her cheeks began to flush. Her immediate thought was not of herself or the new life growing inside her. "My mom and dad are gonna kill me! What am I gonna do, Jess? Mike's parents are going to hate me even more. They already think I'm taking him away from the *family* business."

"Well, first you gotta go and get a blood test and make sure." Jessica's hazel eyes looked at her friend with sympathy.

Anna jumped from the counter, turned, and looked in the mirror. The only thing she could see was the reflection of shame.

Jessica's mother interrupted the girls' whispering, calling through the bathroom door: "Girls, supper is ready."

"Jess, I can't stay… I gotta go somewhere… I can't eat… I gotta call Mike. Oh, what am I gonna do?" Anna's lip quivered, her hands trembled.

"Come on, I'll tell Mom you have to go meet Mike, 'cause his car broke down or something. I'll make up something. Just act calm."

Anna grabbed her coat from the kitchen chair. "Thanks for inviting me to dinner, Mrs. Kitterage, but I have to run and meet Mike," she said, trying to keep her voice even.

"Are you sure? I have a place set for you," Jessica's mom replied with a furrowed brow.

"Yeah, thanks. But I really gotta go," Anna quickly replied.

Jessica walked Anna to the door. "Everything's gonna be okay. Don't worry," she whispered to her friend as she gave her a quick embrace.

Anna sat in her car to let it warm. The windshield was covered with a sheet of ice. She watched as it slowly began to melt. Her heart was as frozen as the windshield. How long would it take for this new reality to set in? she wondered. Anna pulled out of the driveway and drove aimlessly for miles not thinking about her destination. Pulling over on the side of the road, she looked at the house in front of her. It was Mike's. In the darkness she could peer into the lighted living room window. Mike's dad sat slouched in his chair watching TV. She noticed Mike walk by and hand him something, probably popcorn. Anna observed them through the window for what seemed like an eternity. *If I walk in there now, my life will change forever.* She pushed the thought from her mind and opened the car door. With her heart in her mouth, Anna slowly walked up the icy sidewalk and rang the doorbell. Mike opened the door.

"Hey, what's up? I thought you were eating at Jess's tonight?" Mike stood casually in the doorway, one arm outstretched on the door casing and one on his hip. His dark hair tossed, and a smile showed pure white teeth.

"Mike…will you go for a ride with me? We need to talk."

"Gee, sounds serious. Are you breakin' up with me or somethin'?" he joked.

"No, nothing like that." Anna's eyes fell to the icy sidewalk.

Mike saw the seriousness in her face and reached into the closet for his coat. "Dad, I'm runnin' out for a while with Anna. I'll be back," he hollered.

He grabbed her by the hand and went in for a kiss.

"Not now, Mike."

He looked at Anna as they walked to the car. He noticed her dark eyeliner had been smeared as if she'd been crying. He rolled his eyes in exasperation.

Anna sat in the driver's seat but refrained from starting the car. She looked straight ahead and blurted, "I'm pregnant, Mike."

"That's impossible, Anna. What kind of joke are you pulling here?" He laughed nervously and banged his open hand on the dash.

"No joke."

"Just drive," Mike insisted. His breath was audible.

Anna started the engine. "Where do you want to go?"

"I don't care, just go. Anna, you must be crazy? What are you talkin' about?" His anger was palpable.

"What do you mean, what am I talking about? I'm *pregnant*, Mike!" she screamed. Tears prickled her eyes and threatened to flow.

"Wait a minute. You said you were just late. You said you had all the crabby symptoms. I don't get it? We only… That one time…and you went to the bathroom after…and you said you jiggled it all out!" he yelled at her.

"Jiggled it all out? That's birth control? You idiot! Apparently you have great swimmers! One for the team!" she shot back at him.

"Calm down, Anna," he replied, looking at her fearfully.

"*Calm down? Calm down?* Are you serious? What are we gonna do?"

"Anna, calm down! Seriously how accurate are those damn tests anyway?"

"Ninety-nine percent," she shot back, taking her eyes off the road to glare at him.

"Well…you have to go to the doctor tomorrow and verify it. I have a final exam in my AP business marketing class. I can't get out of that test." He ran his hand through his hair.

"Are you kidding me? You're worried about a stupid exam?"

"Do you want me to screw up my future?"

"Your future? *Your* future? What about *my* future?" she spat at him.

"Anna, fighting isn't gonna solve the problem, is it?" He softened. "This is not a problem, Mike. This is a *baby, your baby*!" Anna was shaking now.

"Pull over. Over there." Mike pointed to the side of the road where a dim overhead light tried to illuminate a baseball park.

Anna pulled the car into the parking lot and put it in park but left the engine running. She turned to Mike now, tears falling freely from her eyes. He reached for her hands and held them in his. His dark eyes looked fearfully into hers. His jet black hair tossed as he shook his head nervously. "Anna, I love you," he stated. "We will be okay. I promise." They embraced as snow streaked down the windshield and the wipers squeaked rhythmically.

CHAPTER 2

Anna stood fearfully in front of a two-story brick building. The sign on the lawn read: Planned Parenthood. *What a joke*, she thought. *This is anything but planned.*

She stepped inside and was greeted by a rush of warm air. Her eyes roamed the room. Cheap plastic chairs lined the walls and scratches showed where they had rubbed. Magazines were carelessly strewn about a rickety, worn coffee table. It was not the clean doctors' office she was accustomed to. Behind a glass window a woman sat, round glasses perched on her nose.

Anna knocked and the woman slid the window open. "Yeah, can I help you?"

"Well, I need to see a doctor...I think...I maybe...well..." Anna stammered.

"You want birth control or you need a pregnancy test?" the woman questioned.

Anna looked around the room to make sure no one could hear as the shame bore down on her.

She leaned closer to the glass. "A test, please."

The woman passed her a clipboard. "Fill this out." She handed Anna the clipboard as she abruptly slid the glass window back shut as if to say, "Don't bother me."

Real friendly, Anna thought.

Anna sat down and carefully read the instructions. She filled out the family history as best she could and checked "no" on all of the possible physical problems then returned to the window and handed it to the woman behind the glass. "Doctor will be with you shortly," the woman responded curtly and immediately went back to the paperwork in front of her.

Anna took a torn magazine from the table and tried to focus on reading. She couldn't. She put it back down and gazed out the window at the fresh fallen snow. The sun shone brightly, and Anna saw dust particles swimming in the light that cast a glow on the dirty floor below.

"Anna Lynn Bertram." She jumped at the sound of her name.

She rose to meet a young woman dressed in light blue scrubs and followed her through a long hallway to a weight scale. "Let's get your weight, Anna. I'm Judy, by the way. I'll be your nurse for today." She smiled sweetly.

Anna stepped on the scale and removed her heavy coat. "One-hundred and twelve pounds. Does that sound right?" Judy noted the weight to the chart.

"Guess so," Anna replied as fear clutched her chest making it hard to respond.

Judy led her into a room and handed her a paper gown. "Take everything off and here's an extra gown to place over your lap if you'd like. Dr. Jones will be with you shortly." Quietly she closed the door.

Anna removed her clothes, quickly put on the gown, and sat on the table. She looked around the cold white room and shuddered. Fear again gripped her heart as she waited for the expected knock. The knock at the door admitted a man in his midforties. Anna noticed that under his crisp white jacket he wore jeans and worn cowboy boots on his feet.

"Hi, Anna, I'm Dr. Dennis Jones. What brings you here today?"

"Well, I think… I maybe… I took a test…" she stammered as embarrassment flushed her cheeks.

"You think you may be pregnant?" he asked. "How old are you, Anna?"

"I'm nineteen."

"You married?" he prodded.

"No," she responded flatly. *Why doesn't he ask me all the personal details of how this happened?*

"You here alone today?" he asked.

"Yes," she replied.

"Please step inside the bathroom." He motioned to a closed door inside the room. "There's a cup on the back of the toilet. Leave the urine sample in there, and I'll be back in a few minutes." Dr. Jones stepped out of the room and closed the door. Anna did as told and sat back on the cold table. A knock at the door and he again entered the room. "The nurse will test your sample. Now I will examine you. Have you ever had a pelvic examination before?" he asked as he pulled two stirrups up from the table and guided her heels into them.

"No, I haven't," she replied as her legs began to shake. She wanted to cry.

"Just relax and lay back. The tenser you are, the worse it will feel."

Easy for him to say. She lay vulnerable on the table, her legs spread apart. *What am I doing here? How did this happen? Really? One time? And this is what I get?*

"All done, you can get dressed now," he stated, as he pulled her legs from the stirrups and guided her off the table. "I'll be back in a few minutes with your results."

Anna rushed to put her clothes on and wrapped her jacket tightly around her. She couldn't shake the chill of the cold white room. There were posters taped on the walls. One showed the various stages of pregnancy, how the baby grew. Another showed samples of different types of birth control with vivid pictures of the birth canal. Her eyes shifted from the posters to the closed door while she held her breath.

Dr. Jones entered after yet another swift knock. He sat down in the chair beside her. "Well, Anna, the test is positive. You are definitely pregnant, in the first trimester. It's time to start making plans. You are going to be a mother."

The words were like a slap to Anna's face. Although he'd just confirmed what she already knew; sitting in the doctor's office made it all very real. Terror began to clutch her like no other. "A mother," he had said. A mother. Anna had always wanted a family; she loved little ones and had done some babysitting for a neighbor during high school. But now? How would she support this little one when she was still taking college classes? A part-time job would not support a baby.

"Anna?" the doctor questioned. "Did you hear me?"

"Yes, Yes, Doctor, I heard you."

"What are your plans for this baby, Anna?"

"What do you mean?"

"Will you keep the baby?" he asked.

"Of course I'll keep the baby! What kind of question is that?" she answered indignantly.

"You need to consider your options. You could give the baby up for adoption. Some girls your age terminate the pregnancy," he replied coldly.

Anna stood as the doctor handed her a stack of literature. "I'm keeping my baby," she assured him.

"You need care, Anna, prenatal vitamins and a doctor to monitor your pregnancy progress."

"I got it covered. Thank you," she stated and then turned on her heel and walked out of the stark white room vowing never to step in Dr. Jones's office again.

CHAPTER 3

Anna pulled the car into the familiar parking lot and found a spot. Turmoil raced her mind after her visit with Dr. Jones. The news frightened her. Dr. Jones's suggestion of terminating the pregnancy or considering adoption infuriated her. She wrapped her arms around her stomach. No. She was certain. Fear would not keep her from motherhood. With a new resolve, she looked through the windshield of the car. Her eyes met the sign which read: University of Maine Campus Library. She watched as students and professors walked to and fro. She noticed a group of girls talking and laughing near the sign. A tall guy with a loaded backpack walked with purpose. *I'm late too. I'll never make it in time for my speech final. I guess it's pointless anyway.* She sighed. Anna grabbed her bag from the passenger seat and headed toward the admissions office. She closed her coat around her and walked with her head down to avoid the brisk wind and snow.

"Anna! Anna!" She heard the familiar voice but continued to walk toward the office door. "Anna! Wait!" Mike yelled to her.

Anna opened the door to the admissions office, stood just inside the door and turned to face him. "What's up, Mike?"

"What are you doing? Don't you have a final today? I just finished mine. I think I did okay." He was young, handsome, and in control.

"Good for you, Mike. I'm not going to my final. I'm here to withdraw from school," Anna replied with agitation.

"What? Why?"

"Well, why do you think?"

"Did you go to the doctor?" He shuffled from one foot to the other.

"Yes. Yes, I did." She rifled around in her backpack for a tissue. Her nose streamed from the cold wind.

"Well?"

"Well what?" Her frustration began to reach a boiling point.

"Anna, you *know* what? Was the test positive?" Mike asked as he rubbed his hands together to warm them.

"Yes, Mike, I'm having your baby." She watched as the color drained from his face.

"Wow... We'll get married then," he blurted.

"Was that a proposal? It sounded like a statement to me," she retorted.

"I know it's not what we planned, but we can make this work. I want to be there for you and our baby." His voice softened as he leaned into her.

"I am keeping my baby with or without you. You don't have to marry me out of pity." She gave her nose a hard blow.

Mike took Anna's backpack and put it on the ground. He wrapped his arms around her and held her close. "Anna, I love you," he whispered in her ear. "And we will be a family." The two embraced as the college campus bustled around them. *Was she getting a whiff of booze or was it her imagination? Was Mike a little too willing to commit?* The questions whirled in her mind. Anna pulled away from her boyfriend and looked at her wristwatch. "I have to get to work. I'm not going to have time to stop in at the admissions office. I'll have to do it later. I'm going to be late if I don't leave soon."

"All right, we'll catch up after work. We'll have to tell our parents tonight."

"Tonight?" Anna didn't even want to consider the thought of their reaction.

"Yeah, before we lose our courage. Now go!" Mike handed Anna her backpack and nudged her toward the door.

Anna was grateful for the diversion of her new reality as she walked purposely into work. She slipped behind the desk of the dental office and checked the machine for messages. Wanda, the full-time receptionist, never waited for her arrival; instead, she scooted out the door the second the clock struck three p.m. Anna had lucked into this position. Her senior year in high school, she had seen the AD in the classifieds, stopped in the office, gave a winning smile, and was hired immediately. The afternoon hours were perfect allowing her to keep the position when she started college. There were no messages. Sometimes the phones during the middle of the week were quiet. It seemed only toward weeks end did patients fear the upcoming weekend with a tooth ache. She tapped her finger on the counter top and willed the phone to ring. *I need a distraction. I don't want to think about how I'm going to tell my parents I'm having a baby.* She swallowed the lump in her throat that began to form. Brenda, the dental assistant, came out from the back room, and walked toward the desk.

"Is Debbie here yet?" she asked as she proceeded to the waiting room, her eyes darting around the space.

"Haven't seen her."

Debbie, the afternoon dental assistant, had become notorious for being late.

"You realize this is the fourth time this month she didn't show up on time." Brenda flustered as she stomped toward the sterilization room.

The phone jarred Anna to reality. "Good afternoon. Dental Associates. How can I help you?"

The infamous Debbie was on the line. "Hey, Anna. I'm sick... not going to make it tonight. Please let Dr. Miller know I can't make it in."

"Sure, I'll let him know." Anna hung up the phone and walked into the sterilization room where Brenda was scrubbing instruments and placing them in the autoclave to sterilize.

"She here yet? I have to pick up my son from daycare. My husband is working late, and I can't stay much longer," Brenda asked over her shoulder.

"Um…she's not coming in. She just called in sick," Anna hesitated.

"Great! Just great!" Brenda slammed the autoclave door shut.

Dr. Miller entered the room and handed Brenda impression material to send to the lab. "What's wrong, ladies? I feel like I just walked in on something?"

Brenda ripped off her rubber gloves and tossed them into the trash. "Debbie's a no show again today! I can't stay to help you, Dr. Miller. I'm sorry. I just can't keep bailing her out. I have to pick my son up. I can't be late at the daycare center *again*."

Dr. Miller ran his hands through his salt and pepper head. His aging hair made his young baby face look out of place. He had bad genes he had once shared, bound to go white at a young age. Although it made him look older, he was happy with his look as he said it made him look like a grown-up experienced dentist. "How many patients on the schedule, Anna?"

"Three. Two for fillings and one crown and bridge."

"Anna, since the phone is usually slow midweek, why don't you put the answer machine on and come in the operatory and assist." Dr. Miller paced the small room and finally stopped and put his hand on a hip.

"Are you sure? I don't really know what I'm doing?" Anna's anxiety began to rise.

"Yeah, it's the best we can do on short notice. Brenda, please show her where to leave the instruments after we're done. You can clean up whatever mess we make in the morning when you come in."

"Okay, but I literally have five minutes, and then I have to go," Brenda rushed.

Anna didn't have time to think about her pregnancy, Mike, or her parents, as she was thrust into the dental assistant role. Brenda gave her a crash course on what to do with the instruments, and then Anna rushed to the waiting room to greet the first patient. The afternoon passed quickly as she learned to properly hold the suction and concentrated on how to hold the instruments the best she could. By the time the last patient left, she took a sigh of relief. Dr. Miller smiled at Anna as she wiped the chair clean.

"I think we have a natural here! You saved me, Anna. I really do appreciate your hard work." He patted her on the shoulder. "Oh and, Anna, we might be letting Debbie go. Seems she's more absent then reliable. Would you be interested in becoming a dental assistant? I could train you. I saw great potential today."

Anna blushed. "Sure. I would be interested. It beats sitting by the phone waiting for it to ring. The time flew by."

Dr. Miller chuckled. "Great. In the meantime, we'll have you work both reception and assisting as needed until we find a replacement. I'm going to go lock up. Let me know when you're ready to leave."

"Oh Dr. Miller, one more thing…wouldn't I need formal training to assist you?"

"Not at this time. You'll need a radiology class to take x-rays, but we'll not concern ourselves about that just yet."

Anna turned out the light in the room and proceeded to her final close routine. "I guess I'm moving up in the dental field." She smiled to herself, one small step in a positive direction.

CHAPTER 4

Olivia Gallo moved around the kitchen island chopping and dicing onions and peppers. She reached for a mound of dough and placed it on a floured cutting board. Anna watched mesmerized as she expertly worked the dough back and forth with her chubby fingers. "What did you kids want to talk about?" She reached for a rolling pin and began to stretch the dough into a large rectangle.

"Is Dad comin'?" Mike asked nonchalantly.

"Yeah, he'll be here. He went out to the garage for a few minutes. We both know what he's after." She rolled her eyes as she wiped her hands with a kitchen towel. "Are you kids staying for pizza? I'll make a salad to go with it if you're going to stay."

"No thanks, Mrs. Gallo," Anna replied softly.

The short, plump woman had steely dark eyes, a round face, and straight dark hair pulled back at the nape of her neck. A stained apron covered her purple velour leisure suit. She reached for the door leading to the garage. "Al, kids are here. They want to talk to us about something," she yelled into the garage.

"Coming, I'm just getting a beer," he replied irritably.

Mike held Anna's moist hand beneath the kitchen table as they sat nervously side by side.

Al Gallo brushed the snow from his coat as he entered the kitchen. He leaned down stiffly to remove his boots with one hand while balancing a can of beer in the other. Turning with a groan he hung his coat on a garage door hook. His medium-sized shoulders barely filled the door frame. Anna noted the strained look on his face. Chronic pain, she knew, was a constant reminder of a long-ago car accident that had left him with a permanent limp.

"What brings the pleasure of your company tonight? Need more beer money, Mike?" Mr. Gallo said, dripping sarcasm.

"Al! He just turned twenty-one. Don't encourage him to be a drunk like you!" Olivia scolded as she sent a glare her husband's way.

"That's enough, you two," Mike interrupted. "Actually, Anna and I need to talk to you about something important. Can you please sit down?"

Olivia reached for a glass near the kitchen sink and filled it with tap water. "You kids want a soda?" she offered.

"Sure," Anna replied as Olivia reached into the cabinet for two more glasses. She filled them with ice and then placed them on the table along with two cans of soda.

Anna filled Mike's glass with a shaky hand and then one for herself while Olivia placed her finished pizza into the oven. The four then gathered around the kitchen table.

Mike breathed deeply and began. "I have some news for you," he said hesitantly.

"Don't tell me you failed that final, Mike! I told you I'm not paying for you to party at that school!" Al interjected.

Mike lowered his eyes. "No, Dad, it's not that, umm… Anna's pregnant." The words hung strangled in the air.

Olivia raised her pudgy hands to her face and in a ragged whisper she breathed, "No."

Al Gallo, his face contorted in anger, slammed his fist onto the table so hard that the table vibrated and the drinks spilled over. "You whore!" he shouted at Anna "You did this! You planned this! You wanted to hook my son! Look at what you've done!" He raged on. "I've heard about girls like you." He pointed an accusing finger at Anna. "You've crushed our dream! Mike won't be able to finish school with you and brat to look after. What *were* you thinking! You won't get away with it. I'll see to that!"

She felt herself sinking into the kitchen chair. Her stomach twisted in a knot as she curled her hands around her torso to protect the baby growing inside of her. Weakened and shocked, she sat in stunned silence.

"Dad, stop! That's not true. Don't talk to my future wife that way!" Mike screamed. He reached for his dad's opened beer and chugged it like it was cold water on a hot day.

"Future wife! What are you talking about? No way. Over my dead body will you marry her! We have plans for you, plans for a future!" Al yelled at the top of his voice, while pacing back and forth he would stop only to bore his eyes on Anna.

"Look, you're only early in your pregnancy. Right?" Olivia asked.

Anna cleared the lump in her throat and barely whispered, "yes I'm only a few weeks along."

"Then you can do whatever needs to be done, right? There's no restrictions on you." Oliva stared intently at Anna's stomach.

"I really don't know what you mean," Anna stuttered.

"You haven't told anyone else, have you? You could declare that you are going to put the baby up for adoption right now. Or you could have an abortion. You still have options. We won't tell anyone about it. This will be our little secret. We promise we won't tell anyone." Olivia was begging now, her face white with shock.

Anna pulled away from the table. "This is not a little secret. This is our baby, and we've decided we are keeping it. We're getting married, and Mike will finish school. I have dropped out for now, but I'll go back someday. This baby is a blessing."

"You ignorant little whore," Al railed. "You know nothing about it. All you know is how to screw up my son's life!" He shot an ugly glare at Anna. She cringed. His cruel accusations cut her to the core. Never had anyone talked to her like this.

"That's it, Anna. I've heard enough. Let's go." Mike took his future wife by the hand and led her to the door.

"Wait, Mike!" Olivia clutched her son's arm desperately. "Where are you going?"

"We are going to break the news to Anna's parents. I'll be home later tonight, Ma. Don't worry."

Mike opened the passenger door of his truck for Anna. Shakily she slid into the seat and pulled the seatbelt around her. "Should you drive, Mike?"

"What do ya mean?"

"I saw you with your dad's beer in there."

"One beer, seriously?" He threw his head in frustration and then softened. "You okay?"

"I don't know. Your parents want to blame this all on me! They want me to pretend our baby doesn't exist!" she cried, large tears spilling down her cheeks.

"They are in shock, that's all. I hope your parents don't react that way. I'm not sure I can handle it." Mike rubbed his temples to relieve the stress.

Mike drove into the long driveway leading to a typical New England farmhouse where Anna lived with her parents and older sister, Holly. The outside light illuminated the snow making it sparkle. He turned to Anna as the truck came to a stop. "You ready?"

"Ready as I'll ever be," Anna said with a weary sigh. She dug her keys from her purse and unlocked the front door. The smell of cookies baking in the oven led the two into the kitchen.

Sarah Bertram stood by the counter with a tall glass of milk in one hand and a chocolate chip cookie in the other. She cleaned the chocolate from the side of her mouth with her slender fingers. "You caught me!" She chuckled. "I love baking when it's cold outside, gives me such a cozy feeling."

"Is Dad around?" Anna questioned as she looked toward the living room and noticed the television flickering.

"Yeah, he's about asleep in the chair, but he told me to wake him when the cookies are done. Notice I'm indulging without him!

He really doesn't need cookies with his so called diet," she rolled her eyes.

"He's probably jealous. You never have to worry about that." Anna looked at her slender mother. From the back one would think she was still a teenager.

Mike stood awkwardly in the kitchen and cautiously reached for a cookie.

"What are you kids up to this chilly winter night?" Sarah asked, reaching for the oven mitt to remove a second batch.

"Can we talk, Mom? I mean to both you and Daddy?" Anna asked softly.

"Sure, honey, let's go see if Dad's awake." Sarah led the two into the living room and tenderly touched her husband's shoulder, "Donald?"

Donald Bertram gazed up at his wife. "I heard you trying to keep those cookies from me." He chuckled. "How about bringing me a few with a glass of cold milk?"

"In a minute, Daddy," Anna interrupted. "Mike and I have something important to tell you."

Anna motioned Mike to sit beside her on the sofa. She bravely turned to her parents. "This isn't going to be easy...so well...I'm just going to say it... Mike and I are getting married. I'm pregnant."

Anna watched as the color drained from her mother's face. Her smile quickly faded as she absorbed the news. She turned to her father who was now sitting upright in the chair. Mike reached for Anna's hand and gave it a squeeze. The hiss of the radiator in the corner was the only sound to be heard aside from the TV which had been turned down low.

Mike broke the tension. "I will do right by your daughter," he said tentatively.

"What about adoption? Would you consider giving the baby to a good family?" Sarah suggested.

"No, Mom, Mike and I have already made our plans. We will get married in a few months."

"Sounds like you have it all figured out," Donald said as he wiped his brow so hard a red mark appeared. "I don't know what to say. What about school? What about jobs? Where will you live? You're both working part time. How do you plan on supporting a family?" Donald's questions began to roll now, his concern palpable.

"We have a plan," Mike replied. "I'm going to work full time at the auto shop. My boss already said he would take me on and I'll finish my degree part time at night. Anna is going to see if she can work full time at the dental office until the baby comes, and then we'll figure it out. She's quit school already, but I'm gonna finish so I can get a better job. My boss said I'll even get medical insurance when I start full time so the baby will be covered. I'm not sure where we will live yet." He shrugged his shoulders. "I guess we'll get an apartment."

Tension hung thick as fog. Anna felt her parents' disappointment like a heavy weight bearing down on her, so heavy that she was frozen in place. Her legs were like rubber. Mike, unable to deal with the pressure, stood up and reached for Anna. Together they walked out of the living room leaving Sarah and Donald amid a haze of disillusionment.

CHAPTER 5

After the initial shock of Anna's pregnancy, a cloud of acceptance fell among their family members. A small wedding was planned a few months later. Anna worried about her attire due to the fact that at almost five months along, her tummy had rounded and her waist had expanded several inches. Her concerns were allayed, however, upon venturing into a small bridal shop with her mother and Holly. A doll-like oriental attendant approached them with a pleasant smile. Upon appraisal of Anna's situation, she clasped her delicate hands together.

"I have the perfect dress fo' yo'," she said.

She led Anna to an unadorned full-length satin gown that gathered beneath the bust and fell in soft folds to the floor.

"I love it, Anna!" Sarah exclaimed as Anna twirled in the full length mirrors, her cheeks flushed in excitement.

"It's perfect," Holly chimed in.

"I'll make something for you to wear in your hair," Sarah offered.

Anna rolled her eyes. "No veil, Mom, please!"

"All right then, I'll find something appropriate." Sarah smiled and kissed her daughter on her cheek. "You look lovely, sweetheart," she whispered.

"Okay, enough with the mushy stuff! Let's get on with the bachelorette party," Holly quipped. She grabbed her purse and sprinted to the exit door.

"Where are you going?" Sarah questioned.

"I'm the maid of honor, remember? I have a party to plan!" And away she darted on her mission.

"What will she wear? I thought she too would find a dress today," Sarah mumbled in exasperation.

"Holly's wearing one of our old prom dresses from high school. I think we still have the green one. No sense in spending extra money, it's just a small wedding."

"Oh."

Holly hired a female stand-up comedian to entertain for a night of pre-wedding girls only. The young woman, Lila, so exaggerated the rudiments of marriage and motherhood that everyone present became hoarse from laughter. When the final guest departed, Anna closed the door and let out a sigh. She walked into the kitchen and found her sister loading the dishwasher.

"Thanks, Holly, the party was fun and just what I needed—comic relief." Anna grabbed a dish rag and wiped the counters as she continued, "I can't believe I will be married soon."

"Are you excited?" Holly turned and stole the rag from her sister's hand.

"Yeah…I think so. I have a lot running through my mind." Anna wiped her brow.

"Like what?" Holly stopped cleaning and looked into her sisters eyes. "Is something bothering you?"

Anna looked away from her sister. She hesitated before her response. "Mike and I went to pick out rings today."

"Oooo! How fun! Did you get gold or silver?"

"We picked out gold bands. Mike just didn't seem into it. I guess I was thinking it would be romantic and exciting and it was like picking out cereal from the grocery store. I'm not even sure he cared what we picked." Anna looked at her growing abdomen.

"That's just how guys are." Holly lifted her sister's chin so their eyes would meet. "Didn't you hear Lila tonight? Guys and girls are different. Remember what she said about the remote control and the TV?"

"Yeah, she said one day she decorated a cardboard box to look like a TV and put it over her head and stood in front of her husband and said, 'Now will you listen to me?' That *was* funny. Her facial expressions were hilarious."

"Not that I know anything about it. I always thought since I'm older I'd be the first one to walk down the aisle. I guess you are going first on this one." Holly winked.

"Yeah, they say the romance ends when you get married. I guess I'm wondering if we *ever* had romance. It's just not what I expected. No big deal. I'll get over it." *And he drinks like a frat boy,* Anna was afraid to add. She didn't let the thought linger.

Sarah entered the kitchen carrying glasses and a half a bag of chips. "Wow, girls, you have the kitchen almost finished!"

Holly reached to her mother and took the dishes out of her loaded hands. "Anything left in the living room?"

"Just a few things scattered here and there."

Anna walked out of the kitchen as she spoke over her shoulder. "I'll get the rest." She walked into the living room and picked up napkins and dishes scattered randomly around the room. She stopped at the fireplace and looked at the large family photo depicting her parents, Holly and herself. The photo was taken outside in the fall, and they all wore jeans and crisp white shirts. The more she studied the picture, the more the fear trickled down her spine. Her life was going to change in a very big way; the big question: Was she ready for it?

———— >•‹ ————

The wedding day arrived. Anna, resplendent in her satin gown with a halo of tiny purple flowers and baby's breath upon her upswept hair, walked slowly down the aisle. She gripped her Dad's hand as her legs threatened to buckle.

Donald leaned into her ear and whispered, "You're beautiful, Anna. Everything will be all right, you'll see."

Anna smiled weakly and nodded. She floated toward Mike who was handsome in his black suit, though the color had drained from his face. He looked terrified. Anna's heart ached for him and herself. *If only we'd waited for this baby*, she thought and the hand that held her bouquet automatically found her rounded tummy. As if in a dream, Anna mouthed the vows and she and Mike were husband and wife. It was over too quickly, and Anna's breath caught in her throat, and fat tears rolled along her cheeks. Outside the church, Sarah plucked tissues from her purse and dabbed her daughter's face.

"No tears today, my sweet. It's your wedding day."

Anna forced a smile, a lump still thick in her throat. She looked around for her new husband. "So where has Mike disappeared to?" she wondered out loud.

"I saw him headed behind the church there," an elderly uncle offered. "He was with a couple of his buddies."

"I'll find him." Donald stomped off in the direction of a thick corpse of trees behind the church.

Anna threw her hands in the air. "We've been married less than ten minutes and already he's gone off with his friends. I don't believe this!"

Mike showed up several minutes later followed closely by Donald. Sheepishly, Mike kissed Anna on the cheek and whispered, "Sorry." He reeked of alcohol. Anna's stomach tightened as she met her father's eyes. Donald looked away.

An informal reception took place at a local restaurant where guests ordered from the menu. Purple and white helium-filled balloons danced above the tables, their matching curled ribbons dangled prettily.

A champagne toast was offered and Mike's best friend Ted gave a short, slightly slurred speech. Anna smiled sweetly, though apprehension swept over her when she noticed Mike's eyes drooped and he struggled to focus. Ignoring her concerns, she graciously thanked her family and close friends for sharing their special day. When the guests had dispersed, Mike and Anna drove to a hotel less than a half hour away in the next town. Upon arrival, Anna freshened in the bathroom and drew a soft pink nightgown over her head. The youthful face that looked back at her in the mirror blushed. "*I'm married*," she whispered aloud. Excitedly, she stepped into the room and was dismayed to find Mike sprawled on the bed, still dressed in his wedding attire. When she slipped the shoes from his feet, he groaned and rolled to his side. As the lingering rays of daylight slid behind the hills, Anna pulled the heavy drapes and prepared for a long night of TV and a shared bed with her new husband, who didn't care enough to stay awake.

A sliver of light through dark green drapes revealed the break of dawn when Anna awoke the following morning. She yawned and stretched; her body still tired from the previous day's events. Mike was in the bathroom. She could hear the toilet flushing, the water running. Butterflies danced her stomach as she sat up on the side of the bed, followed by a wave of nausea.

"Mike, I need the bathroom!"

Concerned, he immediately came to her. Anna brushed past him and closed the bathroom door.

After several moments Mike knocked and inquired. "Are you okay?"

"Yeah, I'll be out in a few minutes." She made her way back into the room and sat in an armchair near the bed and held her stomach.

"Are you sick?"

"Morning sickness, it'll pass after I sit for a bit." Beads of perspiration broke out on her upper lip and forehead. She dabbed it with a wash rag.

"About last night," Mike began, and knelt beside the chair.

Anna looked into his red irritated eyes; his pallor closely matched her own. Unshed tears began to flow as she explained how his behavior had disappointed her and spoiled their special day.

"I'm so sorry; I've been a jerk, a total jerk. I was so nervous yesterday; overwhelmed really, everything is happening so fast. That's why I drank too much."

"What, you think I wasn't nervous?"

"I know, but you're stronger than me." He hung his head. "Will you forgive me? Please? I'll make it up to you. I promise."

Like a sad little boy he laid his head on her knees and Anna ran her fingers through his hair and kissed his head. Leaning over she rocked him.

"I forgive you. It'll get better, you'll see."

Please God, she silently prayed. *Help Mike and me stay strong for our little baby.*

Mike sat upright, "can I get you anything?"

"Yeah, I have some saltines in my bag. Can you grab them for me?"

Mike ruffled through the bag and handed her the crackers. "If you're alright, I'm going to take a shower."

Anna nodded. After the snack took effect, she changed her clothes and packed their things. Feeling less queasy she smiled as Mike came out from the bathroom combing his wet hair.

"Are you better?"

"Yeah, much thanks for asking." Anna leaned her head on her husband's shoulder.

"Good. I have a surprise for you." His eyes twinkled.

They packed the remainder of their belongings and left the hotel. As Anna belted into the seat of Mike's truck, he handed her a blindfold.

"What's this?"

"Just wear it," he smiled at her mischievously.

Anna felt the truck moving and after it seemed an eternity she asked,

"Where *are* we going?" She laughed as she adjusted and tugged at the fabric covering her eyes.

"It's a surprise, Anna. Hold on, we are almost there." Mike looked over at his wife to make sure she wasn't peeking.

Finally Anna felt the truck come to a stop. "Can I look now?" her tone thick with impatience.

"Not yet," he replied as he led his bride to the front door of a white-sided townhouse. He removed the blindfold from her eyes. "Welcome home," he said as he lifted Anna through the doorway.

"Really?" Anna squealed with delight. "But how?"

"Mom and Dad own this half. Remember my uncle Tony?" Mike pointed to two doors side by side. "He lives next door. The other renter left, so it's vacant for us to rent!" Mike exclaimed. "I hope you like it. I've been busy repainting it for us. It's pretty clean, just a few things left to fix. Oh, and one more thing… Mom and Dad put a washer and dryer in the basement for us for our wedding present!"

"Wow, I can't believe it. That was really nice of them. I'm glad they've come around Mike. I'm really glad." Anna looked at her husband with relief.

"Well, they know I'm in l-o-v-e." Mike lifted Anna in his arms, spun her around, and kissed her passionately.

"I love you too, Mike. Thank you. This is a wonderful surprise!"

"Come on, let me show you around." His excitement was contagious.

Mike led Anna into the living room. She looked around the bright open space and admired the large picture window. To the left, behind the front door, a stairway led to the second floor. She walked through the room to a kitchen that had been lined halfway with wainscoting. A small half bath finished the first floor of the townhome. Anna ran back to the stairs.

"Where's the baby's room?" she asked, as she climbed the steep staircase. She stopped and peered into the two bedrooms on the second floor. "Soon our baby will be here," she said softly as she stepped inside the yellow and white nursery. Her husband wrapped his arms tenderly around her.

"Yes, Anna, only a few months left." The two stood quietly in the empty room as their individual thoughts filled it.

CHAPTER 6

The scent of summer roses along with thick humid air greeted Anna as she left the dental clinic. Her feet ached and her ankles were swollen. She wobbled to her car. The thought of putting her feet up to enjoy the cool air conditioner enticed her to keep moving. Barely able to fit the seatbelt over her belly, she spoke aloud, "I can't wait to see you, Little One." She felt a kick to her side and rubbed the lump protruding from her stomach. "I know, I know, not much room in there for you anymore." She wiped the sweat from her brow and rolled down the windows. *Ugh, I need air in this car.*

The drive home was exhausting, and she welcomed the sight of the little white townhouse. Gathering the mail on her way through the side door to the kitchen she shuffled through a stack of bills. "These will have to wait," she said aloud as she carried herself upstairs to her bed and blasted the air conditioner. The hum of the air lulled her to sleep.

Anna awoke to wetness between her legs. She pushed herself from the comfort of her bed and proceeded to the bathroom. "My water broke!" As she realized what was happening, she shrieked "Mike!"

The sound of his footsteps running up the stairs gave her a small sense of relief. She reached for a bath towel and jammed it between her legs as she attempted to walk toward him.

"What's wrong?"

"I think my water broke, it's not stopping. I think I'm in labor!" Their eyes met and held with a mixture of fear and joy.

"Oh, aw!" Anna cried. Mike took her by the arm and led her downstairs to sit in a chair while he ran back up to the bedroom to retrieve the pre-packed hospital bag.

"*Hurry!*" The expectation of impending labor rattled Anna's nerves.

The two rode silently to the hospital but for a few moans from Anna. Mike's fast driving, usually an issue with her, was now gratefully welcomed. When an orderly at the emergency door saw Anna trying to walk with a towel between her legs, he quickly grabbed a wheelchair and pushed her immediately to the labor and delivery floor while Mike parked the car. The pain of the contractions increased and the doctor suggested an immediate epidural. By the time Mike returned Anna was comfortably resting in a room, waiting.

A young petite woman with a blond ponytail and green scrubs entered the room. She bustled about and finally arrived at Anna's bedside.

"Hi, my name is Joy. I'll be your nurse today. Can I get you anything?"

"No, I'm okay."

"Dr. Eng will be here in a few minutes. He said your baby is coming soon! When I come back, you get ready to push." She looked over at Mike and smiled. "And, Daddy, you be ready to give ice chips when needed and coach her along, okay?" She threw him a wink and scurried from the room.

"You ready, Anna?" Mike looked over at his wife, his face as green as Joy's scrubs.

"Ready as I'll ever be. I'm tired of being uncomfortable, and I'm so ready to see our little tyke." She smiled weakly.

Dr. Eng and Joy came into the room, and Anna began the pushing process. Beads of sweat lined her forehead. Her arms gripped the bedside as she tried to bear down. Suddenly Dr. Eng got up from the stool where he was sitting on to catch the baby. "Hold it, Anna," he said calmly.

"I can't. I... It's just such an urge to push. I...don't think... I can't..."

Suddenly the doctor clapped his hands loudly and yelled, "Trauma!" Within seconds a bevy of green scrubs entered the room.

"What's…what's going on?" Fear froze Anna's heart. She looked at Mike who had turned deathly pale.

"Anna, I have to push the baby back in. We're going to prep for surgery." Dr. Eng moved quickly and calmly as he pushed the baby from the birth canal back into her body.

"Owww!" Anna screamed in pain and terror.

The epidural did little to ease the pain of the baby being pushed back inside her. There were tubes flying around her head. Quickly, she was taken out of the room. Several nurses and doctors surrounded her bed as they ran it down the hallway. Anna watched the ceiling lights fly past her like lights through a tunnel.

Dr. Eng leaned into Anna as they reached the operating room. "Anna, we are going to perform a C-section. You will be awake, but you will feel pressure, no pain. We are adding meds to your epidural. We don't have time to put you to sleep. Your baby is in distress." He patted her on the arm. "Trust me; we have everything under complete control."

"The baby, is the baby okay? I'm going to be awake? Will I see anything? Where's Mike?" Anna cried.

Joy came beside her head and put an oxygen mask over her nose. "Just relax, Anna. Mike will sit right here by your head, and there will be a curtain up so you won't see the surgery. It's okay, Anna," she soothed. She rolled a stool to Mike so he could sit by his wife.

"You're a tough girl, Anna. You can do this."

The blue curtain separating her head and torso, hung from the length of the ceiling. The realization that only a thin fabric was between her and surgical instruments made her panic. Every sound was magnified. Her eyes widened with fear as she waited in anticipation.

Anna could feel the release of her baby and began to feel her eyes tearing and leaving wet pools on her pillow. Within seconds they heard the sound of a baby cry. "It's a boy!" A boy! A beautiful boy! She looked up at Mike who in his excitement rose up from the stool and looked over the curtain.

"Whoa," he exclaimed. "You don't want to see what I just saw." She heard a loud thud as she saw her husband fall in a heap on the floor beside her.

After taking Mike from the room, Joy came to check on Anna. "Good job, Mama," she winked merrily.

"Joy, what happened…what happened back there? Why did I need a C-section?"

"I can tell you now because you delivered a healthy boy. The cord was wrapped around his neck and he was coming out posterior first. This is a miracle baby, Anna. We almost lost him. As for your husband, he'll be fine. A dose of smelling salts, and he'll be good as new!"

The words were mystical, a miracle baby. Yes, this baby boy was God's little miracle. "I promise God, I will do my very best by him. I promise," Anna prayed as complete exhaustion overtook her.

Sometime later Anna groggily opened her eyes. Colors faded in and out. She wanted to wipe them away, but she could not move her arms. Alarmed she looked down to see her arms braced to the hospital bed. Through a drugged haze a vision of Mike standing at her holding a blanketed bundle emerged.

"Mike," she moaned. Her mouth felt like it was holding cotton.

"Anna, you're awake! Meet our son!" he said proudly. He brought the baby's soft silken cheek close to hers.

"Why…my arms…what?"

"Dr. Eng said you began trembling after the C-section. He says it's very normal; they have you tied to the bed so you won't fall. You're okay, Anna."

She studied her baby as Mike brought him close. The soft pink bundle was wrapped tightly in a blue blanket, his head covered in a miniature knit yellow and white stocking hat to keep him warm. A little fist poked out from the blanket, and Anna noticed his tiny fingers clenched tight. His eyes were closed while he peacefully slept. A wave of pure love engulfed her as a single tear spilled from her eye.

"We have to give him a name," Mike said excitedly. She rubbed her newborn cheek to cheek and reveled in his perfection. Anna asked him to unwrap the swaddled baby, and she inspected all of his fingers and toes.

"He was a miracle, Mike. We almost lost him. They got him just in time. We'll call him Justin."

And so, Justin Michael Gallo was welcomed into the world: August 20, 1983, eight pounds twelve ounces, twenty inches long.

CHAPTER 7

Justin lay snug in his stroller wrapped in a warm blanket. Anna pushed it carefully along the rutted sidewalk so not to waken her sleeping baby. Colorful autumn leaves surrounded her as she soaked in the afternoon sun. Breathing the cool crisp fall air, she expelled a deep sigh. Not sure of her destination, she found herself standing in front of the large church where she and Mike had been wed. She saw through troubled eyes the old stone building with its stained glass windows and was drawn to the front door. She allowed the quiet overtake her as she rolled Justin to the back of the church near the last pew. She knelt and peered down the aisle as tears began to stream down her face. She noticed an older woman lighting candles at the side altar and quickly wiped the tears with the back of her hand. As the woman approached, Anna noted the wooden cross that hung around her neck. On her head she wore a veil that covered and revealed only the outline of her face.

"A beautiful sleeping baby, such peace," she whispered to Anna.

Anna nodded. She felt the nun's tenderness and noticed the wrinkles around her mouth as she smiled down on Justin.

"What is troubling you, child? You look sad. What hurts your heart?" She let the words linger and waited for Anna to respond.

"I'm having marriage problems," Anna whispered, her eyes downcast.

"Come with me. There is a room down the hall. We can talk without having to whisper. I may be able to help you," she said as she laid her hand upon Anna's shoulder.

"But I'm not Catholic, how can you help me?"

"God doesn't look at religion, child. He looks at your heart. Come with me."

Anna rose from the pew. She followed the nun and pushed the stroller into a small office. The nun pointed to two seats where they could sit face to face. She tenderly took Anna's hands in hers, looked intently into her eyes and waited for her to speak.

"I'm trying to be a good wife," Anna began. "But I'm worried about my husband. He…well… he drinks a lot and… I've tried talking to him about it… One day last week, I came home from work and he was supposed to be watching our son… There were cars lined up the street. A party was going on at our house." She gazed over at her sleeping son. "Justin was asleep upstairs; but that's not the point. My husband is not being the father I thought he would be." Anna's eyes left the intensity of the nuns and looked down at the blue tweed carpet.

The nun tilted her head and asked, "How does that make you feel?"

"Well…" Anna sighed. "Disappointed. I've tried talking to him, but he just doesn't get it. I want to have a safe home for our son, and I want him to want the same things. Am I asking too much?" Tears threatened to flow.

"No, dear," the nun agreed gently. "You are not asking too much. I think you need to learn to communicate your and Justin's needs and also understand your husband's needs. How would you feel about coming here for marriage counseling? We have a wonderful counselor that I'm sure could lead both you and your husband in the way that God intends. Sometimes the new responsibilities of parenting can be hard on a marriage. But there's nothing God can't mend, Child. Pray about this and talk with your husband and call me if he is willing." She reached for a piece of paper on the desk behind her and scribbled her name and phone number on it and handed it to Anna. "My name is Sister Mary Catherine. Just ask for me when you call, and I will point you in the right direction. I think you will find the counseling very helpful. I don't believe I caught your name?"

"Oh, I'm sorry, my name is Anna Gallo." She extended a hand to the nun. "Thank you." Anna rose from the chair and looked at Justin who stirred in the stroller. "I'd best be on my way. My little guy will be ready to eat soon, and when's he's ready, I better be ready or the peace you see now will be long forgotten." She smiled warmly.

Anna stepped out into the crisp fall air. She was lighter now, and grateful for releasing her concerns to someone else. With a plan to work on her problem marriage and a sense of renewed hope, she headed home.

Entering the small white townhouse, Anna went immediately to the kitchen to prepare formula for Justin. Her baby was beginning to fuss now, and she chided herself for not coming home sooner. Efficiently she warmed the bottle, lifted her sweet bundle, and cradled him in her arms. "There, there," she soothed smiling at him while he hungrily began to suck and drool formula down his cheek.

"You're a hungry little guy," she whispered as she wiped away the drip. "You'd better slow down; you're going to get a bellyache." His aqua eyes like deep pools looked up at her intently. As if he understood he began to slow his eating. She sat in the rocking chair in the living room and held him close while he filled his tummy. She caressed his soft pink cheek and placed him on her shoulder to burp. He smiled and giggled as she held him in her arms. "Oh, how I love you, my boy. You are a happy little guy when you're fed," she said aloud as she smiled at him. Anna loved this time with her son, when he was happy in her arms, his fingers wrapped tightly around her index finger. Anna rocked back and forth and began to sing to her baby, "Jesus loves me, this I know, for the Bible tells me so. Little ones to him belong, we are weak, but he is strong." Her song was interrupted by the slam of a car door.

"Oh, Daddy's home," she whispered to Justin. Mike banged into the room holding a pizza in one hand and a six pack of beer in the other. Immediately Anna began to feel the familiar knot in her stomach.

"Hey, how's it going?" Mike put the pizza and beer on a side table and reached for Justin. He picked his son up and kissed him on the cheek.

"He needs his diaper changed, and I was going to give him a bath," Anna implied.

"I'll change him. He can sit in the swing while we have supper. You can bathe him after we eat."

Mike headed to the changing table while Anna picked up the pizza and brought it to the kitchen table. She plucked paper plates, napkins, and glasses from the counter and set them down. When Justin was comfortably in his swing, the two began to share their meal.

"What did you do today?" Mike questioned as he pulled melted cheese away from his mouth.

"I took Justin for a walk. It was such a nice day," Anna hesitated. "Um, there is something I wanted to talk to you about." Anna put the pizza on her plate and folded her hands in her lap.

"What now?" Mike asked with resignation. "It seems ever since we've been married you've had one problem with me after another. What is it now? And where's my beer?" He jumped from the kitchen chair and went for the six-pack.

She could feel the tension begin to rise. "Do you really need that tonight?" Anna questioned.

"Need what? The beer? Anna, beer is good with pizza." He shook his head in disapproval. "Don't make problems where there aren't problems," he stated in annoyance.

"Actually, I think your drinking is a problem, Mike. I went to the church today and I spoke to Sister Mary Catherine. She suggested maybe some marriage counseling for us," Anna began.

"*What?*" The tenor of his voice elevated. "Anna, why do you do this?" He roughly ran his fingers through his thick hair and paced the floor. "Why do you make problems where there are no problems? *Everything* is a problem to you. You are ridiculous!"

"I'm not ridiculous," Anna stated quietly. "If we don't get marriage counseling, then I'm afraid this isn't gonna work."

"Well, you're finally right about something…this isn't gonna work!" Mike turned on his heel and stomped toward the stairs to the second floor.

Justin, who was sitting quietly in the swing, began to cry. Anna reached for him and rubbed his cheek. "It's okay, baby," she comforted. "It's okay." Anna placed the pacifier in his mouth, and he closed his eyes again to sleep. Anna looked at the pizza turning dry and cold and was no longer hungry. As she cleaned the table, she turned. Mike stood in front of her with a duffle bag.

"I'm leaving," he stated as he continued to nervously rub his hand through his dark curls.

"What do you mean you're leaving? You can't leave!" Anna tried to absorb the shock.

"You said, Anna… Marriage counseling…or this is over. Well, I'm done. This is over." He walked through the kitchen door into the dark night and slammed the door as he exited.

Anna stood motionless. She looked at Justin who had spit the pacifier out of his mouth and began to fuss again. She put it back into his mouth and then sunk into a kitchen chair. With her head in her hands she sobbed. After several minutes had passed, Anna heard a knock at the front door. *Mike, you're back!* She thought as she sprang from the chair and raced to open the door. Sarah Bertrum stood smiling at her daughter as she juggled two shopping bags.

"Diapers were on sale! I picked some up for Justin. And where is my precious grandson," she said enthusiastically, peeking over Anna's shoulder.

Anna stood aside and watched as her mother dropped the bags and moved toward Justin in the swing. He spit the pacifier out. His little legs kicked, and his arms flailed as he cooed at her. She tenderly lifted him up and nuzzled his cheek. "Hi, precious," she whispered as she held him close. Anna watched as Justin tugged at his grandmother's hair. She gently pulled it away.

"Thanks for the diapers, Mom." Anna put the diapers on the changing table.

"You're welcome, sweetheart. Where's Mike?"

"Oh, not home yet," Anna lied, looking away from her mother so she would not see the truth in her eyes.

"Well, this may be a good time for us to talk. I have something important to share with you." She sat at the kitchen table holding Justin and waited for her daughter to join her. Anna sat beside her and nodded for her to begin.

"Your dad and I are moving, Anna. The bottling plant is closing and is being moved to Tennessee. Dad has to be on the job there in less than a month. I can't believe this is happening so fast." She waved her arms dramatically. "I just hate the thought of being so far away from you and Justin. I knew this could happen, of course, there were rumors. But with the wedding and the baby coming, I just didn't want to worry you, sweetheart."

Anna sat speechless. Everything around her was falling apart, and she had no control. It was if she was in a speeding car, and she desperately wanted to hit the brakes.

"I know this is sudden," Sarah continued. "I have so much to do before the move," she spoke her concerns aloud.

"Wow, Mom! I knew Dad's job was on the line, but this? A move to the south, and within a month, I can barely take it in."

Sarah stroked her brow. "I can barely take it in myself. Doing this is a risk for us. We don't know how long this plant will stay open either."

Anna breathed like the wind had been knocked out of her. She reached for Justin as he began to wiggle in his grandmother's arms. She held her sweet baby and put his head to her nose as she drew in the scent of him. This act of love centered her somehow as she stood with Justin on her hip and moved around the kitchen. She filled the deep sink in preparation for his bath. With her mind in a whirl, she needed a physical task to focus on.

"I'm going to get Justin ready for bed," she spoke to her mother over her shoulder.

"I'm sorry, Anna. This is a bad time for you. I wasn't thinking. I wanted to stop by and tell you what's going on with Daddy and me so you wouldn't be surprised by the for sale sign. We're having a real estate agent come tomorrow." She reached around her daughter and Justin and gave them a squeeze. "I love you, honey." She kissed Anna on the cheek and turned toward the door. "Life is changing for all of us, I guess. Oh, and Anna? Say hi to Mike for me."

When she opened the door, Anna cried. "Wait, Mom. Please!"

Sarah turned back to her daughter and noted her distress. "Sweetheart, what's wrong?"

"It's Mike. He's walked out on us a few minutes ago, and I don't know if he'll be coming back. I didn't want to tell you that we have been having problems."

"My sweet. What will you do if he doesn't come back?"

"I don't know." Anna sobbed quietly as she rubbed her baby's back.

"You could come with us to Tennessee?"

Anna embraced her mother. "You know that isn't an option, Mom. I have to try to work things out with Mike. I have a good job here that I love. Holly's here too and all my friends."

Sarah shrugged her shoulders. "I'm sure everything will work out with Mike. He just needs a little break. You both have had to handle a lot of responsibilities so quickly. He just needs to learn how to deal with all the stress."

"You're right. Maybe he just needs time to figure things out. He's my husband. I love him."

Sarah threw up her hands. "The best I can offer you then is this, know that the door will always be open if you need your dad and me."

"Thanks, Mom," Anna mumbled through her sniffles.

After her mother had left, Anna returned to the task at hand and dressed Justin for bed. A lullaby, a kiss good night, and he went to sleep. With Justin tucked in safe and warm her mind wandered. *What am I going to do? Mike left; Mom and Dad are leaving. What is going to happen to me and Justin? Mike will be back; he's just mad at me right now, but he'll be back.* She comforted herself. After a long day, she drew a warm bath and retreated to bed early.

CHAPTER 8

Days moved quickly as winter approached. The fallen leaves lay covering the ground, and as Anna gazed out the window, she felt like the stark trees, alone and vulnerable. It had been three and a half weeks, and Mike had not contacted her. With most of her salary going to day care, the household bills surrounded her like a pile of leaves. Her hopes of Mike returning to work on their marriage faded as autumn turned to winter.

Anna sat on the shag carpet floor beside Justin. He was lying on his back swatting the toy gym that dangled over his head. He giggled with gratification as he banged the toys back and forth. A knock at the door brought Anna to see who intruded on their play time. She was greeted by an older man, dressed sharply and wearing an overcoat. She looked at him confused as he addressed her. "Mrs. Anna Gallo?"

"Yes…I'm Anna Gallo."

"You are being served an eviction notice." The stranger handed her a crisp white envelope and turned on his heel, leaving her stunned.

She closed the door and tore open the envelope. The enclosed letter read:

> Dear Mrs. Gallo,
>   Due to your failure to pay last month's rent, notice is hereby given to you in accordance with the provisions of Maine's General Laws, Chapter 186, Section 12, as amended to quit and deliver up possession on the 31st

day of January 1984, the premises presently occupied by you and described as 15 Oak Lane, York, Maine, owned by Allen and Olivia Gallo of 132 Cranbury Court, York, Maine.

Please note that if you have not received a notice to quit for nonpayment of rent within the last 12 months, you have a right to prevent termination of your tenancy by paying or tendering to your landlord, your landlord's attorney or the person to whom you customarily pay your rent, the full amount of rent due within 10 days after receipt of this notice.

Allen M. Gallo and Olivia Gallo

By their Attorneys: Berkinwitz and Rostien

Anna read the words over and over on the page. *Evicted*!? She couldn't believe this was happening. Running her fingers through her soft golden curls, she looked over at Justin who still played with his toys. "What will become of us? How could Mike let this happen?" Anger welled inside of her. "How dare they!?" Anna reached for the phone and dialed her lifeline, her sister.

"You have reached Holly. You know what to do… Wait for the beep!" Anna hung up the phone when the answering machine message picked up. She then dialed her sister's cell phone.

"Hi, Anna!" her sister said. "You'll never guess where Chris and I are headed. We're going to New Hampshire to start the ski season! I'm so excited!"

Anna's heart sank. Not wishing to deflate her sisters' excitement she avoided telling of her quandary. She was quiet for several seconds.

"Anna? Are you there?"

"Yeah, I'm here. That's awesome!" She tried to match the excitement in her sister's voice.

"Chris ran into the gas station to get a few things, so I guess I can tell you. I think he may pop the question this weekend. I'm not sure but he's been acting funny, ya know? Do ya think I'm right?"

Anna could feel the animation in her sisters' voice though miles between them. She thought about Holly and her long-time boyfriend Chris. They had dated all through high school and parted for a brief six months to find themselves. Unable to stay separated for long, they were inseparable again.

"I don't know, Holly. He didn't mention anything to me, but then he probably wouldn't want to spoil the surprise."

"I'm so nervous! I'll call you if he proposes. Here he comes," she whispered secretively. "I have to change the subject."

"Yeah, keep me posted."

"So what's up with you? What are your plans for today? Is my favorite nephew being a good boy? Anna, you're so lucky. He's such a love. Kiss him for Auntie!"

"Oh, not much," Anna lied. "Just wanted to check in on you, see what was up." She walked into the kitchen and began to pace as she spoke.

"Chris says hi! I've gotta go, okay? We're almost to the slopes! Yipee!"

"Have a safe trip, sis, and have fun." Anna tried to keep her voice even as she hung up the phone.

Anna prepared lunch for Justin, all the while thinking about what she should do. After feeding the baby, she wrapped him warmly in a soft blanket and packed a diaper bag. *I have to see Sister Mary Catherine*, she thought and headed to the church hoping to find some answers. Anna cradled her baby close to avoid the chill that heralded winter's approach. Upon entering the church a deep solace engulfed her. The door was open to the office; Sister Mary Catherine sat behind a desk shuffling paperwork. Upon seeing Anna she came to her.

"Anna! I've been wondering about you. Did you want to sign up for the marriage counseling I suggested?"

Anna looked away from the gentle nun as she reached into the diaper bag and pulled out the letter. "I'm afraid not. I suggested it to Mike but he left and I think he is staying with his parents. I don't know. He hasn't contacted me, but today I got this." She handed the envelope to the nun.

Sister Mary Catherine adjusted her glasses and read the letter. She looked squarely at Anna. "He refused counseling? I think you may need a lawyer. I happen to know one; she is one of our parishioners here at St. Paul's. You need to get in touch with her right away."

Anna looked at her, shocked. "But how will that help me?"

"Anna, you can't make a person stay who has decided to leave. You must protect yourself and your sweet baby. I'm not saying divorce necessarily, what I am saying is you should not be held responsible for your baby alone and be evicted from your home without cause. Mike needs to handle his financial obligations to his child as well."

"But… This is all wrong! This can't happen, I don't want a divorce!" She sobbed. "I'm a person of faith!"

"Sweet child, God loves you and will protect you. Let your faith guide you. Pray in all things, and you will find the answers. Do call the lawyer to discuss your options. These people cannot evict you." She handed Anna a card that read: Teresa Jackson, Attorney at Law. Anna accepted the card with a trembling hand while Sister Mary Catherine patted her arm encouragingly.

Divorce was not what Anna had in mind when she walked through the church door. She thanked the nun and went on her way back to the little white townhouse. While rocking her baby in her arms her mind raced wildly. She stopped the negative thoughts and uttered a word of prayer. "Please help me, God. I don't know what I'm supposed to do. Lead me in the way you want me to go. Amen," she pleaded in desperation.

CHAPTER 9

Anna stood in front of a small brick building. The inscription-carved door read: Teresa Jackson, Esquire. Jessica was watching Justin, Anna had lied about having to run an errand. This was not happening! Mike would come home, and it would all be a distant memory. Tilting her head back and lifting her shoulders, she let out a quick breath and opened the door. Rich brown leather chairs lined the wall, and burgundy striped wall paper greeted her. A beautiful young woman sat at a large reception desk. Anna stepped to the desk and was welcomed by her smile.

"May I help you?" she greeted Anna warmly.

"Yes, I'm here to see Teresa Jackson. My name is Anna Gallo."

"You can wait in her office." The receptionist led Anna along a short hallway and motioned her to an office with similar rich décor. "Have a seat, and she'll be with you shortly." She turned and left Anna to study the room. A Tiffany desk lamp sat on the massive mahogany desk. Neatly organized stacks of files lay to one side. The walls held college diplomas, one stating Teresa Jackson had graduated from Harvard Law. *Well, at least I'm in good hands*, Anna thought. A tall thin woman with a short blunt haircut and sharp features entered the room. She extended a hand to Anna.

"Hello, Anna. Teresa Jackson. Pleasure to meet you." Her deep voice threw Anna off guard.

"Hi," Anna recovered.

"So, tell me what brings you here today? Sister Mary Catherine mentioned you have some troubling issues. She did not elaborate but did say you would be calling me." Teresa Jackson smiled revealing perfect white teeth.

Anna reached in her purse and handed the eviction notice to the attorney. She watched as her dark brown eyes scanned the document. Upon finishing, she looked at Anna. "So who owns this property?"

"My in-laws own it and are renting it to my husband and me," she stuttered. "Well, just me and my baby now, I guess." Anna's stomach growled; she hadn't eaten all day accept for a slice of toast.

"Is your husband living at this property?" Teresa Jackson pressed.

"No, he left a little over a month ago. I'm not sure. I think he's living at home with his parents." Anna's eyes dropped to the floor. She studied the interlocking wood beneath her.

"Anna, we'll need to file a temporary order if your husband has left and not assisted you financially. I understand you have a baby. Has he visited the baby?" the attorney queried.

"No, he hasn't contacted me, not even once. Our son, Justin, is four months old. What is a temporary order? What does that mean?"

"It is the beginning of divorce proceedings. A temporary order ensures that child support is paid until the divorce is final. You cannot be evicted from this property as long as rent is paid on time—that's illegal."

Anna sighed and allowed the words to sink in. "I don't want to live there any longer if they want me out. I don't want a divorce either. I don't believe in divorce. I married for life. I can't believe this is happening!" Her hands trembled and nausea swept over her.

"A temporary order is not final; however, it will ensure protection for you and your son. I know someone you can contact for other living arrangements if you feel the need. Her name is Jillian Sax. She's the property manager at an apartment complex and may be able to help you." Teresa Jackson handed Anna a business card with the woman's name and phone number on the back. "Give her a call; she's a great lady. In the meantime let's get the paperwork together for that temporary order." She handed Anna a clipboard holding several legal documents. "Oh, by the way, I know money must be tight for you right now. I will charge you a flat fee of five hundred dollars. We can work out a payment plan after you get settled."

"Thanks, Ms. Jackson," Anna said with a weak smile. She took the card and put it into her purse and began to fill out the papers all the while wondering if this was the right thing to do.

CHAPTER 10

The following day, with Justin bundled, Anna went to meet Jillian Sax. She had greeted Anna so warmly on the phone it gave her the courage to pay a visit. Jillian had suggested they meet at her apartment since she lived in the complex as well as managed the property. As she drove into the parking lot, she noticed a swimming pool covered for winter and a park nearby. Beneath snow covered oak trees, swings and slides sat idly waiting for spring thaw. Anna smiled. Soon she could bring Justin there to play. Anna held her baby in his carry seat in one hand and a diaper bag in the other. It took all the strength she could muster to make it to the brightly painted red door. As she lifted her hand to knock, the door opened to reveal a beautiful woman in her midforties with upswept blond hair, slight wisps cascading down her cheeks. Anna noticed that her eye makeup was tastefully applied accentuating her crystal blue eyes and her smile was radiant.

"You must be Anna." The tenderness in her voice beckoned Anna inside the apartment. "I'm Jillian. I'm happy to meet you in person." She bent down to take a closer look at the sleeping baby in the carry seat. "This must be your little boy. Teresa told me about him. He is adorable," she added quietly.

Anna introduced him proudly, "His name is Justin Michael."

A delicate scent of vanilla candle permeated the pastel apartment. An ocean scene of a pink and violet sunset hung above a striped couch. Muted floral curtains hung at the windows. A vase filled with white silk hydrangeas sat on a round table between them. Jillian led

Anna and Justin to a dining area separated from the kitchen with a half wall. She motioned her to sit at a table. Inside the glass table glittered sea shells were scattered haphazardly reflecting the dining light. Subdued piano music played in the background.

"Would you care for herbal tea?"

"Sure," Anna replied. She watched the woman float into her kitchen to heat a kettle of water. "This is a beautiful apartment," she admired as Jillian approached with a plate of chocolate-covered cookies.

Jillian smiled and pointed out the window. "Out there is stressful. This? This is my sanctuary."

Anna nodded in agreement. "I know what you mean. Life sure can be hard sometimes. I don't know how things got so messed up."

"What do you mean messed up?" Jillian inquired.

"Well, I feel so alone. I feel like I don't know where to turn. I don't know what decisions to make. Pretty lost I guess," she confided. Anna lowered her eyes.

"When I get in those situations, I surrender to God's will," Jillian stated matter-of-factly.

"I don't think God wants anything to do with me right now."

Jillian gently raised Anna's chin with her hand so their eyes met. "Honey, there is nothing you can do that will separate from his love."

"But…" Anna interrupted.

"No buts." She smiled warmly. "It's why Jesus died for you and me; he's waiting for you to ask."

"No, I screwed up. My husband and I…well, our baby was not planned…" She began to stutter, and the grief of all she had been though released as large tears dropped from her eyes. "I'm headed for divorce. God hates me!" She sobbed.

"Oh, Anna." Jillian placed her arm gently on Anna's shoulder. "You couldn't be more wrong. It's not about you. Don't you see? And it's not about religion. It's about relationship. You feel you sinned against God; well, who hasn't? That is why Jesus died to freely take our sin so we can commune with him. You only have to ask His forgiveness and release the rest at the cross. He's there to carry it for you if you let him. I promise." She reached for a Bible on the bookshelf behind her. Opening it she began to read, Ephesians 2:8-9, "For it is by grace you have been saved, through faith—and this not from yourselves, it is the gift of God- not by works, so that no one can boast." She pointed to the words on the page for Anna to see. She then flipped the pages and read another passage, Romans 2:22-24, "This righteousness from God comes through faith in Jesus Christ to all who believe. There is no difference, for all have sinned and fall short of the glory of God, and are justified freely by his grace through the redemption that came by Jesus Christ."

"That's what grace is all about, Anna."

Anna allowed the words to pierce her heart. She looked at her new friend with a heightened sense of clarity. Her shoulders began to relax and her lips turned upward in a smile. "You mean I've been getting this all wrong? I thought if I did the right things, made the right decisions, God would love me," she said aloud, although more to herself than to Jillian.

"Anna, you are loved regardless. We will never lack sin, it's impossible. The good news is, you can ask God's forgiveness and ask him to fill your heart and mind with the Holy Spirit. God wants to open the door to your soul, but only you have the key to let him in. Would you like to pray with me?"

"I would love to." As the two women prayed aloud, a new found peace washed over Anna and released her burdened heart.

CHAPTER 11

Time had passed and Justin had grown from baby to toddler. It didn't take long for the two to settle in their new apartment. The emotional baggage on Anna's shoulders had lessoned as her faith increased. She had heard about the peace that surpasses all understanding in church but now understood what that really meant. Her life became manageable in the roles of dental assistant and single mother. Dr. Miller had taken Anna under his wing and sent her to a radiation class. She was now officially licensed. They worked so well together that Dr. Miller had given her a raise and told her he would be hard pressed to work without her. One particular day he asked Anna into his office for a meeting. Anna was nervous because they never met in a formal setting; it had always been between patients or in the sterilization room.

"Have a seat." He motioned a long, thin finger to the chair in front of his desk.

The pause caused Anna to fidget in the chair while she waited for him to continue.

"Thank you for meeting with me today. We have something important to discuss. I know we don't often do this and I'm not trying to make you feel uncomfortable." He sat behind his desk and folded his hands leaning toward Anna.

Her heart quickened. *Oh no, what did I do wrong?*

"I noticed you have been through a great deal of stress for someone your age. You've carried yourself well. I don't know too many young people who could have been so brave in all of your circumstance. I've never told you this before, but you amaze me with your strength and resilience." His eyes were sympathetic. "I've watched how attentive you are with your son, when you bring him to the office from time to time, and I must say you're growing into motherhood beautifully." Dr. Miller rose from his chair and sat on the corner of the desk near Anna.

Anna blushed.

"Where does that come from?"

"A great deal of prayer." She smiled.

"Actually I've been praying about this conversation and how to talk to you about this." He walked back to the chair and folded his hands on the desk. "I'm going to ask you something now that I want you to think about seriously. It will affect your future and that of your son."

Her heart quickened.

"Things are changing drastically in my life. I'm going home to Minnesota to live. My father's health is deteriorating, forcing him to retire. He asked if I would take over his dental practice. If he closes the doors, there is not another dentist for miles. It's a nice community and my father has been extremely loyal to his patients. I feel like I need to do this for my father."

Anna felt the blow straight to her stomach.

"That's not all though. I want you to give serious consideration to relocating to Minnesota as well. I want you to come and work for me there. I can hardly function with other assistants. Without you, I feel like I'm missing my right arm. I promise I will help you with details and make it lucrative for you. I understand this is a big move."

This was not what Anna was expecting, and the news made her catch her breath.

"What about Brenda? Will she be coming too?"

"No, she's staying here to work with Dr. Peters."

"So, if I don't move to Minnesota and Dr. Peters won't need me…" Anna filled in the blanks in her mind. *…I will be out of a job.*

"Will you think about it? I know this is a lot to take in. Take some time, and we will revisit it soon. All right?"

"Yes. Sure Dr. Miller. Thank you. You have given me a lot to think about."

He rose in the chair, and Anna followed suit, as she aimlessly headed out the door.

⸻

Anna welcomed the weekly visits with her newfound friend, Jillian. They would sit together in the evenings after work and drink tea while Justin played on the floor or watched cartoons. They talked, laughed, cried, and sometimes Anna felt the years between them melt away as she soaked in Jillian's wisdom. Justin was growing before her eyes, and before she knew it he was walking and talking.

"Mama?" the little boy questioned as his pudgy finger pointed across the street.

"Yes, sweetheart, we are going to see Jill-Jill." Anna smiled. She kissed his hand and then held it. The two walked safely across as Justin began to pull and tug. Anna let go and watched as her little boy ran toward Jillian's door. His blond curls bounced, and his little legs could barely carry him. The doorbell was too high for his reach, so he stretched up with all his might and pressed as he stood on his tip toes. Jillian greeted him with a cookie. His hands shook with excitement.

"How about we go to the park, Jillian? Gone are the days where we could sit and occupy Justin with a few toys. Besides, it's a beautiful day," Anna suggested.

"Sure," Jillian replied as she put on her tennis shoes and closed the door behind her.

The three headed to the nearby park where Justin ran toward the sand box. Anna exhaled audibly as she sat on a bench alongside Jillian.

"Are you tired, Anna?" Jillian asked her friend with concern.

"No, just weary today I guess. I have a lot on my mind."

"Oh?"

"I don't know if I really want to tell you, because if I do then it will be real." Anna took the rubber band off her wrist and pulled her hair back into a ponytail. She didn't take her eyes off Justin as she spoke.

"What is it? From the tone of your voice it sounds serious." Jillian raised her hand to block the sun as she turned toward Anna.

"Remember I told you about the dentist I work with? How he is thinking of going to Minnesota to take over his father's dental practice because his dad is not well and is being forced to retire. Well, he's definitely going to move."

"Yeah, I remember you mentioned that, but he's only one associate, right? How many dentists work with you?"

"There are two who work at the office besides him but they are not going to need as many assistants. I'm afraid one of us is going to be let go. But that's not all..." Anna let out a deeper sigh. "Dr. Miller asked me to go with him."

"What? He wants you to move to Minnesota with him? Anna, you don't have *feelings* for this dentist do you?" Jillian sat upright and turned her shoulders to face her.

"Dr. Miller? No, it's nothing like that." Anna laughed. "We work well together. It takes a lot of experience to be able to do four-handed dentistry and not consult during the procedures. We have great *working* chemistry. Yuck, Jill. A romance with Dr. Miller, yuck!"

"Well, you say yuck, but I'm sure this Dr. Miller sees you as more than just his dental assistant. You're an attractive young woman. You have a lot to offer. Don't be so naive." Jillian's hand flew in exasperation.

"Oh Jillian, I'm really going to miss you. Who's going to beat off all the bad male suitors that come along?" Anna exaggerated.

"Miss you? You're determined to move Anna, aren't you? You've already decided. What about Mike?"

"Jill, Mike hasn't seen Justin in over eight months. I can't put our life on hold and wait for him to be a Father. I have an opportunity for a job, and Dr. Miller said I can rent his dad's old lake cabin indefinitely. Justin needs someone to provide for him. I guess that someone is me."

"What about Holly?" Jillian asked gently.

"I'm really going to miss her," Anna acknowledged sadly. "I already told Dr. Miller I'll need to come back for her wedding this summer. She's so excited."

Justin interrupted their conversation as he ran toward them covered in sand.

"Mama, me have juice?" He stood before them wiping his sandy hands on Anna's jeans.

"May I have juice? Is that what you would like?" Anna reached into a diaper bag and pulled out a Sippy cup and handed it to Justin. He sat in the grass beside them and took large gulps until he hiccupped.

"Easy there, big guy. Are you all right?" Jillian asked.

Justin smiled, dropped the cup on the grass, and ran back toward the sandbox.

"Oh, he's fine, Jill. He doesn't stop! He's a ball of energy, and sometimes I don't know if I will be able to keep up with him. Single parenting can be exhausting! I love him so much, he's so sweet, and I love those moments with him cuddling on my lap but now he wiggles off my lap instead of cuddling. He's growing so fast I just can't believe it."

"Before you know it, he'll be in school. And I'm going to miss all of it. I'll miss you, Anna. I'm happy for you though if this is what you want." Jillian placed her hand on Anna's shoulder. "I'm proud of you, girl! You've come a long way since the first time I saw you timidly walking into my apartment," she said wistfully.

"Words can't express how much I'll miss you. Justin will miss his Jill-Jill and her cookies! I have to thank you for everything. I don't know where I would be—"

Jillian held up her hands to interrupt Anna as she spoke. "Anna, don't even say it. You are like a younger sister to me, and I love you and Justin. I always will."

"We can't talk like this anymore, or I'm going to start crying!" Anna slid off the bench and walked over to Justin, picked him up from the sand box, and swung him around as he giggled and dirt flung from his body. She led him to the swing set, put him in a seat, and gave him a push. His legs kicked, and he smiled from ear to ear as she swung him back and forth. Anna swung Justin over her head as she ran beneath the swing doing an underdog and then back in front of him. "Peek-a-boo, baby," she teased. Justin giggled and laughed.

Jillian walked alongside her friend and put her arm around her. Anna rested her head upon her friend's shoulder as the two watched the toddler enjoying his play.

CHAPTER 12

Anna stood in the empty apartment and wiped her brow. Jillian had taken Justin for the morning while the moving truck packed their belongings. As she looked around the stark living room, anxiety began to pull at her heart. "Oh dear Lord, I'm scared. I hope I made the right decision. I know with you I'm never alone. Please help me. I *feel* so lonely." She began to clean the empty apartment in preparation for the next tenant. As she bent to pick up the dustpan, Holly walked through the open door.

"Hey! The truck is loaded already?" Holly bounced into the room and brought energy into the starkness. She handed Anna a paper bag. "I brought a muffin and bagels. Which do you want?"

"Thanks, I haven't eaten yet with all this going on." She wiped her hand across her forehead and then opened the bag to find a sugar coated blueberry muffin. She took a large bite. "Yum, this is good," she mumbled, as crumbs fell from her lips.

"Hey, check this out." Holly grinned as she attempted a cartwheel in the open room. "This apartment is huge with nothing in it!" She swung her arms around as she did a twirl.

"You're a goof ball." Anna laughed as her sister grabbed her hands and began to do the twist with her.

"I have decided to have a positive attitude. I'm trying to hide the fact that you're breakin' my heart by moving away, and you're not helping by making fun of me!" She grinned.

"I know, Holly. I appreciate it. You know I can't go through with this if I leave with red, swollen eyes. After all, I might scare off the other passengers on the plane," she teased back.

"Well, we are not saying good-bye. We are saying see ya soon! You'll be back for the wedding in a few months anyway. By the way, about the wedding, I have something to ask you. Do you think Justin could be our ring bearer?" Her olive eyes twinkled.

"That would be so cute! I hope he would behave though? You're putting a lot on the line if you expect a two-year-old to be responsible for your rings."

"Well, I was kind of hoping you would walk down with him as my maid of honor?" she asked tentatively.

Anna hugged her sister. "That would be awesome, and we'd love to. But please understand; I'm not responsible for Justin's behavior if you're looking for a perfect wedding." She shrugged her shoulders and then pulled her sister to her as the tears began to fall down both their cheeks. "Love you."

"Love you too." Holly pulled away and did another cartwheel, trying desperately to lighten their mood.

"Come on. Let's pick up Justin and get you both to the airport!" Holly grabbed her sister by the hand and headed to the door.

"I need to finish this cleaning. I can't leave it like this," Anna fretted, as she looked around the room.

"I'll take care of it Anna. I promise. When we pick up Justin, I'll tell Jillian I'll leave the keys with her when I'm done. Please, don't worry about it. I got this." Holly led her sister out the door and closed it before she had time to change her mind and not let her sister go.

The two walked across the street to Jillian's apartment and retrieved Justin. After a tearful farewell, they headed to the airport. Anna sat in the back seat of her sister's car with Justin beside her in the car seat. He chewed on a bagel that left lumps of dough between his fingers and rubbed it in his hair. Anna took a wet wipe from her purse and cleaned his fingers which made him fuss. "Let's get you cleaned up, baby. We have a long journey ahead," she whispered in a calm voice as she tried to stop the escalating fuss that was turning into a tantrum.

"No! No!" he screamed as he wiggled and cried while she wiped his cheeks.

Anna gave up and turned her focus to the car window. She watched as all the familiar scenes passed by. The New England clapboard houses along the Maine coast were fading from sight as they headed to the highway. She tried to swallow the fear that clutched her chest as tears rolled softly down her face.

"Do you want me to take the coastal route? We can go by and take a look at the beach one more time if you wish?" Holly asked cautiously.

"Sure," Anna replied as she dabbed her cheeks with a tissue.

Holly exited the highway and turned onto the coastal route. The sun was shining as they came to a clearing of vast beach and sky. Anna watched as the seagulls dove among the rocks to fetch their catch of the day. She rolled the window down and breathed in the salt air and pungent kelp.

"Oh Holly, I'm gonna miss the flowers blooming. Do you think Minnesota has hydrangeas? You know how I love hydrangeas."

"I don't know, but I'm sure you'll find a new flower to love. Besides the cabin that you are moving into sounds adorable. At least you won't be in an apartment. You'll be right on a lake!"

"So like you to encourage me. Thanks, Holly. I know this move is best for Justin and me." She gazed over at her son who was now smiling and kicking his feet. "We'll be fine. I just hate good-byes."

"Well, it's not good-bye. It's see ya later. Remember?" Holly turned her eyes from the road and looked over her shoulder at her sister and winked. "How about some music?"

Holly popped in a CD, and before she knew it the two were singing along to Journey. "*Don't stop believing…hold on to that feeling… street lights…people…oh oh oh!*"

The three arrived at the airport, and Holly found a cart to drag the luggage, baby bag, and car seat. Anna carried Justin, kicking and fighting. He had a way of being fussy at the most inconvenient times; Anna also realized he was like a sponge. When she felt anxious, he too became afraid and acted out. She talked soothingly to him as he kicked and wailed, and finally she placed him on the floor.

"What's wrong with him, Anna?" Holly questioned as she pulled the baggage cart behind her.

"This is what is known as the temper tantrum twos? He does this sometimes when he doesn't get what he wants," Anna replied as she ran her fingers through her hair. "I just let him throw a fit until it's over." She lifted her hands in defeat. "I must say his timing is impeccable. We need to get on that plane. Maybe taking the coastal route wasn't such a good idea. We didn't have time for that."

Holly leaned over and whispered in Justin's ear. He smiled and his hands shook with excitement.

"What did you tell him?" Anna questioned her sister.

Holly picked her nephew up and placed him on the luggage cart.

"Come on. Let's goooooooooo!" Holly held him as she pushed the cart faster.

"Holly! Airport security will freak if they see you doing this!" Anna tried to keep up with her sister and Justin as she skipped alongside the cart.

"Well, it's this or you will miss your plane?" Holly shouted over her shoulder.

The three trotted through the airport until finally reaching security. Holly kissed her sister on the cheek and pushed her forward. "Go, get outta here!" Anna reached for her and gave her a quick hug.

Anna was secretly grateful for the diversion rushing through the airport gave them. There was no time for a tearful good-bye. She wasn't sure she could handle any more tears. As she pushed through security, she waved her sister farewell and headed to the gate. The plane was boarding and the stewardess assisted Anna and Justin to their seats. Anna reached into the baby bag and gave Justin a sippy cup filled with juice. She patted his leg as he drank, leaned over, and whispered, "We're on our way, sweetheart. We're going on an airplane ride." He dropped the cup onto his lap and laid his head on her shoulder and closed his eyes. His temper tantrum had exhausted him and as the drone of the airplane started he fell fast asleep. The plane rolled away from the airport, and she watched out the window as they moved into take off position. When the plane rushed forward and the wheels left the tarmac, Anna felt a rush of emotion pass over her. Out the window the familiarity left and a rush of excitement to what their new life would bring filled her.

Her mind reflected back to the court room, the sound of the gavel as the judge proclaimed: "I hereby give Anna Bertrum full custody of Justin Gallo with said father Michael Gallo visitation one month in the summer." Justin was now her total responsibility.

She had silently prayed to God. "*I will do the best by him, Lord. I promise.*"

She didn't know how she would manage to leave Justin for a month in the summer. His father would be a virtual stranger to her young son as he hadn't seen Mike in months. Anna's thoughts were interrupted by the captain's voice over the intercom. "Thank you for flying with us today. We should arrive in St. Paul at four p.m. central standard time. You may remove your seatbelts at this time..." Anna glanced out the window at the dots of houses and snaking rivers that lay below. She laid her head back on her seat and closed her eyes.

The jolt of the plane's wheels touching ground woke Anna. She looked over to see Justin with his mouth agape, drooling and still asleep. She smiled and nudged him.

"Hey, big guy, you're gonna have to wake up. We're in St. Paul, Minnesota!"

Justin stirred in the seat. Anna freed him from his seatbelt, lifted him on her lap and covered his cheeks with kisses. He was giggling now, and she was relieved that he woke in a good mood. The two descended the plane hand in hand and walked into their new world. When she arrived at baggage claim, she was surprised to see an older man holding a sign with her name on it. She was puzzled as he came toward her.

"You must be Anna?" He leaned over to Justin. "And you, der',must be Justin?" he said with a thick Minnesota accent.

Justin twisted and turned as his mother tried desperately to hold her grip on him. She dropped her bags and lifted him protectively in her arms.

"Yes, I'm Anna," she answered the older man with thick gray hair sticking out of a Minnesota Vikings hat.

"Tom, I mean Dr. Miller, sent me to pick you up and drive you to the cabin. He knew with the baby and all, you might need some assistance, eh? I'm a friend of the family—grew up with the Millers. My name's Paul." He extended his hand to shake hers. "I help the family out from time to time and do odd jobs for them. In fact, if you have any problems at the cabin, I'll be the one to fix it." He leaned over and picked up the bags and car seat that Anna had dropped.

"Thank you so much. It's so nice of you to help us."

"Don't thank me, ma'am. Thank Dr. Miller. He would of come himself for yer', but he's busy getting settled."

The three struggled through the airport dragging luggage and coaxing Justin along. Anna noticed the log beams throughout the airport and taxidermy heads of moose, deer, and elk. It had a Northwood's motif, and she smiled to herself at the immediate change to her environment. As they drove along, she learned that Paul lived a few houses down from the cabin where she and Justin would reside. She learned that the fishing was fantastic (not that she cared), and the ice was melting on Eagle Lake. It had been a long winter. Sometimes the ice would last until after Memorial Day weekend, but this year they were in luck. As Paul pointed out, it was the perfect time to move as people began to come out after their long hibernation. The car began to slow as it wound through a long winding road where large pines and spruce canopied the blacktop. Paul pulled into a gravel driveway and announced, "Here we are!"

As Anna exited the car she was immediately greeted by the scent of evergreen. She stretched her arms to the sky and breathed in her surroundings. Justin lifted his arms imitating his mother, which made Paul chuckle. She leaned down and tickled him under his arms and he wiggled and laughed.

Anna knelt to Justin's level. "You stay close to Mama. Don't run off while we are looking at our new house. Understand?" she said firmly.

Justin nodded his head and hung on her leg in agreement.

Anna took Justin by the hand and led him to the one story red-stained cabin. She reached into her purse and pulled out the keys that Dr. Miller had given her. Inhaling deeply she opened the door to the warmth of a knotty pine mudroom. Paul came behind her dragging her luggage.

He dropped the bags by the door. "Let me show you around," he encouraged as he led her to the front of the home.

"This is yer' living space." He swept his arm around the room.

Anna glanced at the open space, kitchen and family room combined. One wall was flanked by a river rock fireplace with knotty pine paneling on either side. She looked above to see the sun shining through a skylight.

"I just fixed that," Paul commented. "After the winter thaw it began to leak. You'll have to let me know if it leaks fer' ya again."

Anna noticed a large sliding door, and she was drawn to the light. She looked out to see an attached deck and a breathtaking view of Eagle Lake.

"Oh, that's beautiful!" She clasped her hands with glee.

"Yep, you got one of the best views der'," Paul agreed. "One hundred fifty feet of frontage, and one of the best fishing spots. You'll see a lot of boats out there, eh real soon."

She picked Justin up and pointed out the window.

"Ocean, Mama," he said.

"No, Justin. Not ocean. Lake! That's Eagle Lake." She watched as a great winged bald eagle swept down over the water and flew away with a large fish hanging from its talons.

"Well, now we know why they call it Eagle Lake." She turned to Paul with a grin.

He smiled and led her to a wooden kitchen table. "You got a note der'." He handed an envelope to Anna.

> Dear Anna,
>
> Welcome to Minnesota! I hope you find the accommodations to your satisfaction. My parents left all the furnishings for you to use until your things arrive so make yourself at home. You should find everything you need. I had Paul load the refrigerator. Be sure to call on him if you need anything. I've enclosed a check for this week. Consider it a moving bonus. We won't be starting work until next week. I think we both need some time to settle in. I'll give you a call and take you for a tour of the new office soon.
>
> Welcome home,
> Dr. Miller

Anna swept her hand along the smooth kitchen table with four white ladder back chairs neatly tucked around it. Her eyes inventoried the rest of the room. A stuffed plaid couch separated the kitchen from the living area and faced the fireplace. A large TV hid behind a cabinet in the corner. A simple willow rocking chair sat in the opposite corner with a red pillow tossed haphazardly upon it. Anna smiled with satisfaction.

"I think we're gonna like it here!" she yelled to Paul as he went back to retrieve her luggage.

Carrying the large load he came into the room and led her to a hallway with three bedroom doors. "Where do you want yer' bags dropped?"

She peeked in each of the rooms as Justin hung from her leg. One had a queen-size bed. One had a set of twins and the third had two sets of bunk beds.

"Justin and I will share the room with the twin beds. Thanks, Paul."

"Well, I'm goin' to show myself out. You let me know if you need anything eh? My wife, Mary, I'm sure, will stop by with a casserole. She's like that there eh. She'll be curious to meet ya. She means well." He winked. "Oh, I'll write my phone number on yer' note here before I go, in case you need anything."

"Thank you so much, Paul. You have been so gracious. Thank you."

"No problem. Don't be shy. If you or the boy needs anything, we're two houses down on the left," he said and lifting his hat with a nod he left them.

Anna looked down at Justin still clinging to her leg. She pulled him into her arms and gave him a kiss on the cheek. "Wanna go see outside? Wanna go look at the lake before the sun goes down?"

He nodded his head excitedly and then laid it on her shoulder as he sucked his thumb. It had been a long day for both, and she hoped he would sleep well in their new home. They stepped through the sliding glass door onto the deck and she put him down to walk. The evening sun slid down, and it sent a shiver through her. She rubbed her chilled arms. They walked on the grass toward the lake. A few remaining speckles of sunlight danced on the water as the breeze rippled them away. A wide dock stretched out where a bench sat empty at the end. She picked up a few rocks, took Justin by the hand and walked him toward the bench.

"Now, Justin, you never come out to the lake without Mama, you hear?" she said firmly.

"Yep, yep, yep," he agreed as he grabbed the rocks from her hands and threw them into the lake. He smiled as one dropped close and gave a big ripple. "More rock, Mama," he encouraged.

"Okay, just a few more, but then we have to get inside before dark."

She watched Justin toddle along the shore looking for the biggest rock he could find. He dropped it, soaked his clothes, and then stepped in the water.

"All right, Justin, time to go in and get cleaned up." Anna reached her hand for him.

"No, no, no!" He dodged from her hand.

She swooped him up and carried him kicking and screaming back to the cabin. Struggling, she brought him to the couch, removed his wet shoes, and sat him down where he wiggled himself off into a heap on the floor.

"Justin," she said firmly, "I know it's been a long day. Hang in there, buddy."

Anna prepared a light supper and turned on the TV to help Justin settle down. She called Holly and her parents to reassure them that she'd made it to Minnesota safely. After filling their empty stomachs, Anna readied Justin for bed and read his favorite book. He pointed to the pictures on the pages as she read the words. They snuggled in the twin bed, and she stroked his head until he closed heavy eyes. Exhausted from their trip, she crawled into the twin bed beside him. Fully clothed and tired, she said her prayers and fell fast asleep.

CHAPTER 13

Dawn awakened Anna as the sun streamed through the window. She had forgotten to pull the shade; she was so weary the night before. Rolling out of bed, she pulled it down hoping Justin would sleep a little longer. She grabbed a sweatshirt, sneaked out of the room, and headed to the kitchen. *I'm sure Dr. Miller has coffee here somewhere*, she thought as she rummaged around in the kitchen cupboards. Finding it in the pantry, she smiled a sigh of relief. When perked, she took her mug of coffee out to the deck where the sun was streaming down. She found it utterly calming, feeling the warmth touch her head. "*Thank you, dear Lord*," she prayed. "*Thank you for taking care of all the details and for this beautiful place.*" It was different from the ocean, and she knew she would miss the salt water, but this was a new kind of adventure and it excited her to think of it. New place, new people; she wondered about this move for so long and now she was here. "I'm proud of you, Anna," she told herself. It was one of the things Jillian had taught her—be good to yourself. She remembered Jill saying, "The world will beat you up if you let it. Talk to yourself kindly, Anna." She could almost feel Jillian's presence. *She would love this place,* Anna thought. Her musings were quickly interrupted by a little boy who sleepily walked through the patio door dragging a blanket.

"Good morning, sweetheart," Anna said as she lifted him onto her lap and wrapped him in the blanket. He snuggled into her shoulder, and she smoothed the hair from his eyes. "You're still a tired little guy, aren't you?" She hugged him and rocked back and forth. They sat together while the morning sun dried the dew from the grass. Soon the rumble in their stomachs prompted Anna to move from their comfort and start the day. Justin followed behind clinging to his blanket. After filling his tummy with cereal, she kissed him on the head and turned the TV on while she took a closer inventory of their surroundings. She checked all cupboards and cabinets, closets, nooks, and crannies in the house. She found an old checker board, a rain slicker, a photo album, and a few other miscellaneous things. Most of the cabin closets were empty save for some cleaning supplies. Anna began to unpack their luggage and place their clothes in the empty drawers in the bedroom when she heard a knock at the door. She looked at a clock that hung on the bedroom wall. It was ten o'clock. She tripped over the empty suitcase and banged her knee on the dresser.

"Ouch!" She uttered out loud as she crippled from the bedroom. Justin came and clung to her leg, and she dragged him along to the door. Upon opening, she was greeted by a plump short older woman in an apron holding a dish with hot pads. Her round face was lit up with a grin as beads of sweat dripped from beneath her gray curls.

"Hello!" she said with enthusiasm. "My name is Mary Hutchinson. I'm your new neighbor. I brought you a breakfast casserole."

Anna lifted Justin into her arms and moved aside while Mary bustled to the kitchen to place the dish on the stove. "Oh thank you. I'm Anna. This is my son, Justin." She smiled.

"I've heard all about you, little guy! My husband, Paul, was right; he's a sweet little fella. Well, I hope you both are hungry. I brought a favorite recipe. It has eggs, cheese, bacon…well, I'm not going to give it all away…you'll have to try it yourself." She clasped her hands together. "I'm just so tickled to have you both here! You know, this cabin hasn't been used much lately. It just seems so lonesome over here. Kids don't come 'round here much anymore," she said sadly. "Well, I'm glad you're here!"

"I can't imagine why the Millers don't use this place. It's a beautiful spot," Anna agreed.

"Well, dear, you know, since Dr. Miller's caught ill, well that's part of it but you know they have a big ole mansion on the lake. What do they need this place for, I guess," she said wiping her sweaty brow with her hot pads.

"They live on the lake? I assumed they only had this cabin?"

"Oh no, dear, since Dr. Miller Sr. became a big dentist in the area, you know, *everyone* goes to him. Well they have money. This is a cottage that's been in the family for years. I think they just hang onto it for nostalgic reasons. They don't come around here much anymore. They own a property way down the other side—you know a big ole place. I'm so glad Tom came back. You know I don't know what we'd do without a dentist out here. We'd have to travel forever to find one," Mary said as she placed her hand on her cheek. "Well, you'll stay here for a while, no?"

"Well, I'm not sure how long I'll be here. I thought I would stay until I find an apartment or maybe they'll let me rent it indefinitely?" Anna questioned more to herself than Mary.

"Well, I should say so! No reason for this place to sit empty when it can be filled with love." She looked adoringly at Justin. "So tell me, little guy, what you think of Minnesota?"

Justin smiled at the older woman and then hid behind his mother.

"Well, I didn't mean to scare you with my bustling about." She knelt down next to Anna and played peek-a-boo with Justin.

Justin came around and gave Mary a hug. She instantly wrapped her plump arms around him and ruffled his curly blond locks.

Anna was surprised. "He never does that. He's usually very shy."

"Well, dear, he knows a good thing when he sees it." She winked. "Ah, I've had years of practice. My kids are all grown and gone, and now I have three grandchildren. Unfortunately they've all moved away, you know, jobs and such. I don't see them like I used to. Of course Paul knows I'd like to have them every day. It's hard for me. I was a teacher for thirty years. Retirement is not what it's cracked up to be. It gets lonely, you know, when all your husband wants to do is fish."

"How long have you lived here?" Anna asked with curiosity.

"Oh, I've lived here all my life. These used to be all summer cabins 'round this lake. We all used to come here as kids for vacation. When our parents left us these places most of us came back and built a life for ourselves. You know, the best days of our life were growing up here, eh."

"Yes. I would imagine," Anna answered wistfully.

"Well, dear, I must get back home. I have another casserole in the warming oven. I'm sure my husband is going mad waiting for me. Hey, I just thought of something. I have an old stroller left from the grandkids if you'd like to borrow it and take your little fella here for a walk. There's a nice park down the lane with swings and such."

"Oh, that would be wonderful. The moving truck isn't supposed to arrive until tomorrow."

"Well, you just come over when you're ready; second house on the left." She rustled Justin's curls before heading out the door. "We'll see you later."

Anna lifted Justin to her hip and waved good-bye. "Isn't she nice, Justin?"

"Yeah! Yeah!" he replied as he ran back toward the TV and the cartoons.

Anna took a spoonful of the delicious casserole. She picked out the bacon and handed a dish to Justin who devoured it within minutes. She wrapped the remaining casserole and went back to unpacking. After she finished her chores and Justin was washed and dressed, they headed out to the Hutchinson's to retrieve the stroller. The idea of exploring her new surroundings excited her. She couldn't wait until the moving truck would arrive with her car.

Paul was working in the yard as the two approached. "There she is, and she brought the little nipper with her too! How ya doin' today der', Anna?"

"Great, thank you." She smiled. "Mary mentioned a stroller we could borrow?"

"Ah, let me see now where dat would be? Hum?" He rubbed his hands along his unshaven gray shadow. "Oh yes, I think der' it's over here." Paul led the two to retrieve the stroller and dusted it off with an old towel that hung in the shed. "Well, it's a bit rickety, but I think it'll do the job, eh?"

"Yes, it will do just fine. Thank you so much. Justin is getting too big for me to carry these days." Anna said as she patted the top of her son's head.

"You keep it as long as ya like. Grandkids won't be here anyway," he said as he grabbed his branch trimmer and went back to work. "Oh and ,Anna, the park is down there off Cherry Lane, eh.'"

"Thanks!" The two waved good-bye and headed off for their walk. Anna breathed the scent of tall pines that crowded the dense woods alongside the road. The aroma reminded her of Christmas. Justin banged and kicked his legs back and forth as the stroller pushed forward. They walked until they found Cherry Lane. The road opened up to a large grass clearing overlooking the lake. Picnic tables and fire pits stood on one side of the park with a play area for children on the other. A closed beach area sat idle, awaiting summer fun. Justin began to pull and tug to get out of the seat. Anna set him loose, and he ran toward the swings. It was a quiet day. Anna had hoped to see kids and parents, but she realized after all, it was a workday. She pushed Justin on the swings until he tired out. Aware that it was his nap time she still wanted to explore. He willingly got back into the stroller and they ambled back down the street. A convenience store on the corner had a sign that said closed until Memorial Day. She noticed a paved cyclist nature trail, and the quiet and smell of the woods enticed her forward. Not long on the peaceful trail she heard a rustle in the trees.

"Oh my!" Anna uttered aloud. Every cell in her body tensed at the stark realization they were in danger. Behind the tree, too close for comfort, stood a small black bear. She looked down at Justin who also caught a glimpse of the bear. Not being fond of dogs, he let out a piercing scream. Anna stood paralyzed with her arms wrapped around the stroller holding Justin's shoulders. *How could I be so dumb as to put us in harm's way?* she chided herself as her heart pounded in her chest and the hair rose on her neck. Suddenly the bear turned and ran off into the dense woods. Trembling Anna slowly turned the stroller around and quickly walked home. It wasn't until she was in the driveway that she released her fear and started to cry.

Justin looked up at her and asked, "Mama, what wrong?" He reached his chubby finger to touch her.

"Mama is okay, Justin. You have to stay close to Mama. Don't go walking off by yourself *ever*, you hear?" She lifted him from the seat and held him tight. As she entered the safety of the cabin, Anna put her son down for a nap and lay down in the bed next to him. Overwhelmed from the bear experience, she cried herself to sleep.

The sound of the cell phone woke her with a start. She was still jumpy after her afternoon encounter. "Hello?" she answered, walking into the kitchen.

"Hey, Anna. It's Dr. Miller. I wanted to check on you and see how you're adjusting to the cabin?"

"Oh, hi, thanks for calling. The cabin is adorable. Your friends Paul and Mary have been wonderful. Thank you for the groceries and, well…everything!"

"No problem, Anna. It's a big move; I know. I'm still unpacking. I'm thinking maybe I can give you a tour of the office on Friday. Will that work for you?"

"Yes, that sounds great."

"Okay, I'll give you a call concerning the time. See you then."

"Bye."

Anna was glad the conversation was short. She didn't want to admit to Dr. Miller how naive she had been on the trail. She massaged her temples to reduce the headache that threatened as she rustled through the cupboard to find something for dinner. While she did so, she heard a knock at the door. She was greeted by a man holding a bouquet of blue and pink hydrangeas.

"Delivery for Anna Gallo?"

"Thanks," she said with a weak smile. She set the flowers and the pretty blue vase on the kitchen table and hurriedly opened the card, which read:

> Just wanted to send you a piece of New England in case they don't have these in Minnesota.
> Love ya,
> xoxo Holly

Anna sat in the kitchen chair and wept. Her brave facade melted like an ice cream cone on a hot summer day. "Oh, Lord, I'm scared. I know you have done so much for me, but I feel like the world is on my shoulders. Justin depends on me and only me. Please help me protect him and give me the strength to stay strong. I miss all that I know," she whispered as she glanced at the beautiful bouquet.

CHAPTER 14

The moving truck arrived early. Boxes and furniture were being coordinated and filling the floor of the cabin. Extra furniture was put in the basement until Anna could determine how to rearrange the space. She was having a hard time keeping track of Justin with all of the commotion. Anna found him hiding behind a box on the bedroom floor playing with a toy.

"There you are!" She leaned down and gave him a cup of juice.

"Mama, we throw rocks?" he asked in between sips.

"That's a good idea, Justin. I think we are in the way here." Anna reached for him and lifted him over the box. The two worked through the maze and meandered to the edge of the lake. She watched as he threw the rocks in the water and giggled with glee as the splash wet his pants. It was a beautiful day, and Anna reveled in it. The sun left glittering diamond specks upon the water. In the distance, fishing boats trolled the lake seeking the perfect spot. One came especially close, and Anna looked to see Paul pulling up to the dock. Justin dropped the rocks and ran down the wooden pier. Anna grabbed his hand as she waved to Paul.

"Hey der', little nipper," Paul greeted as Justin jumped up and down excitedly on the end of the pier.

"How are you this morning, Mr. Hutchinson?" Anna smiled as Paul held up a large fish.

"Well, today's the first day of fishin' season, so I couldn't be better! I see your stuff has arrived der', eh?"

"Yes, I'm just trying to keep out of the way at this point. I'm excited to get my car so I can run some errands. Nice fish by the way!" Anna shaded her eyes with her hand.

"Oh it's a beautiful day on the lake. You two want to go for a little ride? I have some life jackets just waiting for you to fill 'em."

With slight hesitation, Anna agreed and the two boarded the sixteen-foot fishing boat. She held Justin on her lap as they trolled around the lake. The wind whipped through her hair, and Anna felt an immediate rush of freedom. Paul pointed out great fishing spots on the lake and an inlet where loons nested and fed their young. He took them to see a huge pine that held an enormous eagle's nest. A great bald eagle stood stoic on a branch protecting its young. The lake was much larger than she expected. The south side displayed properties with large expensive homesteads. Paul pointed out Dr. Miller Sr.'s home, a large auspicious building nestled on a peninsula and set back from the shore. Anna noted the entire front was covered in glass.

"What a view they have!" she commented as Paul slowed the engine.

"Ah, yep, she's a beauty," he said, as he throttled the motor for fear he'd disturb the owners privacy.

Paul gave Anna a tour of the entire lake. She was grateful for the new perspective of her surroundings. When they arrived back, Paul invited her and Justin to dinner, and she graciously accepted. She walked into the cabin to find the boxes unpacked from the truck and she was left with a sea of disarray. She found a box of Justin's toys and busied him so that she could begin organizing. The day moved swiftly, and as Anna looked around, it seemed like she had hardly made a dent. She breathed a weary sigh, left the work behind, and headed for the Hutchinsons' for dinner. Relieved that she didn't have to cook after a long day, she uttered a prayer of thanks for her new neighbors. Mary greeted them enthusiastically as she wiped her hands on her apron.

"I've made pasta. Will your little fella like that?" she asked kindly.

"Oh yes, it's one of his favorites. His father is Italian. I think the love of Italian food runs in the blood." Anna chuckled.

The four sat around a large round table in the kitchen. Paul and Mary's home was decorated in country motif with dark quilts displayed on the walls. The kitchen was clean but well worn with dark, outdated cupboards and black appliances. Justin interrupted Anna's mental exploration by banging the silverware on his plate.

"Justin! No! That is not good manners." Anna took the silverware away, and he sat back in the chair, a pout on his cherubic face.

"Oh he's fine, Anna. Don't worry yourself. We know all about little ones, don't we Paul?" Mary winked at her husband. "So are you all packed in?"

"Like a sardine." Anna laughed. "I really didn't think we had that much. It will take me awhile tomorrow, but hopefully I will be all finished. I have to take a tour of the office with Dr. Miller on Friday. I'd like to be settled before I start work next week."

"What are ya goin' to do with the little nipper here?" Paul questioned as he reached over to put pasta on Justin's plate.

"I don't know yet," Anna replied softly. "Now that my car is here, I thought I'd look into some day care centers in the area." She rubbed her brow in concentration.

"Anna, I can watch him while you are at work if you'd like, at least and until you find a sitter for him," Mary suggested. "Now that fishing season has started, I won't see my husband for a few months, and I get lonely. Plus I could use a little extra spending money. There is a new hutch I've been eying at the furniture store, and well…Paul thinks we don't need it."

Paul cleared his throat. "I'm right here, Mary. I can hear you!"

The three laughed in unison while Justin looked at them perplexed.

"Really? You would consider taking care of my son?"

"Oh, I would love it." She looked over at Justin. "We'd have a great time together. Just as long as you can bring him here for me to watch; that way I can still do some housework while he's napping and such. I know I'm a stranger to you, Anna, but I have references from my teaching days and you can contact Dr. Miller Sr. to verify if you like. I know how hard all this must be for you, a big move and all." She leaned over and touched Anna gently on the arm.

"You both have been so gracious." Anna looked at her new neighbors with sincerity. "The thing I fear most is your ability to keep up with him." Anna relayed the encounter of the bear in the woods to her new friends and how scared she had been.

Paul interjected. "Yer' lucky the bear ran off, eh. They say the best thing to do in dat' situation is ta' play dead." He wrinkled his brow. "I don't know how many people could do dat' though," he said with a shake of his head. "I'd carry bear spray if I was you."

"Oh you poor dear," Mary empathized. "You must have been terrified." She took Anna's hand. "I know my limitations, Anna, and I wouldn't offer if I didn't think I was capable of taking care of your little one. I may be retired, but I have a lot of energy. Just wait until you see my garden this summer. I would love to have Justin help me work on it. Take the next few days to think about it, and if you find a nice day care nearby, I won't be hurt. I know you want the best for your child. You may be young but I see what a great mother you are."

Anna blushed at the compliment. "Thank you. With the help of God, I try my best."

Mary smiled and squeezed her hand.

Paul added his opinion. "You'd be doing us both a favor, eh. Justin would keep Mary from giving me grief 'bout fishing, and he would fill her empty nest at the same time. You need never worry about your boy when Mary's around."

Mary leaned in and kissed her husband on the cheek.

The conversation continued fluidly around the table with stories of Paul and Mary growing up at Eagle Lake. They had gone to school together and their families were intertwined. They talked of their kids growing up, the three precious grandchildren and how blessed they were. Anna shared a little of her past; life growing up in New England and her hopes and dreams for her future for Justin. All in all, it was nice to get to know her good neighbors, and Anna felt the beginnings of a sense of belonging in her new home.

CHAPTER 15

A routine formed as Mary cared for Justin while Anna worked at the dental office. Although it was a new office, she found stability in working with Dr. Miller and doing a job she knew well. Anna enjoyed meeting new patients and learned a great deal about the community where she lived as she seated each one before their procedure. Most of the patients had been townies all of their lives. She learned there were many popular activities in the area. In the summer fishing, waterskiing, and boating activities were among the popular. In the winter Cross-country skiing, snow shoeing, and snow mobile races were prevalent. As days turned into weeks, weeks into months, Minnesota started to feel like home.

Before Anna knew it, she was preparing to travel back to Maine for her sister's wedding. Holly had called two days previous and assured her that Mom and Dad would be at the airport to pick her and Justin up. It was her last day of work before leaving, and as she pulled into the driveway, the anticipation tugged her heart. She was excited to see her family and show them how much Justin had grown. After parking the car in the driveway she walked over to the Hutchinsons' to pick up Justin.

She smiled as she watched Paul leaned over her son as the two pondered a worm that lay in Justin's hand. They were knee deep in the garden pulling weeds and gently putting the worms back in their "home."

"Mama!" Justin squealed with delight as he dropped the creature and ran to her.

"Oh my sweet! I missed you today!" She covered him in kisses.

"We got 'matoes!" he said as he ran toward the tomato cages to show her the shiny green un-ripened fruit that hung from the vine.

"Wow! Beautiful!" Anna met his enthusiasm and reached out to touch one.

"No, Mama!" Justin said sternly. "No pick yet, not ready!" He looked at her with a furrowed brow.

"Oh sweetheart, I know they are not ready for picking. I was just admiring your work." She smiled at Paul who winked at her.

"You have dis'." Justin ran toward a basket filled with radishes. He rubbed the dirt on his pants and handed it to Anna. "Eat it, Mama!"

Anna looked at Paul who nodded in agreement. She was not a fan of the radish. The bitter taste made her face pucker. Paul laughed as she choked a piece down.

"You try it, Justin," she encouraged him.

"No, no, me no like." He shook his head vigorously as he picked up the basket and trotted toward the house. "I bring to Nana Mary," he said over his shoulder as he left them shaking their heads.

"Not a fan of the radish, huh, kiddo?" Paul chuckled as he laid a hand on Anna's shoulder.

"What we do for our children!" She laughed. "Thank you for teaching him about vegetables, Paul. At least he will try things he never would before."

"Ah yes, the little nipper tasted all kinds of things. It's a funny thing, if you grow it yer' more likely to give it a try, eh?" Paul rubbed his chest, and his brow furrowed.

"You all right?" Anna asked as she watched her neighbors face grimace.

"Ah, I'm fine kid, just a little indigestion. Don't be sayin' anything to the wife der'. She'll be after me to go back to the doc, taking time away from my fishin'," he warned with a weak smile.

Anna was about to respond but kept quiet as Mary and Justin came out of the house hand in hand. Mary held a Ziploc bag with homemade cookies in the other hand, and she handed it to Anna. "Here's a little something for him on the plane."

"You spoil him, Mary!" Anna grinned as she gave her a hug.

"I'm going to miss the little tyke," Mary whispered in her ear.

Anna nodded in agreement. After the wedding Justin would be spending a month with his Father as the court had determined. She had to banish the thought from her mind. Leaving him in Maine for a month was too much for her to digest, and she wasn't sure how she would handle it. Anna inhaled deeply and took Justin by the hand.

"We must get home and finish packing. We have an early morning flight. I'll see you both in a week or so. Thanks for everything."

Paul and Mary stood at the edge of the driveway and waved as Anna and Justin walked toward home.

Anna could not rid herself of the foreboding feeling that washed over her. She looked down at her son who turned his face to her and smiled. Anna tossed her negative feelings aside and squeezed Justin's hand tighter. He released her grip and ran toward the cabin door. She watched his strawberry blond curls bounce up and down as his little legs gained speed. Once inside, Anna put a frozen pizza in the oven and then sat down at the kitchen table to write a list of Justin's routine for Mike; his favorite foods, his nap time, what medicines he took when he had a cold and any other thought that crossed her mind. She folded the paper and neatly tucked it into an envelope. Anna glanced at her son who had plopped himself in front of his plastic trucks that lay on the floor. He banged them together and crashed them into a tower of plastic blocks.

"*How am I going to let him go?*" A wave of concern washed over her as the innocence of her young boy tugged at her heart. She lifted herself from the chair and placed the envelope in the open suitcase that lay haphazardly on the bed in their bedroom. "God be with him while he is away from me…"

After his clothes were neatly folded in, she zipped the finished bags and rolled them out to the mudroom. The two ate their pizza as

Anna heard all about the gardening Justin had worked on that day. Ready for tomorrow's adventure, Anna tucked her son in, kissed his forehead, and crawled into the twin bed beside him. She closed her eyes and prayed for protection on their trip the following day, thanked God for his strength and faithfulness until sleep over took her.

———•◦•———

The following day, Anna and Justin descended the plane into the arms of her parents. Donald and Sarah Bertram were all smiles as they greeted their daughter and grandson.

"Oh how you've grown," Sarah said as she kneeled to take a closer look at Justin. He smiled and shyly hooked onto his mother's leg. Sarah pulled a toy from a bag and handed it to the toddler. He willingly took the truck with both hands and sat on the floor to give it a push.

"Come on, Justin. We need to pick up our luggage." Anna tried to pull him from the floor.

He shrugged her off and continued to play with the truck. He did not listen, so absorbed was he with his new toy.

"Justin Michael!" Anna said firmly. "Get up!" She felt her temples pulsate as she rubbed them with her fingers.

His crystal blue eyes turned to stone as he looked up at his mother and continued to play.

"I hope he won't behave like this at Holly's wedding?" Sarah frowned.

"I don't know, Mom. I never know what mood he'll be in." This was not the reunion Anna had pictured in her mind.

"Mom and I will grab the bags and get the car. We'll pick you two up outside that door." Donald pointed to a door outside the airport terminal."

"Okay, Dad. Mine are the blue bags with pink ribbon." Anna agreed, as she gave Justin a stern look. He turned his head to ignore her.

She pulled Mary's cookies from her purse. "Justin, look… See that bench? We are going outside to sit there and wait for Grandma and Grandpa. When we get there, I will give you one of these," Anna bargained.

"No! Me want now!"

Anna pulled him up from the floor, truck in hand, and practically dragged him outside to the bench. Justin tried desperately to let go her grasp.

"Now you listen to me," she said firmly. "You will behave!" Anna felt her patience wearing thin. With fists clenched she prayed. "God send me your grace, like now!"

Justin sat on the bench and pouted as he reached out for a cookie. She handed him one. He grinned with satisfaction knowing he'd won the battle. Anna sat back in frustration and waited for her parents to arrive. They loaded into the car and headed to the freeway. Anna breathed sigh of relief thankful they were on their way.

"I can't wait for you to see Holly and Chris's new house," Sarah commented from the front seat. "Holly moved in last week, and Chris will move in after they get back from their honeymoon. It's small but adorable."

"Yeah, she told me about it when we talked on the phone. Are we all going to be able to stay there this week?" Anna questioned.

"Your father and I used the pull out couch last night when we arrived. We figured you and Justin could take the other bedroom. There's a twin bed in there along with a blow-up mattress. You'll have to draw straws." She chuckled.

"I'll take the blow up. That's fine. I'm sure Justin will fall asleep before me anyway. It sounds like we have a busy week before the wedding on Saturday."

"Yes, dear, we do. Tonight we have the pre-wedding party for the girls. We are putting center pieces together. Dad can take care of Justin; right, Don?" Sarah looked over at her husband who nodded his head in agreement.

"You'll need our prayers." Anna chuckled as she regarded her son who now had cookie crumbs dangling from the side of his mouth. He sat utterly pleased with himself, which made Anna all the more frustrated with his antics.

The four pulled in front of a tan bungalow with dark brown trim. The front steps led to a glass enclosed porch where Holly waited expectantly and ran down the steps and into the arms of her sister as soon as the car came to a halt.

"You're here! Oh, I can't believe you're here!" Holly pulled her sister away to get a better look at her. She then reached into the car and retrieved Justin from his car seat. "How's my little nephew?" She covered him in kisses and swung him around. "My goodness, you're getting heavy!" She put him down beside her and rubbed the top of his head.

Justin took flight toward the steps and into the house. Holly's eyes followed him as he ran. "He's so big, Anna. I can't believe how he's grown!" She tucked a dark curl that fell from her ponytail behind her ear.

"Yeah, and he's a handful today," she answered. "I hope he calms down before Saturday."

"He'll be just fine." Holly wrapped her arm around her sister and led her into the front porch where she almost tripped over an empty paint can. "Oops. We've been working hard to get the place painted before Chris moves in. Watch your step!" Holly kicked the empty can out of her way.

The two walked arm and arm followed by her parents into a narrow hallway that led to the kitchen. Justin had discovered a tabby cat and sat beside it on the floor holding it tightly on his lap.

"You found Snickers. Don't squeeze too tight," Holly cautioned. She leaned down and petted her cat protectively. Justin released his grip and the cat jumped off his lap and skittered out of sight.

"Juice! Juice!" Justin whined as he pulled on his mother's leg.

"Sis, you have anything for him to drink?" Anna asked.

Holly reached into the refrigerator and pulled out chocolate milk. She handed Justin a cup, which was a mistake, as most of the milk landed on his shirt.

"Holly, what room will Justin and I be using? I'd like to get him a clean shirt and unpack." Anna's energy waned along with her patience.

"Sure, come on." Holly led the two down a narrow hallway. The entire home was painted pure white. The original wooden floors creaked as they entered a small bedroom. "There is a bathroom across the hall." Anna's sister pointed to a door decorated with a cranberry wreath and led them to it. Anna removed Justin's chocolate milk stained T-shirt as she followed Holly into the small bathroom. A claw foot tub surrounded by a cranberry-colored shower curtain occupied most of the room. White octagon floor tiles were met by a tweed mat that Holly confided, "Covered a crack in the tile that needed to be fixed." She then led them to another door and entered the master bedroom which was not much larger than the bedroom she and Justin were sharing. It barely fit the queen-size bed. Despite the size, the home was cozy and clean, a perfect starter home for the newlyweds.

"It's very cute, Holly," Anna said affectionately.

"It's not a castle, but it's fun," Holly agreed. "No more apartment walls. We can decorate it the way we wish. And Chris is so handy, ya know? He already has plans to build a deck out back. We have our own yard, Anna—a yard! Can you believe it?" She placed her hand upon her hip. "You two get settled in. Let me know if you need anything." She leaned down and kissed Justin on his cheek then rushed off.

The family sat at the kitchen table catching up on each other's lives and going over the wedding plans for the week. There were so many details: flowers, the cake, the wedding attire. It would be a busy week indeed. Anna looked around the table at the people she loved. Her life was so different now. Her family was spread over the country, and the closeness they once felt seemed like a distant memory. She wanted to share every detail of the cabin in Minnesota and her new life, but she sensed a minor disconnect.

"Would you all consider a Minnesota Christmas?" Anna suggested.

"What a great idea!" Anna's mother agreed. "We would love to see where you live, the pictures you sent are nice but I'm sure they don't do the place justice."

"I'll ask Chris if we can come too." Holly nodded her head in agreement.

"Maybe we can cut our own tree this year," Donald suggested.

"Yeah, an old-fashioned country Christmas; sounds like fun!" Anna was excited at the thought of sharing a holiday with her family. Maybe they would regain the intimacy she felt slipping away.

After cleaning the remnants of sandwiches, which the family shared the five dispersed. Anna's parents went to buy candles while Holly discussed details over the telephone. Anna put Justin for a nap and chose an outfit to wear for the evening with the girls.

Anna pulled her golden hair back with a barrette. She curled a few strands to frame her face and then applied blush and rubbed her lips with Chap Stick. "That should do it," she said aloud as she looked away from her reflection, pleased. Holly met her in the hallway carrying a basket of clean clothes balanced on her hip.

"The girls should be comin' any second. Oh…I forgot to tell you. I ran into Jessica at the mall. She asked how you were doing, so I invited her here tonight. I figured you haven't seen her in ages and you'd like to catch up."

Anna thought of her high school sidekick. Life had changed so much for both of them since graduation. She wasn't sure if she was excited or nervous as she remembered back to her pregnancy test in the bathroom. "Thanks, Holly. It will be nice to see her," she answered with hesitation.

Holly, preoccupied with the impending events of the evening, continued to her room to get ready. Anna watched her sister walk away. So much had changed in so little time. It had been months since she had been with girls her own age and she was like a fish out of water. She was a Mother now. Justin depended on her. She didn't feel she fit in with the college-age girls that were coming. *Where did she fit? What did she have in common with any of them?*

Her father and Justin approached, jarring her back.

"I'm going to take the little lad for ice cream while you girls do your thing." Justin sat comfortably in her dad's arms with his little arms wrapped around his neck. Donald leaned over and gave her a kiss on the cheek. "You look beautiful, little girl," he admired. "All grown up now."

Anna smiled at her father and rubbed Justin's cheek. "Thanks, Dad."

Sarah rounded the corner and rushed Donald and Justin out the door. "The guests are arriving Don; time for you to get going," she demanded.

"Easy there, Sarah. We're going already," he answered with a shake of his head.

Giggles and chatter filled the living room as the girls arrived. Holly's friends from high school and college, and a few from work soon consumed the small space. Claustrophobia clutched Anna so she moved into the kitchen. A stylish girl wearing a fitted white T-shirt draped with a soft leopard scarf floated toward her. Anna noted her designer jeans perfectly hugged her hips and legs. She watched the girl gracefully toss her red silken hair over her shoulder.

"Anna!" The girl squealed.

"Jessica?" she questioned as she looked into hazel eyes enhanced with deep shadow.

"Yeah, it's me, you goof." Jessica wrapped her arms around her old friend.

"You look so different," Anna said. She detected the scent of sweet jasmine as they embraced.

"We're not kids anymore; it's not like high school. Ugh, I cringe when I see those old pictures. It's amazing what a few beauty products will do." She ran her fingers through her silken hair.

"It's not that…you just look so…well, put together! I remember us in sweatshirts and torn up sweatpants. Maybe I would have recognized you in that," Anna added with a laugh.

"I'm finishing my degree in fashion design." She lifted her shoe to show Anna the newly designed three-inch heels. "I'm almost finished, and I think I may have an internship in the fall in New York. I'm so excited!" She beamed.

"That's great, Jess." Anna looked down at her outdated denim shirt embarrassed. Fashion was the last thing on her mind. As a matter of fact having a shirt without chocolate or food of some sort smeared on it was a rare occasion.

"Oh…and I met this great guy. Anna, he's dreamy. He's studying architecture. I'm trying to convince him to come with me to New York. It would be great for his career. How about you? Are you seeing anyone?" Jessica inquired as she tugged on her gold hoop earring.

"No, I'm pretty busy, and it just wouldn't feel right."

"What do ya mean? Mike had no problem moving on," she quipped sarcastically.

Anna's face flushed. "What do you mean?"

"Oh boy! Did I step over the line? I'm sorry; I thought you knew." Jessica covered her mouth with her hand.

"Knew what?" Anna could feel anger rise in her chest.

"Mike's been seeing someone for almost a year now. Haven't you heard? He's taking over his dad's insurance business soon. You know he graduated right? It sounds pretty serious. I heard he bought her a ring. I'm sorry, Anna. I thought you knew about all this?"

Anna felt as if her face had been slapped. She shook her head "No, I didn't know any of this."

"Everyone gather around!" Anna and Jessica looked to see Holly laying trash bags on the living room floor. Holly pointed her manicured finger to the items that were placed on the bags. "We have sand in this bucket and a bowl of glitter. We're going to mix the two together and place them in these glass candle holders and add a white candle." Holly demonstrated the centerpiece. After many oohs and awws, she proceeded to another demonstration. "For favors we are going to put these mints in white tulle fabric and tie it in bows with these violet satin ribbons," she said as she popped a mint into her mouth. "Thanks, everyone, for the help. I'll be in the kitchen getting snacks ready; we eat when the work is completed," she teased.

As Holly walked by Anna, she nudged her toward the group. "Go mingle!"

"I can help you in the kitchen if you need," Anna suggested.

"Go have fun with the girls. I know you don't get to do this kind of thing often," her sister encouraged.

Anna begrudgingly walked into the living room and stood near her mother.

"You okay, honey? You look a little pale?" Sarah intoned.

"Yeah, Mom, I'm okay. We'll talk about it later." She sighed.

The group joined forces, and before the evening ended, they'd made a box of ten candle centerpieces and fifty wedding favors all packed and ready for the event. Anna did her best to put a smile on her face through it all. The more she was around the young giddy group, the more disconnected she felt. She loved her sister, and they had always been close. The move and changes in her life had put a chasm between her and the ones she loved the most. It seemed they were leading different lives now and the everyday details were missed. It was as if their roads crossed for a brief time and now they were heading in separate directions. Desperate to find a footing she decided to call Jillian before bed.

"Hey, Jill, how are you?"

"Anna, it's so good to hear your voice! How's Minnesota treating you?"

"Actually, Jill, I have a surprise. I'm home this week for my sister's wedding. I was hoping Justin, and I could meet you for lunch tomorrow. You won't believe how big he has gotten!"

"Tomorrow? Oh shoot, I wish you told me you were coming. I completely forgot about your Sister's wedding date. I have a meeting tomorrow. It's a full day and I can't possibly get away. How about later in the week?"

"No, later in the week won't work for me. That's why I didn't make plans with you before I arrived. I'm really on Holly's schedule. She needs a lot of help with the wedding, you know how that is."

"I totally understand. I'm disappointed we won't see each other. You'll be back this way again, I'm sure. We'll catch up then. Well, I don't want to keep you from your family, honey. Have a good visit with them and enjoy yourself. I miss you, Anna, and that little darlin' too. How is the little tyke?"

"He's growing leaps and bounds and getting fresher by the day. I miss you too," she answered sadly as she hung up the phone.

Anna walked quietly into the darkened bedroom.

"Mama?" Justin questioned groggily as he lay strewn across the twin bed.

"Yes, baby, I'm here." She sat on the edge of his bed and covered him with a blanket.

"Grandpa didn't read me 'tory," he mumbled.

Anna turned on a bedside lamp, reached into a bag, and brought out his favorite book. She read her son a story as he cuddled next to her. "I love you, Justin," she said as she kissed his forehead and prayed over him.

"Love, Mama," he replied as he rolled over and fell fast asleep.

Anna lay on the bed next to her son, tired but stimulated from the evening's activities. Her mind darted back and forth as she recalled the lightheartedness of Holly's friends. She lay there for what seemed like hours until sleep finally came.

The following morning, Holly and Sarah were cleaning up the breakfast dishes as Anna brought her son into the kitchen. Justin reached for Snickers who skirted down the hall toward the bedrooms with the giggling toddler in pursuit.

"Would you like to go for a walk with me?" Anna's mother suggested. "Holly will look after Justin while we're gone, won't you, Holly?"

"Yeah, you two go," Holly agreed as she wiped her hands on the dishtowel. "I'd like to spend a few minutes with my nephew this week and this would be the perfect time."

Anna went back to the bedroom and told Justin where she was going.

"Me go too, Mama?"

"No, sweetheart. Auntie wants to play with you, okay?"

"Okay, Mama. I stay with Auntie." He smiled with satisfaction.

She changed into shorts and tied her tennis shoes. The air was hot and humid as she and her mom walked out into the summer day.

"Are you all right, dear? You looked ill last night," Sarah asked with concern.

Anna inhaled deeply. "Physically I'm fine. I'm just out of sorts I guess." Anna swiped her hair from her brow.

"What's wrong?" Sarah pressed.

"I feel like I don't fit anywhere," Anna stated. "All those girls are so different from me. They all have these big plans. Jessica is going to New York to work on her career in fashion. I'm not like that. You know what I dreamed? I wanted a family. That's all I ever wanted— to raise kids. And now I have half a family. Mine is broken." Tears formed in Anna's eyes.

Sarah threw an arm around her daughter's shoulders. "Oh sweetheart, I know your rush to motherhood has been difficult. You were thrust into responsibility while you were a child yourself. You didn't even get a chance to know what you wanted." Sarah stopped on the sidewalk to face her daughter and wiped her wet cheeks with a gentle hand.

"But I do know, Mom. That's just the thing. I want a family that's not broken, and I can't have it. That's not all. Do you know what Jessica told me last night? Justin's father has found another woman, and he's bought her a ring. I think he's engaged, Mom, or going to be soon. Where does that leave Justin and me?" Anna said as she wiped the tears that fell.

"I didn't know, sweetheart. I'm so sorry. How does that make you feel?"

"Mad, sad, hurt, jealous, I don't know how to feel? I hurt for my son who deserves to have a father. When Holly's wedding is over, I have to let him go for a month to a virtual stranger. It kills me inside. I feel like I'm going to break in two. It's just not fair— for me, for Justin, for anyone. Mom, how do I explain to my toddler that I'm not coming with him? That I'm dropping him off. He doesn't understand the concept of time, or when he'll see me again. It's cruel! Justin is going to feel abandoned, and there's not a thing I can do about it." She sobbed.

Sarah wrapped her arms around her daughter as she wept. "I wish I could take all this pain away from you."

"Being a mother myself, I understand what you mean. I wish I could take away every pain that Justin will ever have." Anna hiccupped.

"Ah the joys of motherhood." Sarah sighed as the two chuckled. "Anna, you can't take on all of this. Justin will be okay. Mike is his father and he loves his son. You must give them a chance to build a relationship too." Sara said tentatively. "It really isn't Mike's fault that your job took you away from Maine. I know this may be hard for you to hear. I'm not trying to take sides, you are working so hard. I'm trying to be objective in what is best for Justin. And the truth is a relationship between father and son is important. You are in a tough situation. I never would have wanted this for you."

Anna broke away from her mother. "I know you're right... It's the letting go, and he's so little, Mom. I want him to be safe and secure, and you know how I hate good-byes."

"I know it's hard, but you can't protect your child from life. Do you know how hard it was for me to see you so young and pregnant? I was worried for you because of exactly what you are going through right now. Being a parent has a lot of joy, but it can be tough too." Sarah inhaled deeply as she gently touched Anna's shoulder. "We have a wedding to prepare for. Let's see if we can put a smile on for Holly."

"Yeah, you're right. I'm not going to do or say anything to ruin her special time. I just needed to vent. Thanks for listening."

"Someday you'll be doing this for Justin," she winked. "It's what mothers *do*."

By the time they arrived home their shirts clung to their bodies from the humid sticky air. Justin and Holly played in the backyard with a big multicolored rubber ball. He ran to his mother as they approached. Anna wrapped him in her sweaty arms and swung him around and as she did she noticed the sky had darkened. A storm was definitely brewing.

"I think the heat is going to break. Look at those clouds." She pointed to the threatening sky.

A loud clap of thunder followed by rain bore down on them. They ran for the safety to the little brown bungalow and spent the day working on wedding details while the rain pounded upon the roof. Anna determinedly put her worries aside and enjoyed the time with her family. When the storm receded they drove to the bridal shop for their final fitting. Donald and Justin tried on their tux's first. Anna could not believe how adorable Justin looked in his little white suit. He tugged at the violet bow tie attached at the neck. Sarah came out of the dressing room next. She strolled in front of Holly and Anna and spun around before them.

"I feel like a movie star, *dahlings*." She batted her eyelashes. The full-length aqua gown was adorned with a sequined bust. She lifted her arm to show the girls the sheer sleeves with sequenced buttons holding them in place.

"Stunning, Mom! Yeah, amazing!"

"I thank you, girls," she said as she bowed.

Donald looked at his wife in amusement. "Okay, diva woman, go and put your street clothes on," he said sarcastically. "You and I and Justin are going next door while the girls do their fitting. I want some French fries. I don't want to see the bride until tomorrow, it will ruin the surprise."

Anna went into the fitting room and tried on her violet satin dress. A line of crystal beads formed the neck, and capped sleeves hugged her arms. She looked in the mirror to admire her reflection. Holly joined her to inspect the gown.

"It looks nice, Anna. Do you like it?" Holly questioned with her hand upon her hip.

"Yeah, it's pretty. I think it will look better with my hair up." She lifted her hair to see if it better suited.

"Oh yeah! When we get our hair done tomorrow, you should wear it like that." Holly's olive eyes twinkled with satisfaction.

"All right, your turn bride girl," Anna said as her sister unzipped the back of her dress.

Anna sat in a chair waiting with anticipation to see her sister dressed in white. Holly tentatively entered the room. She brushed her arms along the white satin fabric. The boat neck like Anna's also had a line of crystal beads, which continued along the hem of the full-length gown.

"Wow, Holly." Anna put her hand to her lips. "You're actually a bride!" she said to her sister with glee.

Holly looked at her sister with a frown.

"What's wrong?" Anna left the chair and stood by her sister.

"Can I go through with this?" Holly searched her sister for answers.

"What do you mean?"

"I don't know…am I doing the right thing? Is Chris really the *one*?" Holly's hands shook.

Anna took her sister's hands in hers. "You love Chris… right?"

"Yeah, but…this is so…forever?"

"It's called cold feet. It's totally normal to get a little jittery. You've been busy with all the details and now the big day is here. It's okay to feel a little freaked. It is just a *little* nerves right?"

Holly pulled her hands from Anna. "I don't know. I love him so much. Maybe I'm just tired. Right?" She nervously paced the room.

"Take a deep breath," Anna suggested.

"I love him. I love him," she said firmly. "I'll be okay," Holly said with conviction.

The nervous bride went into the dressing room while Anna retreated to the chair. She slumped down with her head in her hands and prayed. "Dear Lord, please bless my sister's marriage. Please don't let her end up like me. Help me say the right words; show me the way."

CHAPTER 16

The car stopped in front of a small white church. The doors stood open to welcome the wedding party and guests.

"Looks like everyone's here judging by the cars," Donald said with a wide gesture of his big arm. He opened the passenger side door, and Sarah stepped out clutching the skirt of her gown.

"You look fetching, my love," he teased in an animated voice.

"Stop the nonsense, Don, and give the girls a hand. It's getting late." She glanced uneasily at the dainty silver watch at her wrist.

"At your service, ma'am," he continued with his antics. He opened the back seat door and lifted the white-suited Justin into one arm and helped Anna out with the other.

"Thanks, Dad," she said as she brushed wrinkles from her dress.

Justin tweaked his grandfather's nose and squealed with delight. Donald laughed heartily and tweaked him back.

"I'll take him, Dad. You help the bride, okay?" Anna encouraged.

"You look lovely, my beautiful Anna," he said seriously. She looked at her father with love.

He rushed to the other side of the car and held both her hands as his oldest daughter struggled to alight gracefully in her long gown. "You, my daughter, are the essence of beauty today."

Holly hugged her dad as she cajoled. "You're being goofy, Dad. Keep it up." They both chuckled.

As Anna watched her family interact, a wave of joy mixed with sadness overcame her. Tears welled in her eyes.

"Mama!" Justin tugged on her gown. She looked down into two blue pools as he mumbled, "I hungry."

Anna bent to his level. "Listen carefully, Justin Michael." She pointed to her father. "Grandpa has animal crackers in his pocket. When we get into the church, he'll give you some. You must use your soft voice inside the church. Can you do that for Mama?"

Justin leaned into her and whispered, "I try, Mama."

Holly overheard the conversation between her sister and nephew. She whirled around, picked him up, and planted a lipstick kiss in the center of his forehead. He giggled and squealed.

"Swing me, Auntie!"

"Not now, Justin," Sarah interrupted. "Everyone, can we go into the church?" She threw up her arms. "The guests are waiting, the ceremony is ready to begin, and poor Chris is standing in wait thinking he's been left at the altar!"

"Sarah, my love, calm down," Don said in a condescending tone.

"Donald Arthur Bertram!" She exclaimed with her hands on her hips.

"Okay, okay, we're going! Come on, girls. Hop to!"

Even Justin obeyed. He held his mother's hand and walked into the church.

The guests were seated in anticipation as an usher escorted Sarah to her seat. Holly's makeup was flawless, her summer tan made the pure white gown dazzle. Her dark curls were upswept and met by a veil that delicately touched her shoulders. A flute played melodiously as Anna hugged her sister. "You look absolutely amazing. This is your day!" Both girls' eyes misted.

"Don't make me cry, Anna. My makeup will be in ruin." Holly dabbed her eyes with her manicured finger tips. "Shoo, Anna. Get goin'."

Anna held Justin close and walked proudly down the aisle. The wedding march played, and Holly floated toward the altar, her arm tightly entwined in her father's, her eyes glued to her soon-to-be husband. Her beaming smile soared like a tidal wave over the entire congregation. Don gave his daughter away, took Justin from Anna's arms, and joined Sarah in the front pew. Anna smiled to see her child crunching contentedly on the much anticipated animal crackers.

The age old words "I do" were spoken, and Mr. and Mrs. Watson were introduced as the couple waved the crowd. A soloist sang "Ave Maria," accompanied by a lone violin. The new husband and wife along with family and guests spilled out of the church. Anna looked back at the empty church with its pews decorated in fern and baby's breath, the baskets of hydrangeas adorning the altar. "My sister is married," she whispered as Justin ran to her.

"Mama, I talk outside voice now?"

Anna lifted him into her arms and smothered his face in kisses. "Yes, yes, you may. You've been a very good boy for Mama."

"Swing me, Mama," he squealed.

And swing him she did, 'round and 'round until they were both spent. Tired and dizzy, he lay on the grass in his pure white wedding suit, the bow tie hanging askew.

"Justin!" Holly called. "Come, Auntie wants to take your picture." He rolled to his feet and ran laughing back into the church with the bride in hot pursuit.

The reception was held at a beach side restaurant. The massive room sported a full wall of glass with an attached outdoor patio overlooking the sea. The lovingly made centerpieces glowed on tables dressed in white linen. Sea shells were scattered around the centerpieces adding to the seaside motif. A long table also dressed in white linen boasted cold salads, lobster rolls, fruit, and cheeses. The room was beautiful, and Anna was impressed with the details that her sister had artfully chosen.

Donald took a flute of champagne and clicked the side of the glass. "I'd like to propose a toast to the happy couple. May God bless you and fully enrich every day of your married life." He raised his glass to cheers. "Here, here!"

Chris raised his drink with a long, slender arm and added in his deep voice. "I wish my parents could be here. Most of you are aware they died in a car accident five years ago. I toast my dad and mom, I feel them celebrating with us in spirit. Thank you all for coming near and far to be a part of our special day."

Holly stroked her husband's blond spiked hair and looked at him adoringly as he spoke. When he finished he turned to his wife and kissed her which made the guests cheer and whistle.

Anna could sense Justin becoming antsy. She backed away from the crowd and led him through the glass doors onto the patio. The wind off the water whipped at their hair as they stood looking upon the Atlantic. *I wish I'd had time to visit my peace place,* she reflected silently. The week had gone so fast. Anna lovingly watched Justin run around the patio picking up insects he discovered. She was grateful they had gotten through the ceremony without incident. Donald joined them on the patio and sighed thoughtfully. "Beautiful out here, little girl."

Anna chuckled aloud. "When are you going to stop calling me little girl? I'm a mother now, ya know."

"Listen, you'll always be my little girl." He wrapped his arm around her shoulder. "You got a cute kid there too," he added.

"Yeah, takes after his grandpa," she teased.

"Well, of course, you didn't think his looks were from you did you, little girl?" He leaned down as Justin begged his grandpa to pick him up.

"Let's get back inside," Anna encouraged. "I don't want to miss the cutting of the cake. You don't want to miss cake, right, Justin?"

"No! No! Me want cake," he said excitedly as Donald carried him in.

Every detail of Holly's wedding had been perfectly orchestrated. The food was delicious; the room glowed as the afternoon turned into early evening. The family was cheerful, and Anna was grateful for the time she spent with her loved ones and friends. Holly and Chris would be spending the night in a honeymoon suite at a local hotel, so this would be her last opportunity to say good-bye. Anna kissed her sister's flushed cheek and gave her new brother-in-law a hug.

"We'll see you at Christmas, okay?" Holly encouraged. She knew her sister hated good-byes.

"Don't worry, I'm not going to cry all over your dress," Anna teased. "I'm so happy for you both. Be happy today and always. I love you."

Donald lifted Justin to give his aunt a kiss. "I'm going to take these guys back to the house; your nephew has had quite enough. He was a good little fella today, but I think he's ready for bed."

Holly and Chris said good-bye to Anna and Justin as they left for their last night together in Maine.

CHAPTER 17

Anna surveyed the room with her hands on her hips. Her clothes were folded and packed for the trip home to Minnesota. Justin lay strewn across the bed petting Snickers.

"Mama…we take Snickers home?" he whined.

Anna sat on the edge of the bed and ran her fingers through the silken ball of fur.

"Your auntie Holly would miss her cat. Besides, Justin, remember what we talked about. You are not going home with me now. You are going to spend time with your daddy." Anna struggled to keep her voice even.

Justin sat up on the bed. "Me go home! Nana Mary said 'matoes will be red I get home!" He pounded his fists on the bed. The startled cat darted off the bed and out the door.

"That's right, sweetheart. When you come home, they will be ready to pick. They need more time." She laid her hand upon his arm. "It will be fun to visit with your daddy. I bet he'll take you to the beach." She encouraged with more excitement then she felt.

"I want Snickers!" He jumped off the bed and skittered out the door after the tabby cat.

Anna breathed deeply. She could feel anxiety creep in. She would have to face Mike. She would have to let her son go. She didn't want to deal with either situation. She heard her father bellow from the kitchen "Anna, it's time to go."

Sarah and Donald drove their daughter and Justin to the airport. Anna was to meet Mike at the coffee shop and hand his son over before boarding the plane to Minnesota alone. She looked at Justin who was buckled safely in his car seat as he sipped juice from a box. She rubbed her hand along his cheek. He pushed her away and looked out the window.

"We'll drop you at the baggage area, Anna," Donald said from the driver's seat.

"Yes, honey. We don't want to make this awkward for you." Sarah dabbed moist eyes with a tissue. "We'll see you in a few months at Christmas," she reminded them as she blew her nose.

"Time will fly, and we'll be together again," Anna replied.

She waved to her parents as she watched their car pull away from the curb. She grasped the filled baggage cart in one hand and tightly griped Justin with the other. As they approached the airport coffee shop, her heart pounded in her chest. Her hands began to tremble and sweat as she felt Justin loosening from her grasp.

"Don't let go of Mommy's hand, Justin. This is a big airport; you could get lost."

She lifted her head from her son to see Mike sitting nearby. He immediately got up as they approached. Anna noted an air of new confidence in her ex-husband. His looks had not changed since she'd last seen him. Mike held a large swirl lollypop, which he handed to his son. Justin took it willingly.

"Hey, buddy!" he greeted. "Anna." He nodded his head in acknowledgement.

Her heart beat so hard in her chest, she looked down at her rumpled T-shirt, certain the garment would be pulsating. Mike opened his arms to give his son a hug. Justin tentatively moved toward him as he looked up at his mother. Anna stood stoically wearing a forced smile even though her legs were jelly beneath her. She reached to take Justin's bags from the cart and handed them to Mike.

"There's a list in the side pocket; medicines he takes, his nap schedule, favorite foods. If you have any questions, please don't hesitate to call." She cleared a lump that formed in her throat.

"I think we'll figure it out," he quipped sarcastically as he ran his hand through his dark hair. "Say good-bye to your ma, Justin. We gotta get goin'."

Anna wrapped her arms around her little boy one more time and held him tight. "Have fun with Daddy," she whispered in his ear. "I love you, sweetheart."

Justin kissed his mother on the cheek as Mike reached for his son's hand. The child looked at her intently before taking his father's hand in his. She watched the two walk away from her as Justin's little legs tried desperately to keep up with Mike's long stride. Justin watched Anna over his shoulder as he propelled farther and farther away from her. She waved to her son and blew him kisses as they turned the corner, and she could no longer see them. Anna clenched her fists, inhaled deeply and proceeded to check her bags to board the plane.

"Good morning. How many bags today?" the attendant questioned.

Anna, dazed, barely registered the simple question.

"Excuse me? What did you ask?" She rubbed her hand across her forehead.

"Are you all right, ma'am?"

"Yes, I'm fine," Anna responded.

The attendant repeated the question. Anna numbly handed her bags over as her head spun and she felt faint.

Somehow she managed to board the plane, weak and spent. The seat next to hers was unoccupied, and Anna was relieved. What she desperately needed was privacy to deal with her emotions. Soon after she'd buckled her seatbelt, the pilot's voice spoke over the microphone. "Good morning! Weather looks good for the flight. Make yourself comfortable, and thank you for flying with us on Midcontinent Air today." He clicked off, and a perky stewardess began the mundane instructions for survival in the customary sign language. Survival was the least of Anna's concerns; her pain and emptiness was so great that nothing could compare; not even a downed airplane. The drone of the engines took her farther and farther away from her Justin. She averted her eyes from the signing stewardess and peered through the tiny window. Gossamer clouds like ragged angel wings, surrounded the plane. All was white. Mesmerized by the ethereal scene outside, Anna's rage erupted as tears streamed unabated down her cheeks.

How could you allow this to happen? You have control over everything, yet you allow my son to be ripped away from everything he knows. You could have prevented this in court, but you didn't. Anna's fists were clenched so tight, the knuckles on her hands were white. She sobbed. *What kind of a God would allow an innocent child to be separated from his mother and send him to a father that he barely knows*, she hissed inaudibly. *I am so angry, God, so angry!* She pounded her clenched fists on her own thighs while her rant continued and seethed inside.

Suddenly, a thunderous voice rebuked her as it roared. "*He's not yours he's mine!*"

Anna instinctively covered her ears with her hands as she cringed into a ball in the seat. Terrorized, she sat deathly still, afraid to open her eyes. After several moments passed and nothing happened, she turned away from the window and shifted in her seat. As she rationalized her surroundings she was convinced she alone heard the Voice. She glanced to the aisle to see the stewardess pushing a serving cart toward the other passengers. All was normal. Individuals watched their miniature TV's, worked on their laptops and chatted. Anna sat back in her seat, released her taught fists, and breathed deeply. She turned again to the window and beheld a vast sea of bright blue, so brilliant that her eyes squinted. She looked for clouds but could see not a whisper of white. The tears had dried on her cheeks making her face sticky. As she inhaled a ragged breath, Justin's face appeared in the watery blue sky. A cherubic face wearing a mischievous grin came to her and just as quickly faded.

"My Justin!" she cried softly.

The Voice called to her again; this time, however, it was gentle and loving.

"He's not yours; he's mine."

Goosebumps and chills claimed her flesh. Again she peered around the plane. All was quiescent.

Oh my God, my Lord, I'm so sorry. Anna cried from her heart. *Yes, he is yours. Forgive me for claiming him as my own. I know that Justin is your gift to me to care for and to love. Forgive my lack of trust; my God I know you will watch over Justin Michael. Please God help me to fully surrender him into your loving care.* Warm tears flowed freely, cleansing tears, as a beautiful tingling sensation of peace filled her from the top of her head to the bottom of her feet. All the anguish released and she was left with pure unconditional love.

CHAPTER 18

A sense of relief filled Anna as she pulled her car into the driveway leading to the lake side cabin. She was physically and emotionally exhausted from the trip. *Maybe a hot shower would ease my sore muscles and cramped legs.* As she entered the empty cabin, a wash of loneliness came over her. She flicked the light on to reveal the toy truck and blocks that Justin had left scattered on the floor. With her hand upon her heart, she whispered, "I miss you, baby." The quiet was deafening. Anna took her bathrobe from the back of her bedroom door and retreated to the bathroom. She allowed the warm water to rain over her body and found relaxation. Feeling refreshed, she walked into the bedroom that she shared with Justin. Sitting on his bed, she began to pray, "Please God help me with my loneliness. I know Justin is in your hands. I trust you will watch over and protect him."

Anna dressed and walked to the kitchen. After she looked into the cabinet, she realized she had no coffee for morning. Too tired to go to the grocery store, she decided to pay the Hutchinsons a visit and borrow some. Anna walked out into the warm summer Minnesota evening. She could hear the cicadas chirping in the trees. As she approached, she wondered if the Hutchinsons were at home. It was eerily quiet as she knocked on the back door. When no one answered, Anna looked into the driveway and saw the car parked. She took the path that led to the side of the house facing the lake. Mary sat on an Adirondack rocking chair in the screened-in porch with a handmade quilt covering her legs. Her eyes were fixed on the lake in front of her and as Anna came closer she barely moved.

Thinking she was almost asleep and not wanting to startle her, Anna whispered, "Mary?"

"Anna." Mary barely moved her lips to respond; so different from the enthusiastic older woman of whom she was accustomed.

"Are you all right, Mary? Why are you out here by yourself? Where's Paul?"

"He's gone, Anna," she choked.

"What do you mean he's gone?" Anna reached for her neighbor's hand. It was cold to the touch.

"He had a massive heart attack the day you left...out there...on the lake that he loved." She pointed listlessly toward the water.

"Oh my, no!" Anna could hear her own voice crack. Stunned, she sat in the chair next to Mary. It was quiet for several minutes before her neighbor continued.

"Yes, Anna." Mary sighed deeply, her eyes moistened and in a monotone voice she revealed the details of Paul's death. "A policeman came to my door and gave me the sad news. My stomach knots when I think of it," she added sadly.

"Oh, Mary, I'm so sorry you lost Paul."

A thin smile creased Mary's lips. "He was a good man, my Paul—a good, good man."

"I'll miss him too," Anna replied sadly. "He was always so kind to me, and Justin loved his Grandpa Paul. He'll be heartbroken when he comes home and his best buddy is missing."

Mary smiled weakly. "Little ones forget. We older folks don't, unfortunately." She raised reddened eyes to Anna. "I'm not sure how I can go on without Paul. It's so hard."

"God will sustain you." Anna wrapped her arms around her grieved neighbor.

"Sweet child, I know you're right. I'm still in shock. With all of the busyness of the kids here this week; I really haven't had a chance to properly grieve." She placed her hand aside her cheek. "I'll be all right. The pain of losing the one you spent all of your life with..." She trailed off wistfully.

"I have an extra bed in my room. If you get lonely or afraid, you're welcome to come and spend the night with me," Anna suggested.

"No, dear, you're sweet to offer. I need time to adjust. I'm used to spending time alone during fishing season. The nights are lonely, but knowing you're a few houses away brings me comfort." She weakly smiled at Anna.

"Would you like me to stay awhile?"

"Actually I'd like to take a bath and go to bed. I'll read for a while, that seems to help me tire enough to sleep. Thank you anyway, Anna, for your offer to stay. I must ask before I retire to bed, how was the wedding? Did Justin get off to his dad's all right?" she asked as she folded the quilt from her legs and stood.

"The wedding was absolutely beautiful. And yes, Justin is with his dad. My house is pretty quiet too. What do ya say we have dinner tomorrow night when I get home from work? I can make you that chicken recipe we talked about before I went on vacation?"

Mary started toward the door. "Sure, that would be nice, dear. I'll see you then. I'm sure you've had a long day too and you're back to work tomorrow. You need your rest."

Anna hugged her neighbor tightly before walking home. Normally hearing the death of a loved one would be a blow to her, but her experience on the plane had changed her perspective. She knew God was in control and would give her and Mary the strength and peace they needed, which brought her immense contentment.

The two women spent a great deal of time together in the next few weeks. Mary bought the hutch that she had wanted, and the two spent many hours perusing antique markets and yard sales on the weekends searching for the perfect treasures to adorn the shelves. They broke bread together and grocery shopped and although there was an expanse of years between them, their combined loneliness became their common bond. Somehow helping Mary through her grief took the sting from Anna's own, as she put her trust in the Creator who was infinitely greater than herself.

CHAPTER 19

It was Justin's tenth birthday. Anna had planned a surprise party for him and was ready to pull it off. Every year on his birthday, she would take him out to lunch to celebrate. This year would be different. As they drove the car into the roller rink parking lot, Justin's crystal blue eyes looked at his mother, puzzled.

"Why are we here, Mom? I thought we were going for pizza. Besides this place is closed today."

It was a Sunday, and Anna had secretly rented the entire rink for his party. She suggested he get out of the car as she wanted to read the hours posted on the door so they could go skating the following week. As they came closer, Anna jumped in front of him and swung the door open.

"Surprise!" a group of school age kids shouted in delight.

Justin stood with a shocked look on his face as he rubbed his hand through his short strawberry blond hair. He turned to his mother, who smiled from ear to ear.

"Happy birthday, Justin," she said happily.

"Thanks, Mom! This is awesome!" Anna watched with delight as Justin and his best friend Scotty took off their shoes and ran to retrieve their skates.

Justin had met Scotty the first day of school, and they'd been inseparable ever since. It had helped that Scotty's mom, Rae, and Anna became fast friends as well. They would meet and take the boys to the park and on play dates. They'd carpool for soccer team as well.

Rae came up behind Anna and tapped on her shoulder.

"We did it! I thought for sure Scotty would spill the beans and tell. Did you see the look of surprise on your son's face? Priceless!" Rae tucked her short black hair behind one ear.

"Well, I have you to thank. I never could have pulled it off if you weren't here to open the place up for us. Did you give the owner the check for me?"

"Yep, all taken care of." Rae smiled.

Anna looked at her tall slender friend. Her features were striking, with straight black hair cut in a bob, and a flawless dark completion. She was a beauty with little makeup. Rae was unaware of her attractiveness and laughed when Anna would tell her that men ogled her. She loved Rae because she was grounded and they parented in much the same way. Their boys were their life and they were content with that. Rae's husband, Chad, travelled a great deal with his job which left Rae like a single mother as well. Anna never felt like she was interrupting their family life because he was always away. And so, like their sons, the two became inseparable.

Justin and Scotty rolled by on the carpet and gave their moms a high five before entering the rink. Justin was surrounded by kids, and Anna could hear the chatter from where she stood.

"What a cool party, Justin!" they stated.

"Yeah, my mom is the best," she heard him say. Anna was so pleased to make her son happy, it warmed her heart.

Rae motioned Anna to the tables on the side of the rink. The two readied the area for the kids to eat their pizza, and Anna moved gifts to another table to make more space. As they worked, Rae asked if Anna would carpool the following week as she would be away.

"Where are you going?" Anna asked inquisitively.

"Chad wants to take me to Jamaica for a few days."

"You don't sound too excited about this trip, Rae." Anna placed a present on top of the already huge stack.

"I don't know. I guess I should be. I hate to leave Scotty, ya know? And honestly, I can't remember the last time I spent time alone with my husband. What if we have nothing to talk about? You want me to be perfectly honest? I'd rather be going to Jamaica with you than him," she said dejectedly.

"Sounds like time away is what you need," Anna encouraged. "I'll help with Scotty any way I can."

"Thanks. I have a sitter for after school and at night while we are gone. Maybe he could spend Friday night with you?" she asked with hesitation. "I'd never want to impose, Anna, you know that," she confirmed.

"He is absolutely welcome. Justin will be thrilled, whatever you need." Anna nodded her head in agreement.

The hot pizzas arrived at the table, and as the smell wafted through the air, the kids skated to the table laughing and chatting. Justin came by his mother and gave her a half hug. "Thanks, Mom." He smiled up at her showing dimples on his flushed cheeks.

The kids dove into the pizza like vultures as Anna lit the candles on the racecar cake. Everyone gathered around and sang "Happy Birthday" to Justin. Her son beamed and blew out his candles to make a wish.

Be happy always, Anna thought as the smoke from the candles drifted upward. Justin ripped through his presents to find games, a new soccer ball, and Legos that had been on the top of his list. He squealed with pleasure as he ripped the paper off each present. Anna watched her son beam as he talked excitedly to his friends. She smiled at Rae who was taking the discarded paper and tossing it into a garage bag. The boys scattered back onto the roller rink leaving a path of destruction. Anna picked up the paper plates and napkins and began to clean the mess.

"Thanks for your help, Rae. I couldn't have done this without you," Anna said to her friend with gratitude.

Rae continued to work around the table cleaning up the demolition. "No problem. I know you would do the same for me. Anna...?" She hesitated.

Anna stopped cleaning and gave her friend her full attention.

"What if this trip to Jamaica doesn't go well? I know it's been a long time for you, but how did you know when you were ready for divorce?"

Anna blinked her eyes as she heard the "D" word come from of her dear friend's lips. "Oh Rae. Are you considering divorce? I didn't know it was that bad?" She laid her hand upon her friend's shoulders.

"I don't know. We never see each other anymore. I don't know what the point is. He travels all the time." Rae rambled on.

"I do know this. You probably don't understand this because I am divorced, but it's not something I believe in. I believe in making it work, if you can." Anna encouraged. "Single parenting isn't as easy as it looks. You know that because Chad is away a lot. But imagine if he never came back; it changes everything. Plus, you love Chad, don't you?"

"I don't know, Anna. I don't know what I feel anymore. That's what scares me." Her eyes fell to the floor.

"Well, I think this trip is just what you need." Anna shook her friend's shoulders to jolt her. "I bet a little fun in the sun, and you will be reconnected in no time," Anna said more confidently then she felt. "So, how good are you on skates?" she added, trying to lighten the mood. "Want to try a trip around the rink?"

"I'll beat you to the skate counter." Rae laughed as the two raced like kids to join the party.

———— ◆ ————

Anna closed the trunk as she and Justin loaded the last of the birthday presents into the car. They turned to wave to Rae and Scotty who were the last to leave the parking lot.

"That was the best party ever! And you're the best mom ever!" Justin said to his mom as they drove toward the cabin.

"I'm glad you had fun, sweetheart. Were you surprised?"

"You bet I was! Did you see my face; the guys said it looked like I just saw a bear!" he squealed.

Anna looked at her son through the rearview mirror. He wiped the sweat from his short hair leaving it to spike. Still reeling from the excitement he asked. "Can we try out my new soccer ball at the park?"

Anna looked at her wristwatch. "It's getting pretty late, Justin. We've had a long day."

"Awww, Mom. *Please,* pretty please with sugar on top?" he pleaded, smiling mischievously.

"I guess." She gave in as she pulled into the park off Cherry Lane.

The two kicked the shiny new ball back and forth. Justin then dribbled the ball and tried to keep it away from his mother.

"Come get it," he teased as he scrambled around his mother's legs.

She chased him and played until they were out of breath. Anna wrapped an arm around her son's shoulders. "Okay, you win," she said as she held the other to her chest.

The two sat on a nearby picnic table before heading home.

"Remember your last soccer game?" Anna asked.

"Yeah. How could I forget? We lost!" Justin said as he bounced the ball on the top of the table.

"I was never more proud of you than at that moment." She smiled at her son.

"Mom, what are you talking about? We lost! Were you at the same game?" His clear blue eyes looked at her, perplexed.

"When that kid on the other team got hurt, you rushed to his side to see if he was okay. You didn't even know him, Justin. You held your hand out to help him up from the ground. That showed great maturity, son. It was better than winning a game," she reminded him.

"Well, it was the right thing to do," he answered humbly.

"Yeah, Justin, it was. But you were the only one who bothered. I want you to know I noticed," she said softly.

"Thanks, Mom." Justin blushed.

She changed the subject, noting his embarrassment. "So what did you wish for as you blew out your candles?"

"You know I can't tell! It won't come true!" He shrugged his mother off.

"Come on," she teased.

He raised himself from the table. "No way, I'm not gonna tell ya," he said as he kicked the ball far away and ran to fetch it. She watched as her son chased the rolling ball. He had thinned and grown taller. His short, spiked hair made him look older. She noted how his waist became thinner and shoulders widened. *He's growing up. Where did the time go?* She wondered. It seemed like yesterday she was watching chubby little legs run from her. Justin kicked the ball back toward her, and Anna dribbled it to the car.

"Let's stop and bring Mary a piece of cake before we go home," she hollered over her shoulder.

Anna tossed the soccer ball into the back seat, and Justin followed. They drove in silence before reaching Mary's driveway. The sun was setting and a cool breeze blew off the lake as the two exited the car. Anna carried the cake to the door. Mary clasped her hands together joyfully as the two walked through the back door. She reached for Justin, and he fell into her arms for a big hug.

"Happy birthday, darling,'" she said as she pulled him away to get a better look. "I think you grew already." She smiled at him.

Justin blushed. "Thanks, Nana Mary," he said shyly.

She handed him a large envelope with a bow. Enclosed in the card was a gift certificate for new water skis.

"No *way!*" he exclaimed as he hugged her excitedly. "This is the best day ever!"

"I know you always use Scotty's skis since you've been trying to learn on his dad's boat. I thought you might want your own. You can get one of those funny boards you put your two feet into if you don't want the skis. What are they called?"

"A wakeboard!" he exclaimed. "Wait until I tell Scotty! He's gonna freak!"

Anna looked at Mary and silently mouthed the words *thank you*. Justin jumped up and down, unable to contain himself. "Can we go tomorrow after you get home from work to pick one out? Can I see if Scotty can come with?" He shook her arm until she answered.

"Sure, we can go tomorrow." She handed him the house key and agreed that he could go home and call his best friend. "I'll be home in a few minutes."

Justin sprinted back to the cabin. Anna looked at her neighbor with a furrowed brow. "That was too much money to spend on a gift. You really shouldn't have."

Mary waved her hand in annoyance. "Nonsense, Justin is like one of my own. How the years have flown by," she said wistfully. "I don't know how I would have made it through Paul's passing without you and Justin to fill my heart and home. You and Justin rescued me. I don't think you realize that. So don't give me grief that I spent too much. What the heck am I going to spend my money on anyway?"

Anna chuckled at her neighbor. As she grew in age, she didn't hold back her feelings. Whatever she was thinking Anna knew it, and she loved that about her.

"We rescued each other." Anna smiled. "Imagine my naiveté to come here as a single mom with a toddler not knowing a soul except Dr. Miller? I look back on it now, and I see how God had his hand in bringing us together."

"Yes, Anna. We've both grown so much, well at least one way. I'm shrinking in my old age," she added with a laugh. "Ooh, this chocolate cake looks delicious." She took a dollop of frosting on her finger. "Did you get a piece at the party or would you like to sit and have a piece with me?"

"I'd better get home. I don't want to leave Justin too long by himself. I don't need it anyway." She laid a hand upon her slender hip.

"Anna, please, you could blow away in the wind you're so thin," she said mockingly. "You could *use* a big hunk of this cake."

"Enjoy, Mary." She gave her neighbor a brief hug before returning home.

Justin was still on the phone when Anna arrived. His hands flew in animation as he talked with Scotty about his birthday present. Anna leaned against the wall watching her son, and as he hung up the phone, it rang again.

"Hi, Dad," she heard him say as he took the phone into the kitchen. She listened as he told his father all about his birthday party. Anna brought the gifts from the car and tossed them into his room. Dr. Miller Sr. had agreed she could paint the room as long she kept the color neutral. She looked at the walls covered in posters of racecars and water skiers. One wall held a shelf of his soccer trophies from the many years he'd played. As she glanced around the room, Justin came to join her.

"It was nice of your dad to call to wish you a happy birthday," she commented.

He flung himself onto the bed after kicking the soccer ball under it. "Yeah, I don't think that's why he called."

"What do you mean? Of course that's why he called."

"Naw, he just called to tell me that I'm going to have a baby brother or sister in a few months," he said dejectedly.

"Tina is pregnant?" Anna asked with a furrowed brow.

Justin's father had married soon after he'd turned four. He was not told of the wedding but merely received a photo in the mail after the fact.

"Yep." He looked down at his feet and rubbed the dirt from his shoe with his fingers.

"Are you okay?"

Justin looked at his mother as his eyes filled with tears. "Dad's new baby will get to live with him all the time, not like me. I only get to be with him in the summer, and all he does is work." A large tear dropped from his eye and rolled down his cheek.

"Oh, baby." Anna wrapped her arms around her son. "You get to be a big brother. You'll still be the apple of your dad's eye," she answered with assurance.

Her heart ached for her son. She hoped that she was right and prayed Mike would not use this new baby as a replacement for Justin. She couldn't help feel that Justin's feelings were justified. His father's timing telling Justin on his birthday irritated her. Could he not wait for another day? He didn't keep in touch with Justin as much as she would like. After their visits in the summer, he'd call regularly, but the calls waned as time progressed.

"I'm going to take a shower." Justin grabbed a pair of clean pj's before stomping off to the bathroom.

She sighed. "Okay, sweetheart." Her thoughts continued. *Mike had to ruin a perfect day. Of all the self absorbed...* she fumed. She sat on Justin's bed and questioned herself. Was she jealous? Was she angry because Mike moved on with his life and had a wife to help him with a new baby? Was she hurt for Justin's sake? Anna really wasn't sure what she felt. *Please, God, help me to support Justin through this,* she prayed as Justin came from the shower to sit with her on the bed. He read a few pages of the book they had been reading then snuggled under the covers. She smoothed his wet hair as they said their prayers together, kissed his forehead, and turned out the light.

CHAPTER 20

After work the following day, Anna collected Justin from Mary's, and together they went to pick up Scotty. She stood in Rae's bedroom and watched as her friend tossed clothes into a suitcase.

"Getting ready for the big trip?" Anna asked with hesitation. She wasn't sure if Rae had changed her mind, and she was unsure if she should broach the subject.

Rae held up a shiny gold bikini. "Look what Chad gave me to pack." She dangled the skimpy suit in Anna's face.

"Oooh. Wow. Not much material here?" Anna giggled, taking the bikini and examining it further.

Rae rolled her eyes as she grabbed the bikini from her friend and threw it into the suitcase. "I haven't worn anything like that since before Scotty. Not sure I want to either."

Anna looked at her tall, slender friend. "Now, Rae, come on, it was thoughtful for him to buy you a gift for the trip. Apparently he loves your body and knows you will look amazing in that. Besides, you don't have to wear it to the beach if you are uncomfortable. Just think of it as lingerie." She batted her eyes.

"Yeah, he has been thoughtful the last few days. He says he's excited for us to spend some quality time together. I'm coming around. I'm going to take this trip and see how it goes." She sighed as she zipped the luggage.

Scotty and Justin popped their heads into the room. "Can we go now?" Justin begged.

Anna wished her friend bon voyage and reminded her that she would take Scotty the following Friday night as planned. Rae agreed to pick him up on Saturday when they returned from Jamaica. The boys chatted amiably on their way to the ski shop. Anna's mind turned to Rae and hoped this trip was the fix her friend needed. In fact she was a little envious. *Would she ever fall in love again and be taken on a tropical vacation?* She tossed the thought out of her mind as they entered the ski shop. The boys were fixated on the variety of ski equipment. Justin finally settled on a bright shiny red wakeboard due to Scotty's coaxing. She watched as Justin ran his hand along the shiny board. His face lit up like a Christmas tree as they went to the cashier to purchase it.

"Can Scotty come over for supper, Mom?"

"No, sweetheart, not today. His mom and dad only have tonight to spend with him before their trip tomorrow. He has to go home."

The two boys sighed begrudgingly.

They dropped Scotty at home and went to the cabin to fix supper. Justin sat at the kitchen table drawing a picture. By the time the chicken was ready, he had finished his masterpiece, and mother and son sat across the table telling funny stories that happened that day. Anna told of one of her patients whose face was so numb from the Novocain that she couldn't talk after the procedure. Anna pretended she had a numb face and drooled water out of her mouth to demonstrate. Justin giggled at his mother's silliness. He told her that he and Mary were making muffins and spilled the batter all over the floor. Mary was angry at first, but then they had ended up laughing and rubbing batter on each other's faces. They cleaned the supper dishes and watched TV before going to bed. Justin held the wakeboard on his lap and would admire it during the commercials. She smiled at her son and rolled her eyes.

"You're not going to sleep with that thing, are you?"

"You bet I am!" He giggled as he hugged his new board.

CHAPTER 21

Justin walked groggily into the kitchen and sat down. He reached for the cereal in a starry haze. Anna wasn't sure if he was sleepwalking or awake until he looked up and saw his Mother in shorts and a T-shirt.

"How come you're not in scrubs? Aren't you going to be late for work, Mom?" He dropped his head and hunched over his cereal bowl.

"I took a vacation day since we only have a few days of summer left before school starts. I thought we'd spend the day together." Anna leaned her arms on the kitchen table.

Justin looked up from his cereal bowl. "Really? Awesome! What are we gonna do today?"

"I have a few ideas," Anna hinted, as she walked out to the patio into the hazy summer morning. The grass was still wet from the rain the night before. She breathed in the heavy air and leaned over her clay pots to dead head the violet petunias that had made it through the summer. As she was piling up the lifeless flower petals, a young duck waddled over and stood by her feet. Anna whispered to Justin through the screen door, "Come quick, son! You gotta see this!"

Justin walked toward her as he rubbed his eyes. He quietly opened the screen door and the young duck waddled closer to his feet.

"Aww, Mom, I think he's lost! I don't see his family." He scanned the lake for other ducks in the area. "He must be hungry!" Justin went back into the house and returned with a sleeve of saltines. He broke the crackers in his hand, and the duck took a nibble from the crumbs. "Mom, look! He likes it! I'm going to call him Quacker. 'Cause he likes crackers!"

Anna giggled as she heard the name he chose. She watched how tenderly he cared for the vulnerable bird. As he walked toward the lake he held it in his hand. "Let's go find your family," she heard him say. Anna stood on the deck with her hands on her hips and watched the event unfold. Justin found the family of ducks behind a rock and let Quackers go to join them. She watched as the duck and its family swam under the pier and out toward the middle of the lake. Justin returned with a smile as he wiped his wet feet upon the deck.

"I'm glad we found Quacker's family, aren't you, Mom?"

"Yes, another duck saved," she answered.

"By the way, where are we going today?" he questioned as he leaned in to help his mother dead head the dying petunia petals.

"I was thinking we'd go to the carnival. This is the last week it will be in town, and we haven't gone yet. What do ya think?"

"*Awesome!*" He opened the screen door and left it ajar as he ran toward his bedroom.

Anna wiped her soiled fingers on a towel and brushed the sweat from her brow. The haze began to burn off to reveal a warm summer day.

Within seconds Justin was dressed in shorts and a baseball hat, and mother and son left for the carnival. The crowd was thick as everyone savored the last days of summer. Lines for rides were long, and the hot day made for some cranky spectators. Justin pointed to a smaller line for bumper cars, so the two jumped at the chance. They slammed each other in separate cars as Justin raced around the track to bump his mother. He was smiling from ear to ear, and the jolt of the collisions only made Anna laugh harder.

Anna led her son to the games to try to win a prize. Good luck prevailed when Justin shot a water gun and hit the target.

"Yes!" He squealed when the alarm went off. He picked out a stuffed frog and held it proudly up to the crowd that had surrounded them.

"Nice shootin', Tex!" Anna flicked his baseball cap and gave him a wink. "I think that win deserves cotton candy!"

He love punched her on the shoulder and said, "I'm good." She rolled her eyes at him smilingly.

They shared a pink fluffy cloud of sugar and licked their sticky hands and lips.

"How do they make this?" he asked his mother.

"I don't know, kid, but it sure is *good*!"

Justin pointed to a roller coaster. That's where Anna drew a line in the sand.

"Sorry, roller coasters are not my thing, but I'll watch you if you if you care to ride it."

"Naw, line's too long, and I'm getting hot." He removed his baseball hat and fanned his face with it.

Anna and Justin enjoyed the shade of a large spruce as they sat Indian style under the tree. They sipped on water bottles as a young man walked along pushing a baby in a stroller. Justin stared intently at the child and looked at his mother with serious blue eyes while posing the question, "Is my dad going to forget about me?" He lowered his eyes and aggravated a hangnail on his thumb.

"No, how could anyone forget this face," she answered as she pinched his rosy cheeks. Anna hoped for her son's sake that she was right.

Justin jumped up and brushed an ant from his bare leg. "I want to go on one more ride and then go home okay? It's too hot!" he whined.

"Yeah. I think maybe a swim in the lake is in order!"

Justin ran toward the fair grounds and pulled his mother along by the arm. They rode the spinning tea cups until Anna felt like she would throw up. Between the heat and the sugar from the cotton candy, she wasn't sure the spinning ride was the best idea and so after getting her sea legs back they headed for home. Upon arrival they immediately changed into their swimsuits. The cool lake water refreshed them as they splashed around and swam. Exhausted, they finished the day sitting on the deck eating grilled hotdogs. Justin wiped ketchup from the side of his mouth and mumbled.

"That was fun! I wish you didn't have to work *every* day."

"Wouldn't that be nice," Anna agreed regretfully. "Soon you'll be back at school," she reminded him. "You'll have plenty to keep you busy then."

"Ugh, don't remind me," Justin said as he poured more lemonade.

The two chatted about their fun filled day while they finished their supper. After cleaning the table Justin went inside to play video games. Anna wrapped up the evening by doing laundry and vacuuming. She was so tired from their day; it was all she could do to finish the chores. She was glad school was starting soon as she found it difficult to leave Justin with Mary in the summer. The pull between work and child was always a battle for her, one that she would never win.

CHAPTER 22

The remainder of the week passed quickly. Friday arrived within a blink of an eye, and Scotty was dropped off with a sleeping bag to spend the night. The boys were a ball of energy, so Anna sent them outside to work it off in a game of street hockey. Sweaty and dirty, they came in for Gatorade breaks and then back to their game. It wasn't until evening that the boys settled down. Anna read in her room while they watched movies and ate popcorn. She could hear them giggle and babble on about school and soccer. It brought Anna joy to hear her son having a good time with his friend. She wondered what it would be like if he hadn't been an only child. Soon he wouldn't be, as Mike and Tina would be having a baby. Justin would only get to see his new brother or sister for a month in the summer. *How would that change the dynamic of his visits?* she pondered. She continued to read until it became quiet apart from for the drone of the TV. Anna pulled on her bathrobe and trotted out to the living room. The boys' heads leaned off to either side of the couch, their feet met in the middle. She covered them each with a blanket and flicked the TV off. "*They look like little angels when they sleep.*" She smiled, as she tucked herself in for the night.

The next morning they all sat around the kitchen table eating pancakes, the boys' hair tussled from their fitful sleep on the couch. The two stifled yawns as they ate their breakfast. Anna half smiled. She hadn't seen her son this tired in a long time.

"Will you bring some of these pancakes to Mary for me? I think I made too many," Anna asked as she cleared the plates.

"Sure, Mom," Justin answered. "Come on, Scotty." The boys darted to Mary's while Anna cleaned the kitchen.

Soon after they left Anna heard a knock on the door. Rae let herself in.

"Hey, look at you!" Anna said as she wiped the syrup splattered table. "You've gotten so tanned!"

Rae spun around the room. Her dark skin glowed against the pale pink shirt she wore. "Anna, I had a wonderful time." Her eyes sought her son. "Where are the boys?"

"They went next door for a moment. Tell me everything! How was the trip?"

"It was great. Chad and I were like honeymooners. It was such a romantic place. One night we had dinner on the beach," she said dreamily. "Can you imagine? Candlelight! Reggae music! Look I even got my hair braided!" She came to Anna and showed her the small braid with tiny colored beads outlining her face.

"I knew this was just what you needed. I'm happy for you, Rae," Anna said with relief.

"Yeah, Chad and I agreed that we have let our relationship take a back burner for too long. We've decided on planned date nights and a trip like this at least once a year. Anna I feel so alive!" Her smile was contagious.

"I think I need a trip like that!" Anna teased.

Rae pulled photos from her purse and displayed all the places they explored. Scotty ran into the room, interrupting them, and hugged his mother. She kissed him all over his face until he told her to stop. Justin was bummed at the thought of his friend leaving. "Aw, Mom, can't Scotty stay a little longer?"

Rae interrupted Justin. "Actually, I was wondering if you two would like to go out on the boat this afternoon. You could try out your new wakeboard," she coaxed.

"Can we, Mom, can we?" Justin jumped up and down and pulled on his mother's arm.

"Oops. I should have asked you first," Rae apologized.

"No, it's okay. I was going to grocery shop today, but I guess that can wait. What time are you thinking, Rae?" Anna glanced at her watch.

"I'll pack a lunch, so can you guys meet us at the dock in an hour or so?"

"Sure, we can be ready in an hour." Anna looked at her son who was nodding his head vigorously.

"Great, we'll see you in a little while then." Rae lifted her son's sleeping bag, tossed his backpack over his shoulder, and nudged Scotty toward the door.

"Can we bring anything, Rae? Sandwiches? Drinks?

"No, just bring yourselves and of course that shiny new wakeboard, don't forget that." She winked.

Justin giggled. "Don't worry, we won't!"

—◆—

It was a perfect day for boating with a light breeze and calm water as Anna and Justin stepped onto the long wooden pier. Justin proudly carried his shiny new wakeboard over his head while Anna lumbered along carrying beach towels, cooler bag, and a backpack of clothes. Rae came toward them and alleviated some of her burden.

"Simply beautiful for water fun." Rae twirled around with her hands to the sky.

"Gorgeous," Anna agreed enthusiastically.

Justin pushed past them and hopped on to the twenty-foot-long speed boat. Chad held the boat in place with a rope in wait for all to board. As they approached the bright yellow vessel, Anna noticed an unfamiliar face. The six foot, bronzed, muscular man handed Scotty a lifejacket. He removed his sunglasses from sun-streaked hair and laid them on the dashboard. As Anna and Rae approached to board, he held out his tan, well-manicured hand. Rae turned to introduce the two strangers.

"Meet Owen Ridgeway." She nudged her friend toward him, and Anna almost tripped.

The man reached for Anna with a firm handshake. She looked into his green emerald eyes and smiled. "Anna Bertram. Nice to meet you."

The two women sat in the front of the boat while the boys and men sat in the back. As the boat slowly eased away from the dock, Rae leaned in to whisper to her friend, "What do ya think?"

Anna looked at her inquisitively, "About what?"

"*Owen*. What do you think, silly girl? Chad and I invited him for you."

Anna glared at Rae as the boat picked up speed. The wind whipped through their hair as they sped away from the pier. Sprays of water tickled their hands as they splashed through wake left by fast moving skiers. Chad brought the boat to a halt in the middle of the lake and turned to Anna's son.

"Justin, you ready to try out your new board?"

Justin stood up from the seat with his wakeboard leaned against him. "I've only tried skis. I'm a little nervous," he said as he adjusted the straps on his lifejacket.

"Get ready, and I'll tell ya what to do," Chad encouraged.

Anna and Rae moved to the back of the boat to help him into the water. Justin shivered from the shock of the cold hitting his warm skin. Chad tossed him a rope and gave him instructions.

"Okay, Justin, when the rope gets taut, that's when the boat is ready to pull you up. Keep the bottom of your board facing the back of the boat here." Chad tapped the back of the engine. "Bend your knees and lean back, let the boat do the work okay? Give me two thumbs-up when you're ready. Hey, and Justin, if you fall, wave your hands as high as you can so other boats know you're in the water. Okay, buddy?"

Anna watched as Justin slowly floated farther and farther away with a hesitant smile on his face. She said a prayer of protection as she held her hand on her heart. The women sat in the back for spotting purposes. Owen sat alongside Chad to drive the boat. Justin gave the thumbs-up and the boat picked up speed. He attempted to stand but fell and dropped the rope.

"He's down! He's down!" Anna yelled to Chad who immediately maneuvered the boat back to Justin.

"What happened?" Chad shouted to Justin as he tossed him the rope.

"I don't know. I gotta get the hang of it I guess," Justin stated.

"Let's try again. Remember lean back, bend your knees, and let the boat pull you up, okay?"

Justin gave the thumbs-up, and the boat picked up speed. Again he fell and the rope went flying.

As they approached him and handed him the rope the third time, he shook his wet hair. "I'm not sure I can do this," he yelled with his hands cuffed around his mouth bobbing up and down in his lifejacket.

"One more time. Try again, Justin!" Chad shouted.

Justin gave the thumbs-up, and the boat picked up speed.

"He's up! He's up!" Scotty yelled as he clapped for his friend.

Anna's heart swelled for her son as she watched him lean over and touch the water.

"Show off!" Scotty yelled.

Justin beamed as he skimmed along the water. He leaned back and took the rope with one hand and waved to spectators on the shore.

"He's a pro, Anna. Look at that!" Rae exclaimed.

Anna reached into her backpack for her camera and snapped a few photos. After several minutes of wakeboarding, she could see Justin adjusting his shoulders. He was getting tired. He dropped the rope and waved his arms for them to retrieve him. As they pulled up close and Chad cut the engine, they all stood on the boat and clapped for him as he climbed aboard, a proud grin on his face. Anna wrapped him in a beach towel and held him while he shivered.

"That was awesome!"

She kissed her son's soaked head and excused herself to the front of the boat so Justin could watch his friend take a turn. She lifted her face to the sun and reveled in its warmth. It felt good to be on the water. Rae joined her and gestured for her to look at Owen who was now spotting for Scotty.

"He's cute, isn't he?" she pushed.

"Yes, but that's beside the point. What are you thinking, Rae? Does *he* think he's here for me because if that's the case I'm going to hide under this seat in embarrassment?" Anna held a beach towel over her head to hide.

Rae chuckled at her antics. "Come on, girlfriend. No, he doesn't think he's here for you. He works with Chad. While we were on vacation, you two became the topic of our conversation. He's divorced, you're divorced… We thought it would be a perfect fit." She ripped the towel from her friend.

"And since when did I say I needed a fit? I have a full life, Rae. I work full time, I have Mary, I have friends, and Justin is the center of my world. You know that," she snipped.

"Anna, you're my friend, and I love you. Justin is not going to be with you forever. You can't make him the center of your world."

"Gee, look at the pot calling the kettle black," she reminded.

"Yeah, well, that's what I learned from my trip with Chad to Jamaica. Maybe we've had it all wrong, Anna. It's okay to have a life besides being Justin's mother."

The words stung Anna. She couldn't believe what her good friend was saying. Who was this new person, and where was the old Rae? The boat's engine stopped and along with it their conversation. Scotty hopped into the boat as his turn was finished, and Anna sat next to Justin. She could feel herself fuming, and she didn't want to ruin a perfectly nice day. Biting her lip, she looked up to see Owen gazing at her. She turned her head toward her son to avoid his advances.

The group pulled into an island to have lunch. Anna was grateful to leave the vessel and get a little space. She reached for her cooler bag and jumped off the side into the water and waddled into shore. The boys were running around the island picking up sticks. Chad and Rae had brought a compact grill, which they were attempting to light. Owen came up behind Anna and reached to take her cooler bag.

"Having fun?" he asked. "Your son sure got up like a pro on that wakeboard today."

"Yes. That was amazing. I'm glad I got the chance to watch. Do you have a boat?" She attempted light conversation.

"Naw, too much work, why bother when you have friends like these to take you around?" he said as he slyly pointed to Chad and Rae. "Although eventually I will have to get one for my girls I guess. I want them to be amazing athletes like myself." He puffed out his chest.

"Are you married?" Anna asked, already knowing the answer.

"No, divorced. I have three-year-old twin girls," he added.

From the corner of her eye, Anna noticed Justin holding a match and attempting to light it. "Excuse me, Owen... *Justin!*" She yelled as she ran toward him, grateful for a reason to leave the man's company. She took the match from her son's hand. "Just what do you think you're doing?"

"I'm gonna light a fire for marshmallows," he said dejectedly.

"Since when is it okay to play with fire?"

Scotty shyly backed away and ran to his parents to avoid Anna's wrath.

"Mom, it's no big deal," he whined.

"It's a huge deal. Don't let me ever catch you with matches again. Do you hear me, young man?"

Justin gave his mother a half hug. "Sorry," he stated half-heartedly.

"Lunch is ready!" They heard the call and went to join the group.

Hamburgers and chips were devoured at the picnic table. They all chatted amiably about the boys' wakeboarding and tips for how to jump higher on the wake. Justin avoided eye contact with his mother, and Anna was keenly aware that her son got the message regarding his use of matches. The boys ran from the table and chased a hopping frog underfoot. Chad and Owen walked to the boat to load the grill aboard while the women were left to pack up the leftovers.

"You're upset with me," Rae commented softly as she emptied leftover soda onto the ground.

Anna stopped wrapping the unused hamburgers. She looked at her dejected friend.

"I'm not angry. I understand your intention, Rae. I just don't like being put in an awkward position without notice."

"Anna, I never want to hurt you, you know that. I feel that you put all your effort into Justin and no effort into yourself. I know, I know, I'm guilty with Scotty too." She raised her hands in defense. "But maybe it's not the best thing." She laid her hand on her friend's shoulder. "I'm sorry for trying to set you up."

"It's okay. You meant well, and I forgive you." Anna smiled at her and sighed. "I don't think I'm ready, Rae. Is Owen attractive? Sure, he is. But he has twin girls, he's obviously recently divorced, and I don't think I could take all that on? Maybe I'm selfish, but I'm happy with my life. I come and go as I please. I have no one to answer to and I have a beautiful son whom I adore. For me right now, that's enough."

"I understand. I won't do this to you again. I know for now it's enough, but will it always be? What happens when Justin grows up and you're left alone? Have you thought about that?"

"Rae, he's ten! Besides, he tells me he's going to live with me forever," Anna teased.

Scotty ran to the table breathless. "Dad wants us to go."

Rae handed several items to the boys, who loaded their bounty onto the boat. Anna washed her hands in the lake and looking to the sky noticed clouds forming. She pointed them out to the skipper who agreed their time on the water had ended. Once more around the lake and they headed for shore. Boats were lined up at the pier to dock as a storm loomed overhead. As they pulled into the pier, large drops of rain fell. Anna and Justin said a quick good-bye and thanked Rae and Chad for the day on the water. Owen reached to help them from the boat.

"Nice to meet you today," he said with a charming smile.

"Yes, nice to meet you too Owen." Anna waved good-bye as mother and son ran for the safety of their car.

Justin laid his head against the backseat and closed his eyes. Anna looked through the rearview mirror and noticed her son's exhaustion. She studied her sleeping angel and smiled as she pondered Rae's words. *It's okay to have a life besides being Justin's mother.* Was Rae right? Did all of her efforts focus on her son? Wasn't that what she was *supposed* to do? Justin was her life; he had become her life when she was twenty. It was herself and Justin against the world, wasn't it? Who was Anna? Anna was Justin's mother, and she was happy with that, she decided defiantly.

CHAPTER 23

Without warning Justin's grade school years ended. The years melted into each other and rushed forward. Anna wished she could slow time. Sometimes it felt like she was on a fast-moving train. It was Friday evening in late August. Anna sat sipping herbal tea on the porch when the phone rang.

"Hi, what's new?" asked Rae in her bubbly voice.

Anna smiled; she always enjoyed hearing from Rae. "Not much," she answered, running her fingers through her bangs. I need a haircut—does that qualify as news?"

"Not really. I could use some TLC myself." She sighed. "The reason I called is to invite you and Justin for a hike tomorrow. The weather is supposed to be really nice, high seventies."

Anna pouted. "I'm hesitant about being in the woods. I'm afraid of the wild animals."

Rae split her sides laughing. Through her chuckles, she explained that they were going to a marked trail that would wind around a lake. "If you'll feel, better I'll bring my animal spray and we can carry sticks. Oh come on, Anna, it's the last weekend before school starts."

Anna hesitated for only a moment then acquiesced. "You've talked me into it. Let me go tell Justin. He's in his room putting his clean clothes away."

Justin yelped for joy upon hearing.

"I take it he's interested." Rae laughed. "We'll pick you up around ten. I'll pack a light lunch for all of us.

"You're the best, Rae."

"I know!" Rae teased back.

The next day the four arrived at the state park. Anna was taken with nature's beauty. Tall evergreens surrounded cobalt blue water under a cloudless sky as a light breeze stirred tall yellow grasses along a pea graveled path.

"It's beautiful here." Anna spread her hands wide closed her eyes and breathed the pungent woodsy scents. "I'm glad you encouraged me to come."

Rae gestured toward a bench nearby. "We'll need to give to give the boys instructions before we embark on our adventure." She rolled expressive eyes. "Come here, boys!" Rae called. They ran toward the bench, punching each other in jest as they approached. "Okay, we're going to walk all the way around." She pointed to the tree with a yellow paint marker. "As you can see the trail follows the lake, you two must stay in eye shot. No running off on your own."

"Got it?" Anna added.

"You guys won't be able to keep up with us," Scotty remarked.

"Hey, smarty pants, we're up for it," Anna quipped.

"All right, let's go." Rae rose from the bench. "Take a stick from that bucket over there just in case."

Anna chose a well-rounded one with a hook on the end. Held it over her head and growled. Everyone shrieked with laughter.

"You look mean, Mom!" Justin chuckled.

They'd been hiking close to thirty minutes when Rae exclaimed, "Ouch! I have a stone in my sneaker," and bent over to remove it. Anna watched as she shook the rock loose. Preoccupied for mere seconds they looked up, and both boys had disappeared.

"Boys! Boys!" the mothers called.

"Justin!"

"Scotty!" they yelled as they searched.

Then Rae stopped short and placed her hands on her hips and growled loudly, "Scotty and Justin, where are you? Come out of hiding like *now*!"

They heard giggling and upon looking up found both boys sitting in a large jack pine partially hidden by its ample branches.

"Come down right now!"Anna yelled. "Now!"

After they jumped, Rae cuffed each of them lightly on their head.

"Don't ever try that trick again, or you'll be grounded for life," Anna told Justin."And what's that on your face?" She held his chin in her hand.

"War paint. Scotty's neighbor gave it to him, and he brought it in his backpack."

She looked at Scotty who shied away from Anna's glare.

"Why did you do that to your face?"

"We're playing war, Ma. We're trying to hide from the enemy."

"Well, we are not the enemy, so you best stay close and do what you're told."

After they'd rested, it was decided the boys would follow closely behind their mothers for the rest of the hike. "Should we treat them to ice cream after the scare they give us?" Anna whispered to Rae at the end of the trail.

"Yeah, they're little stinkers but just being typical boys. Anyway I can't eat ice cream in front of them, and I'm craving a large chocolate dream."

Tired and happy they headed for cool treats and then returned home.

CHAPTER 24

Autumn exploded in brilliant color and cool breezes. It was Saturday morning and Justin came yawning from his room at ten a.m.

"Good morning, sunshine," Anna sang and mussed his already tangled hair.

He pulled away from her touch.

"I thought we'd take a ride and view the foliage after lunch."

"I can't, Mom; I'm going to a movie with Scotty this afternoon. His mom said she'd pick me up and drop me off." He flipped his hand through his hair to put it back into place.

"You've already made plans?"

"Yeah, we planned it earlier in the week. I thought I told you."

"I don't remember discussing it, Justin. Besides, we plan a day every autumn to go leaf peeping. It's our tradition. Maybe tomorrow?"

"Come on, Mom. That's for kids." He grunted and headed to his room.

With Justin occupied, Anna decided to phone Mary and invite her to go view the leaves. Mary was thrilled for an opportunity to view autumn's splendor. They drove along dirt roads in awe of the visage of brilliant yellows bronze and scarlet. After taking several photographs, they stopped at a quaint café for pie and coffee. Small shops displaying their wares, mostly fashioned by local artisans, beckoned the two. They browsed to their hearts content before returning home, each with a small treasured souvenir. Justin had not yet returned, and Anna invited Mary to stay for supper.

"I don't want you to go to any trouble. I'm not all that hungry after the hunk of apple pie we ate."

"No trouble. I'll throw a ham and grilled cheese together. It will only take minutes." Anna rummaged through the cupboard for a skillet.

"You talked me into it. I can't resist a good hot ham and cheese." Mary sat on the chair, folded her hands in her lap, as she watched Anna prepare the food in the kitchen.

The two sat companionably and enjoyed the meal.

"Mary, do you remember when your son was Justin's age?" She wiped the oozing cheese from the side of her sandwich.

"Do I? Good grief. He turned into a different child. Not out rightly bad, you know, but difficult to live with."

"In what way?"

Mary reached for her napkin. "He got mouthy. I used to feel like swatting him but didn't. He also acted as though I was clueless, like I just fell from a turnip truck."

Anna laughed aloud. "That sounds familiar. I guess my boy is only being normal. I miss the old Justin, though, I admit."

Mary nodded in agreement. "Yes, but we must never forget that God has entrusted us with our children. His plans for them are far greater than we could even fathom."

"Hey, Nana Mary," Justin greeted as he interrupted by clambering through the door.

"Hey, yourself. I'll be getting on home now. I'm plum worn out. But thank you for a perfectly wonderful day. I so enjoyed it."

"Want me to walk you home, Nana Mary?"

"No, dear, I'll be fine." She hugged Anna and Justin and then lumbered to the door.

Anna watched her dear friend through the window and was saddened to realize how feeble she had become.

Autumn leaves dried up, twirled in the air and fell in clumps where the wind dropped them. Anna had neglected to root out their winter coats and was glad to arrive to the warmth of the cottage. The place seemed to wrap its arms around her. She started a pot of coffee and plunked down in a chair by the fire. It had been an unusually stressful day at work. An elderly male patient had had a massive stroke while having his teeth worked on. It happened so quickly everyone was shocked. She could still see his pallid face as the emergency team wheeled him away. The recollection made her shiver.

When the coffee was ready, she poured herself a cup and slowly began to relax. Barely had she taken a few sips of the sweet brew when Justin burst through the door with loud exclamation, "Where's my winter jacket, my gloves, and stuff, Ma? I'm frozen. Did my dad call? He told me he would when I talked to him last week."

She turned to her son, and before she could answer, his bedroom door slammed and loud music blared from behind the door. Anna placed the cooling coffee on a table and folded her hands in prayer. *Give me strength, dear Lord, and an abundance of patience.*

CHAPTER 25

Winters in Minnesota were not for the faint of heart, but because Anna had grown up in Maine, she was able to contend with its harshness. Always though, she longed for spring and the first appearance of the brave daffodils, which most times patiently contended with snow on their bright faces. Of course spring led to summer, and as soon as Justin finished school in late June, he'd prepare each year to be in Maine with his dad before the Fourth of July. July was the most difficult month every year for Anna. She would feel lost until her son returned home on the first day of August. In Justin's younger years, he'd phone her every other day, but Anna noted that each July as he got older he'd call her less and less. And so she'd stay at home as much as possible and wait for his call or rush from work to check the answering machine. Rae and Mary scolded her on many occasions but to no avail. She couldn't let him go.

This year when Anna picked him up at the airport, he appeared older. He'd gotten slimmer, seemed to have grown two or three inches, and wore his hair in a buzz cut, which enhanced his expressive blue eyes. Mike had changed considerably also. He'd put on weight, and his thick hair had thinned to a bald spot on the top of his head.

"How's it going?" he asked. "I brought our boy back to you safe and sound. He'll be sixteen next month he can travel alone and I won't have to make this hateful trip every summer."

Justin looked from mother to father. Anna knew he felt the continued animosity between them. She changed the subject. "How is the family?"

"They're all doing fine. Just fine. Well, I'm gonna grab a beer before my flight back to Maine. Talk to ya soon, Justin." He punched him playfully on the shoulder.

Anna tried in vain to make conversation on the drive back to the cottage. Justin sat quietly peering out the window at nothing in particular. She didn't question him but gave him space to readjust to life in Minnesota. Several days later he opened up and began to talk.

"I'll be sixteen soon. Dad says I should be thinking about getting a part-time job."

Anna made no comment but allowed him to continue.

"I met this friend in Maine. He's seventeen. His name's Conor. Anyway, he's joining the army next year when he graduates."

Anna cleared her throat. "He's not planning to go to college?"

"Naw, says he wants to see the world. Says he's sick of school-work. I think he's right."

Anna placed a hand on her hip. "That's no way to see the world."

Justin rolled his eyes and changed the subject. "I'm going out to meet the guys for basketball."

"What guys? Where are you playing? What time will you come home?"

"Come on, Ma, with the twenty questions. I'm meeting up with Tim and some of his friends. I don't know their names yet. We're playing at the high school. What time do I have to be home?"

"Who's Tim? I'd like you home by seven."

Justin ignored her inquisition. "Give me a break, Ma. It's not even dark until way after eight."

"Fine, but not a minute later."

Justin blew a kiss to his mother and ran out the door before his mother could change her mind.

———•◦•———

When his birthday rolled around on August 20, Mary called before lunch. "What have you planned for the birthday boy?"

"Sadly nothing. He doesn't even want a cake this year." Anna sighed deeply. "I think he's outgrown our party with balloons, streamers, and cakes shaped like skateboards. He said he would celebrate with his friends, whatever that means. When I asked him what he wanted, he said cold, hard cash. I don't even have anything to wrap!"

"He's growing up, Mother. Send him over, will you? I have a little gift for him."

Anna knocked on Justin's bedroom door.

"Come in, Ma. I'm going through my closet. Some of these clothes don't fit me anymore, and some I don't even like," he screamed over the music. Anna turned the volume down, and Justin rolled his eyes.

"Mary would like to see you for a few minutes. She has something for you."

"Okay, I'll run over now 'cause I'm going off with the guys this afternoon."

"Where are you going with the guys? Who are *the guys* anyway?"

"Mom, give it up." He moved her aside and bolted out the door.

Anna watched him through the window. Her son ran like a deer, youthful and strong. It was becoming increasing difficult for her to watch him grow up.

Justin always treated Mary lovingly, and when she opened the door, he smiled and embraced her.

"I have a little something for you. I don't shop much anymore, the old bones won't allow me to putter the mall like I used to."

"You didn't have to get me anything, Nana Mary."

She handed him a card containing a gift card for the sporting goods store at the mall.

"Please indulge an old lady and sit with me a few minutes. Will you?" She plucked an ice cream cake from the freezer and cut a hunk and set it before him. "Eat." She smiled.

"Wow, this is the best, Nana Mary," Justin said with a mouthful of cake.

When he finished, she popped a can of cola and gave it to him. "Now you've made an old lady happy, we've celebrated your sixteenth birthday." She sat down with a groan.

Justin tapped the fork on the ice cream–smeared plate. "Can I talk to you about somethin'?" he asked with furrowed brow.

"You can talk to me about anything. You *know* you are like one of my own." She placed her hand over his.

"Well…" He hesitated. "It's my mom. She's buggin' me all the time. She wants to know everything. I feel like she's drivin' me nuts. I wish she'd just leave me alone." He jumped from the chair. "Can you make her get off my back?" His face turned red.

"Goodness me, Justin. Try to understand your mom has built her whole life around you. It's hard to give up parental control. Do be patient with your ma, and I will speak to her, I promise."

"Tell my mom to get a life."

Mary slowly rose from the chair. "I think you need to be more respectful of your mother, Justin. She has been very good to you, and you know she loves you very much. It's your birthday. Calm down. You only turn sixteen once."

"You're right, Nana Mary." He softened. "But can you still talk to her though? She listens to you."

"I told you I would." Mary took his hands to her heart.

———◆◆———

Since Justin had plans, and Anna knew that Chad was traveling, she phoned Rae to meet for dinner. It was a beautiful sunlit evening with a light breeze, and so they bought subs and headed to the park to picnic. The park was quiet except for an older couple walking slowly arm in arm, holding each other up it seemed. A few children swang back and forth on the swings. The rhythmical squeak of the chain reminded Anna and Rae of the many hours they spent here with their boys. They both sighed at the same time and then chuckled.

"I wish I could have Justin back at that age." Anna gestured to the swinging children.

"Not me," Rae countered. "I'm looking forward to Scotty going off to college. Chad and I will have more time to travel. I don't want to rush my son's life, obviously. I guess I'm slowly preparing for that change in my life. That's what we do, ya know?"

"What do you mean?"

"Well, I'm sure you've heard how the ole saying goes: 'We give them roots, now we must give em' wings.'"

CHAPTER 26

All too soon Justin began his senior year of high school. Anna had noticed her son emerge from an awkward boy to a young man. His short, lean legs were sturdy from running track, and broad shoulders stood out from his slender physique. His complexion had cleared, and a soft reddish shadow appeared on his face while his hair had darkened to a light auburn. The only thing that hadn't changed was his crystal blue eyes.

One day shortly after school had begun, Justin stayed home ill. With a high temperature and a raging sore throat, Anna decided to take the day off work and take him to the doctor. She handed him a cup of hot tea with honey and placed her hand on his forehead.

"You're burning up. I'll make toast so you can take aspirin after you've eaten."

She walked into the kitchen while Justin lay lethargic on the couch. He clicked on the TV. News filled the screen, and just as he was about to change the channel he called, "Mom, come quick."

The two helplessly watched as two planes smashed into the twin towers in New York. They were stunned. They didn't speak but stayed glued to what was happening before their eyes. They learned that two of the terrorists had flown from Portland, Maine, to Boston. Anna could not believe they had come from her home state airport. What seemed like minutes became hours as they watched the horror of 9/11 unfold.

The shrill of the phone ringing in the quiet room jarred Anna upright. The voice of her sister pulled the miles between them.

"This is unbelievable," she heard Holly say through long pauses of breathing as they simultaneously watched their TVs.

"I can't believe they were in Maine. Are you guys all right?"

"I know, right? How scary is that? I could have been standing behind terrorists in McDonald's this week. Or at the grocery store. Or at the gas station. Anywhere! Hang on, Anna, I've got call waiting."

Anna continued to watch the updates on the TV as she waited for her sister.

"That was Mom. They are okay. She said she would call you next."

"Thanks. I haven't called anyone yet. I think I'm still in shock. Justin's home too with a temp," she added.

"Perfect timing, at least you guys are getting this news together. Say hi to him for me. I'm gonna go and call Mom back. I'm sure you'll hear from her soon. I love you, sis."

"You too, take care." Knowing they were safe brought little comfort as a sense of vulnerability soaked through the living room of their Minnesota cabin. Anna thought of her long-time friend Rae. She reached for the phone and dialed.

"Rae, are you watching what's happening?"

"Yeah, I'm in shock. I can't believe it. It's horrible."

"Where's Chad? Please tell me he's not travelling this week." Anna paced nervously around the kitchen.

"He was supposed to head out this morning. Thank God he didn't go. Oh, Anna, I don't know how I'm going to let him travel ever again." Anna heard her friend sniffle into the phone.

"I'm so glad he's home with you, Rae. I was worried. Justin is home sick. I think he may have strep. I was going to call the doctor this morning, but we've been glued to the TV. I guess I better go and try to get an appointment for him. I just wanted to check on you."

"Thanks, Anna. Tell Justin I hope he feels better soon. Take care, my friend."

"Yes, and you as well."

Anna joined Justin on the couch as he shivered from chills. He looked at his mother sadly.

"Why is this happening, Mom?"

She sighed. "I don't know, son. I don't know." Sadness mixed with fear hung like a spider web over them.

"Well, what are they going to do? I don't understand. How did the terrorists get away with this? Isn't it somebody's job to be stopping this, like the CIA or somethin'?"

"I don't know. I have no more answers then you. I don't know. All we can do is pray."

The two prayed together for their country, for the families hurt by the terror attack, and for the safety of all.

CHAPTER 27

Antibiotics healed Justin physically; however, emotionally, Anna noted a marked difference in her son. In fact, while watching the horrific pictures played out over and over, week after week was too much. He'd smashed one fist into the other and stated through gritted teeth, "I'm eighteen. I should join up right now."

"Join up?" Anna blurted.

"Yeah, Ma, why not? President Bush'll need ta send more troops out after whoever did this to us. We need to defend our country, don't we?"

"Yeah, right, you're not even out of high school yet." She brushed him off like sweeping crumbs under the rug. The lingering days after September 11 left Anna needing to cling to all that was familiar. It was like walking a tight rope; waiting for it to break. The daily routine gave her a feeling of safety. Anything that interrupted that routine brought on anxiety. Justin became increasingly angry. Little things would set him off and leave Anna confused. She missed the closeness they once shared, and the more she tried to engage him, the more he pushed her away. A bitter winter converged on Minnesota, and it was not only cold outside, it was cold inside as well.

Anna looked out through the mudroom window at the snow-covered driveway. The wind whipped large flakes through the darkening sky. *Justin should have been home from work an hour ago*, she surmised. He'd gotten a part-time position at the town grocery store to help defray the cost of insurance and gas for his car. Anna was unsure if his beat-up Honda would make it through the snow as the tires were balding and he barely had the cash to replace them. She paced back and forth from the kitchen to the mudroom window and then decided to shovel a path for him. The snow was heavy and wet, and the cold wind sent swirls of white around her head. As she worked to move the snow, a set of headlights shone weakly through the storm, and Justin's car approached.

"Where have you been?" Anna asked with concern.

"At work. Where do you think I was?" he said blatantly.

"You were supposed to be home over an hour ago. It would have been nice had you called to tell me you were going to be late. It being the first storm of the season; you know how I feel when you start driving in the snow again." She held the shovel out for Justin to finish the job.

"Yeah, perfect! I'll tell my boss I have to call my mommy right in the middle of my shift," he said mockingly. He took the shovel and began to work vigorously to finish the driveway. "Where's the snow blower?"

"No gas in it yet, I wasn't expecting a storm this early. Guess I should know better." Anna pulled the stocking cap from her head and handed it to Justin to wear.

He gave her an annoyed look, grabbed the hat from her hand, and tossed it into the snow.

"I give up," Anna said as she stomped to the mudroom to take off her boots. She gathered some wood and started a fire in the fireplace. The crackling wood filled the quiet space. Anna rubbed her hands in front of the fire. She heard boots stomping in the mudroom, and soon Justin joined her flicking large flakes from his hair. He took off his wet socks and placed them to dry near the fire.

"Angie called." Justin had recently started dating a girl from his high school that Anna was anxious to meet.

"Yeah, well, I'm not calling her back," he groused.

Anna walked into the kitchen, polished an apple on her jeans, and took a bite. "Why won't you call her back? She sounded like she really wants to talk to you. I was thinking we could have her to dinner this weekend so we can meet."

"Not gonna happen, Ma. She has eyes for someone else. I'm over it." Justin looked into the refrigerator and pulled out a soda.

"Eyes for whom? I thought you really liked this girl?" Anna was confused.

"Scotty, Ma. The two of them were waiting by my locker today whispering and making goo-goo eyes at each other. I'm not blind. As soon as I came toward them, they hushed up. Scotty got a football scholarship to U of Minnesota and was waving it around like he's all that. Angie's going there too—they deserve each other," he said as he took a sip of his drink.

"Oh. I'm sorry, Justin. Are you okay? You didn't get your letter of acceptance to the university yet. Is that why you're upset?"

"No, I didn't apply. And now I'm glad I didn't. I don't want to be there with those two," he said nonchalantly.

"What? I thought you applied? What are you saying?" Anna felt anxious.

"I didn't have my transcript sent. I'm not going," Justin said with conviction.

Anna stood with her hands on her hips, her brow furrowed. "You're telling me you are not going to the U? Then where *are* you going? It would be nice if you would tell me what your plans are. Do you think you are going to work at that grocery store for the rest of your life at minimum wage?" Her hand flew in the air in frustration.

"I have a plan. I'm joining the army," he said as he tossed the empty can into the recycle bin.

"Over my dead body!" Anna's blood boiled. "You are going to university. You are going to do something with your life. You're a smart kid, Justin, and you are not going to throw it all away to be some grunt in the war." She pointed her finger in his face. "You've worked too hard and too long to mess up now. You get that transcript sent tomorrow before it's too late. I don't want to hear any more about this. It's crazy, Justin."

Justin glared at his mother before retreating to his bedroom. He slammed the door and turned the radio volume loud. Anna stood shaking in the kitchen with her hand on the counter to keep her balance and gasped a deep breath. *This is just a phase; let it go,* she thought. *He'll come around. He's just mad at Scotty and Angie. I shouldn't have argued with him about this now. The timing is all wrong,* she chided herself.

She sat in front of the fire and watched the flames flicker. Her mind whirled fretfully. How could she reach her son? What had happened that put such a chasm between them? *Lord, please help me. Touch Justin's heart and show him your will. Help me to know how to communicate with him.*

The week passed uneventfully. The argument between mother and son became a distant memory, although Anna felt like she was walking on eggshells. Afraid to rock the boat, she kept the communication light when they passed each other in the evenings. On Friday night Justin announced that he was going out.

"Where are you going?" Anna asked.

"Out with Tim," he quipped.

"Who's this Tim character you keep talkin' about, and why haven't you brought him over?"

"Mom, I'm not a kid anymore. I'm not going to have him come over for a *play date.*" He rolled his eyes.

"Aren't you going bowling with Scotty?" Every Friday night for as long as Anna could remember the boys bowled in a local league.

"I'm done with Scotty. I told you that." Justin was putting his boots on to leave. "What do I have to say or do to convince you?"

Anna folded her arms across her chest and bit her tongue. She watched as her son walked out the back door. Within seconds he came back into the cabin.

"My car won't start. Can I take yours?" Justin threw his car keys on the kitchen table.

"No, I'd rather you not. I can give you a ride if you'd like."

Justin rolled his eyes at his mother. "Come on, Ma. I'm not having you drop me off at a party."

"What party? Will the parents be home?" Anna searched his face for answers.

"Ma, come on… Please stop. I'm eighteen. When are you going to get over it?" Justin walked past his mother and grabbed the keys for his snowmobile. "Never mind, I'll take the skidoo."

"Wait, what time are you going to come home? It's supposed to snow again later?" Anna grabbed hold of his jacket sleeve.

Justin shook her off. "I'll be home when I'm home," he said determinedly as he walked from the mudroom and into the snow-covered yard.

Anna heard the old snowmobile engine start. She looked out the sliding glass door and watched as her son zipped across the frozen lake, leaving a white cloud behind him.

Placing a few prepackaged brownies in a bag, Anna trudged through the fallen snow and ice to see her neighbor. She couldn't stay in the empty cabin to fume alone. Mary was so happy to see her friend; she made herbal tea for them to enjoy.

Anna tossed the brownies on the kitchen table. "They're not homemade, but it's the best I could do on short notice."

"That's fine, you're a busy woman. I think anything chocolate will do us just fine. How are you, dear?" She placed a cup in front of Anna.

"Ugh, Mary, I'm so frustrated with Justin these days. We're not on the same page like we used to be. He's mad at his best friend. He's frustrated with me. He even intimated that he's thinking of joining the army. I can't figure him out." She blew into the steaming mug.

"The army? He changed his mind about college?"

"I think he's just angry at Scotty and wants to avoid going to the same school. I don't know…" Anna put her head in her hands in frustration. "What am I going to do with this kid?"

Mary placed her hand on Anna's arm. "He's not a kid anymore, dear. He's a man," she gently reminded.

Anna looked at her aging friend. The lines around her eyes had deepened. "Yeah, well, he certainly isn't acting like a man. He doesn't ask my permission for anything. He just does his own thing and waits for me to react."

"Anna, dear, this is perfectly normal. He's pulling away because he's trying to be a man. This is why you raised him. You've done a great job. He's becoming a fine young man." Mary took a slow sip of tea and bit into a brownie and then continued. "Remember back when Paul died? You had to leave Justin with his father for a month. Remember what you told me? God spoke to you on that plane, Anna. God has him; you need to trust and let go. I'm not saying this is easy. I remember back when Paul and I were struggling with our Ben. Oh, he was headstrong; we couldn't give him any advice. I have to tell you though he turned out to be a wonderful man. He works hard and provides for his family. That's what you want, Anna. Justin is kindhearted and strong. He'll do the right thing—you'll see."

Anna allowed her neighbor's wise words sink in. "Thank you, Mary. You always know the right thing to say," she said appreciatively.

Mary laid her thinning hand upon Anna's. "Oh, my dear, you have been like a daughter to me and we mothers understand the woes of parenting. It's a tough job. Your kids are your life and you turn your head for a second and their gone," she said wistfully. "We've all been there Anna. Don't think you're the first to have these struggles, my sweet. You've raised a fine son. Trust in a job well done."

Anna smiled. "He grew up so fast," she said tearfully and then excused herself to leave. "Thanks for the tea, Mary. It was just what the doctor ordered."

Mary smiled. "Anytime, my dear, anytime." She held the door and watched Anna struggle along the snow clogged driveway.

Snowflakes began to fall again, and Anna tightened her jacket for the short walk home. The brisk air made her breath visible. She looked into the sky and watched the sparkling ice forms glisten from a pale moon. The holidays would be upon them soon. She decided to form a plan to lighten her mood. She would call her parents and Holly and invite them for the holidays. A family Christmas was right around the corner and that was something to look forward to.

She tugged the artificial tree from its old, worn box. The mangled limbs looked like it couldn't possibly stand another year. Slowly, however, the Christmas tree began to take form. Anna hummed festive tunes as she strung the white lights. It was well after midnight when Justin arrived home and found his mother knee deep in ornaments that were scattered over the living room floor.

"Oh, perfect timing! You can help me decorate the tree," Anna said excitedly as she hooked a glittered ball onto a branch.

Justin stood in the kitchen eating leftover casserole from the dish. "I'm going to bed. I'm tired," he answered as he put the dish back into the refrigerator leaving the fork on the counter.

He passed by her, and she held an ornament to him. He ignored her. "What about the angel for the top? I can't reach it by myself," she called after him.

"I'll do it tomorrow." His bedroom door slammed behind him.

Anna slumped on the couch. *What happened to the days when Justin was happy and joined in the festivities? Is there any common ground between us anymore?* She picked up the handmade ornament that Justin had made in third grade. The gold-painted macaroni was falling off the shiny silver star. She turned it over and read his hand-printed name and slid her finger across it. Taking super glue from the kitchen drawer, she attempted to put the broken ornament back together. She laid it on top of the box to dry as her eyes moistened and then left the scattered ornaments, turned out the lights, and went to bed.

———◦•◦———

A blizzard blew in from the northwest, paralyzing all flights into Minnesota. Both her parents' and Holly's flights had been canceled.

The food she had prepared throughout the week sat idly in the refrigerator, and she was trapped and lonely inside the Minnesota cabin. She had taken a week's vacation, thinking her family would be with her. Mary was suffering from the flu, and Anna brought hot soup and checked in on her from time to time. Understandably, Mary was not up to the usual festivities. The candlelight service at church had been cancelled for fear no one would show up. On Christmas Eve, Anna sat alone in front of the fireplace as Justin took the snowmobile to visit Tim. She flipped through an old photo album and smiled as she reminisced about their first family Christmas in Minnesota. Her parents, along with Holly and Chris, had come for the holidays and had cut a tree from the woods. Her father had carried it into the small living room, and they laughed when its presence over filled the space. They sang carols together and decorated the tree with strings of popcorn. Justin had been in his footed pajamas for most of their visit and had kept them entertained with dancing and toddler antics. "Those were fun days," she said aloud. Her words echoed in the lonely room.

The long Minnesota winter dragged on, and Anna and Justin saw each other less and less. Justin was either working late at the grocery store or out with his new gang of friends, Tim being the ring leader. Anna was not fond of his new relationships. Justin's personality had changed. He became more disrespectful toward her and the personal goals that he once had fell to the wayside so he could party. Anna thought she had smelled booze on him a few times and when confronted he said she'd overreacted. They became more like roommates rather than mother and son, and Anna was desperate to fix the situation.

She called Rae and asked to meet for coffee with the hope that her good friend would shed light on the disturbing problem.

The bell on the coffee shop door tinkled as Rae stepped in. The sound made Anna look up from her book as she waited.

"Hi, so good to see you! It's been ages!" Anna stepped away from her friend to get a better look at her. Rae was dressed in a well-matched black gym suit with pink pinstripe outlining her figure, her shiny black hair pulled up in a knot. "You look great for someone who just came from the gym."

Rae kissed her on the cheek before sitting at the coffee bar. "Thanks, I've been teaching again—Pilates, yoga, you name it," she answered with a wide smile. "You should take a class."

Anna noted with some envy how happy Rae seemed.

"How are things at Dr. Miller's? You still work there, right?"

"Great, the practice is growing. The addition of Margo has been such a blessing. I think there may be something going on with her and Dr. Miller though."

"Ooh, sounds juicy. Do tell!" Rae leaned toward her.

"Once in a while, I notice the two of them together, stealing glances or laughing in the sterilization room. It's kind of cute to watch actually."

"Do you think there's something more to it than just flirtation?"

"I don't give it much thought actually. I would be happy if they got together. Dr. Miller has been consumed since we moved here between the practice and his father's health. It's been years with no break. Honestly, I think it would be good for him to have something else besides work."

Rae uttered under her breath. "He's not the only one."

"What was that?" Anna leaned in closer to hear.

"Nah, nothing." Rae waved a hand aside.

"If I didn't have my job, I think I would go mad. Oh Rae! I'm so worried about Justin. He doesn't go to church with me anymore, says he doesn't want to run into Scotty. I think he's just using that as an excuse. I'm really hoping you can help me to understand. It's been months since Justin has even brought up Scotty's name. Are they going to throw away years of friendship over a girl?" Anna searched her friend for answers. "Justin really has not been himself. I've smelled alcohol on him. This new gang of friends..." Anna trailed off.

"I know. I heard he's been hanging around with that Tim character. I don't want to scare you, Anna, but I've heard that group has gotten into some trouble with the law. I know the boys have gone their separate ways with Scotty busy with football, but I do think it's Angie that's really keeping them apart. Scotty is broken up about it. He misses Justin," she said sadly. "I guess he didn't realize how much Justin cared for Angie. He knows he made a mistake, but I don't think he knows how to undo the mess, ya know? It's not our place to interfere. Do you have any suggestions?"

"I thought about talking to Justin. I have to wait for the right time, catch him in a good mood." Anna nibbled on a fingernail, a habit she'd long outgrown.

"I've talked to Scotty," Rae said. "He wants his friendship with Justin mended, but he's also smitten with Angie. I don't think he's going to give up one for the other." Rae leaned into her friend across the table. "Please tell me whatever happens it won't affect us. I've missed you Anna," she pleaded.

"Rae, I'm not that way, you should know that about me. The boys will work this out or not. It doesn't change the way I feel about you," she encouraged, although she knew this problem had already come between them. Anna attributed their separation to the busyness of life but knew it was merely a convenient excuse.

The two chatted with a new resolve to speak to their boys and a plan to get together again soon. They bid each other good-bye, and Anna had a new sense of hope that Justin would come around. He was going through a rebellious phase as all teenagers do, she told herself. She hoped it wasn't too late to reach him. Anna waited for the perfect opportunity to talk to her son. Graduation was around the corner, and with no plans in sight for Justin, he needed talking to.

CHAPTER 28

Justin walked into the cabin, wiping grease from his finger tips, and then stepped in front of the kitchen sink and washed his hands. Anna was making a sandwich and offered to make one for him.

"Did you get the oil changed?" she asked lightly.

"Yeah, the car is good for another five thousand miles," he said, smiling.

"Justin." Anna paused as she waited for him to look at her. He glanced at her, his baseball cap turned backwards on his head. Grease was smeared on his cheek, and she reached to wash it off. "We need to talk," she stated.

Anna sat at the kitchen table while Justin stood idly eating near the kitchen sink.

"What's up?"

"I want to talk to you about Scotty," she said hesitantly.

"What? You want to discuss the enemy?" he said gruffly between bites of his sandwich. "What is there to talk about? Scotty is a jerk."

"Justin, he misses you. You guys have been friends for years. It's almost graduation! I know he hurt you, but don't you think this has gone on long enough? It's time to forgive," Anna said softly.

"Forgive? Forgive?" His tone elevated. "*You* are the one telling *me* to forgive? That's funny, Mom." He tossed his food on to the counter.

Anna looked at her son, confused. "Yes. I think this has gone on long enough. I don't understand how you can throw your friendship away like this."

"You're one to talk! You didn't forgive my dad! You took me away from my *father* because you couldn't forgive. Please don't tell me how to act, you hypocrite."

Stunned, Anna shook her head to clear her mind. "What are you saying, Justin?"

"You, Mom. You brought me out here to the Midwest away from my father, away from my grandparents. You stole my family from me," he spat.

"Justin, I moved us out here in order to survive. I didn't leave Maine to take you away from your family. I needed a job to support us. There wasn't a choice." Her hands trembled.

"Oh, you had a choice. Dad said you ran away. You stole me from my real family, and I grew up with you and a neighbor for a grandma instead."

Anna seethed. It was time her son knew the truth. "You want to talk about your grandparents who wanted you aborted, who threw us out into the street by evicting us? Or how about your dear daddy who didn't visit you for months? I raised you by myself. I taught you how to be a man!" Anna screamed the words, and as soon as they flew from her mouth, she was remorseful.

Justin stood motionless. "You liar! You liar! You taught me nothing. I had to learn how to shave from my friends. I had to learn how to tie a tie from the internet. I had to learn how to change the oil from the guys at the garage. You taught me nothing! I'm so glad I'm out of here in a few days. I can't take this anymore!" The vein in his temple protruded.

"What do you mean you're out of here?" Anna's face paled.

"I'm leaving for basic training. I've joined the army where I can be with real men and away from you! I'm tired of being a mama's boy! You're so fixated on me; you don't have a life of your own. Why don't you just get a life?" He stomped out of the room and into his bedroom.

Anna sat motionless as the room spun around her. She grabbed the table to steady herself.

Justin stomped into the room carrying a duffle bag. "Don't call me. Don't contact me. Just leave me alone!" he said as he tramped out of the cabin.

"Justin! Justin!" Anna wailed but it was too late. His car peeled out of the driveway, leaving a cloud of dust and his mother in a pool of tears.

———⊷⊶———

A week passed and she hadn't heard from her son, so she paid a visit to the high school. *He's had plenty of time to cool off.* She walked into the school where teenagers bustled through the hallways. Some stood at lockers gaping at her like she was an alien. She asked one of the students directions to the principal's office and took a deep breath before entering. A secretary sat at a wooden desk, and as Anna approached, she hung up the phone.

"Can I help you?" she asked.

"I was hoping to see the principal," Anna responded.

"Do you have an appointment?"

"No, I'm afraid I don't, but it's urgent," Anna pleaded.

The secretary rose from her seat and popped her head into an office. She turned to Anna and waved her inside. The principal arose from her chair, took her reading glasses off, and laid them on her desk. Silver roots grew from her short blond hair and deep wrinkles creased her face. Unsmiling, she reached her hand across the desk, to shake Anna's.

"I'm Silvia Kruger," she announced. "What can I do for you?" She urged Anna to take a seat.

Anna looked at the poised woman. Intimidated by authority, she softly whispered, "I'm here regarding my son, Justin Gallo."

"Yes, Ms. Bertram, how can I help you?" She sat behind her desk waiting for Anna to continue.

"Well, my son hasn't been home in a week. We had a bit of an argument. I was hoping you might know where he is staying, or if you can call him to your office so we can resolve a family matter."

Ms. Kruger pulled a file from a cabinet. "Justin is no longer enrolled with us. He picked up his diploma earlier this week. He's not participating in the graduation ceremony this weekend because he left for basic training. He said you were aware of his decision."

Anna felt as if her face had been slapped. A burning sensation rose in her cheeks. "Oh no!" She held her hand to her heart. "Why didn't someone contact me?"

Ms. Kruger softened slightly. "I'm sorry, Ms. Bertram, but Justin assured us that he had discussed this with you. The recruiter came in for his transcript months ago. He's been training and working with the recruiter for some time. Didn't you know?"

Anna thought of all the "extra hours" Justin had been quote "working" and finally put it together. "No. I did not," she answered, ashamed that she had missed the clues. "What job will he do in the army?"

"Infantry." The principal checked the file in front of her without emotion.

"How could this happen? He joined without anyone contacting me? This is absurd!" Anna's anger was apparent as she rose from her seat. "I can't believe this," she stated as she paced the small office.

"Your son is eighteen, Ms. Bertram. He has the right to do whatever he chooses. Maybe there was a communication problem between you?"

Anna could not believe this was happening. "Yes. There was a communication problem and one that can't be resolved now. Thank you for your time." She nodded her head, turned on her heel, and walked swiftly out the door.

CHAPTER 29

Days passed with no contact from Justin. His exit from Anna's life was so abrupt, it left her emotions raw. She tried to create a new norm for herself. Instead of making dinner, she would order take-out and pick it up on her way home from work. One evening she decided to leave the loneliness of the cabin and eat her salad out on the pier. It was fishing season. Her thoughts turned to Paul when she and Justin first met him. He was so happy holding up that stinky fish. She laughed to herself. *I wonder if things would have been different for Justin if Paul had lived and stayed in his life.* She sighed as she removed her work shoes and plunged her toes into the lake. The cold jolted her, and she waited for her feet to adjust. Flecks of golden glitter danced along the lake. Pensive, she stared into the water and pondered. *Maybe I should take a trip back home to Maine. Or go and see Mom and Dad. Maybe I should just get away from all of this for a while.*

Her thoughts were interrupted as she caught sight of a boat roughly fifty feet in front of her. The engine had died, and the owner fussed with the motor. She watched as he threw his hands up after checking something and then put ores in the water. With each row, his biceps flexed through his T-shirt as he glided closer toward her. His shoulders were wide giving him an advantage. Each stroke was seamless as he glided toward her with ease. Anna put her salad aside and pulled her feet from the water as he approached.

"Sorry to bother you. Any chance you have a spark plug?"

Anna looked at his sheepish grin. His auburn hair shone in the late afternoon sun. As he smiled showing dimples a shiver shot down her spine.

"No, sorry." She grabbed a rope that he'd tossed from his boat and wrapped it around the pier.

He jumped from his fishing vessel. "How about a crescent wrench. A socket set?"

Slightly embarrassed for not having any tools, Anna shook her head no.

"Well, I'm stuck." He shrugged and held out his callused hand to her. "Steve Henderson, idiot fisherman."

She took his hand in hers. "Anna Bertram, pleasure to meet you." She smiled. "I'm sure you're not an idiot. A wise friend once told me, 'Don't beat yourself up; the world will do that for you.'"

He shook his head. "I told myself to put an extra spark plug in the tackle box before I left. Serves me right for not listing to my instincts." He reached and pulled a cell phone from his pocket. "Excuse me," he said as he dialed a number. Steve rubbed his reddish beard as he waited. Closing the phone shut, he looked at her with tender golden eyes. "I guess my buddy's not home either."

"Do you want a ride to a hardware store?" Anna offered.

"Would you mind giving me a ride home? It's closer; I have a slew of plugs back at my house. I don't want to put you out or anything, but it would be a long walk for me from here." He looked to the sun slowly sinking in the evening sky. "By the time I'd get back, it would be way after dark."

Anna looked at his stature. He was only a few inches taller than her, but his strong build and wide shoulders made him seem rugged and tall. "Sure. I'll get my keys." She picked up her shoes and salad, leaving him to wait at the pier. Entering the cabin, she found them on the table, and she paused to gaze at Steve Henderson through the window. He was bent over his boat looking for something. It was comforting to look out and see a man at the end of the pier.

Part of her wanted him to stay; the stranger filled the emptiness that surrounded her like a cloud. She watched as he brushed his hand through his hair, put his hands on his hips, and looked at his abandoned boat. He turned to look back at the cabin, and she rushed through the screen door, embarrassed in case he'd caught her watching him. Steve walked toward her, and the two got into her car.

"Where to?" She could smell a hint of musk that stimulated her senses.

"I'm on the south side of the lake," he answered, pointing out the window.

The south side. Anna remembered the prestigious area where Dr. Miller Sr. lived.

"So what's with the scrubs?" He noted her work attire.

"I work for Dr. Miller, the dentist. You know him?"

"Ah yes. His dad lives a few doors down from me. Are you a hygienist then?"

"No, I'm Dr. Miller's assistant." She smiled.

Steve pointed to a narrow road that led to his driveway. The tall, perfectly aligned pines gave an air of elegance. He asked her to pull in, and he hopped out of the car. "I'll be back in a minute."

The trees blocked her view, but she saw a hint of a well-oiled log cabin. She wished she had pulled closer to get a better look at his home. *He can't possibly live at this estate alone,* she surmised. He came back with a smile holding up a spark plug and a tool box. "Got it!" he said as he entered the car. Anna noted that he wore no wedding band on his left ring finger. She smiled at him and asked. "Anything else you need? Remember I have absolutely no tools back at my cabin."

"All set." He nodded as they travelled back to Anna's home.

The sky darkened as Steve rushed to his boat to attempt to fix the engine. Anna ran into the cabin, grabbed a flashlight from under the sink, and met him at the pier. She held the light on the motor to assist him. Within minutes the engine was running, and he raised his fist in the air with relief. He wiped his hands on a rag in the boat and then reached to take Anna's hand.

"Thank you, Ms. Anna." He bowed as he untied the rope and pushed away from the pier.

She curtseyed. "Welcome, Mr. Steve." She smiled as she watched him motor away.

CHAPTER 30

Anna had not seen nor heard from Mary in two weeks. Issues with Justin along with her work schedule kept her overwhelmingly busy. Feeling guilty for being inattentive to her old friend, she drove to her house straight after work and was shocked to see a bold red and white *for sale* sign on the lawn. Her heart quickened as she rushed to the door. Mary opened it with a welcoming smile.

"So good to see you, Anna," she said as she threw an arm around her shoulders and led her into a box-littered living room.

"What's going on, Mary? Why is your house for sale? Where are you going?" Her voice raised an octave higher with each question.

"Whoa! Slow down, dear." She gestured toward the sofa for Anna to sit. "Relax, I'll explain everything," she said as she shoved an empty cardboard box to the floor. "I knew I should have called and told you what's going on." She furrowed her brow. "With Justin being a mitt full these past months, well, I didn't want to bother you. The real estate agent visited just today."

"Mary, you could never be a bother. You're like family." Anna hugged the now slender woman.

"Thank you, dear. I feel the same about you; you must know that." Her eyes softened.

"We've been through a lot together these past many years." Anna's eyes filled as her voice cracked.

Mary stood up and straightened her shoulders. "Enough of this sentimental talk. I'm moving; I'm not dying. Want a cup of tea?"

"Sure could use a cup," Anna said with a sigh.

Mary put the kettle to boil and then ambled to the window. As she peered out, she said wistfully, "I'll miss this place." With head bent, she cleared her throat and went on. "I'm going to live in the newly renovated apartment building on Willow Street. They call it an extended-care facility," she said as she rolled her eyes. "I'll have my own space with a small kitchenette. It's quite lovely really."

Anna joined her at the window. "But why, Mary? You love this house and the lake and all the wild critters and your garden."

The two women gazed fondly at the lake as the last of the daylight lingered on the calm water. Mary smiled into Anna's eyes and said. "Anna, dear, God has been very good to me. I've had a wonderful life here with a wonderful husband, my Paul," she whispered. "This house, Eagle Lake, has been mine to enjoy for so many years, I'm grateful."

The tea kettle whistled shrilly. Mary hurried to the kitchen to turn the burner off and set the tea to perk. Anna followed, speechless, and surprised at how quickly things changed.

"It's time for me to move on now," Mary continued. "The kids say the house is too much for me to keep up. I don't eat properly. They are concerned for me." She shrugged her shoulders dejectedly.

"But, Mary, how do *you* feel about moving?" Anna asked

Her neighbor brought her into a motherly embrace. "It's time, dear. I'll be okay. I'm sure it will be strange at first, but I'm sort of looking forward to being with folks who are in the same boat, so to speak. It's for the best, Anna, you'll see."

Anna was perplexed. She noted, however, that Mary had lost a considerable amount of weight and the house that she'd kept scrupulously clean in the past had taken on a lackluster appearance. Mary's family had reason for concern, she admitted.

"I'll pour the tea," Anna offered as she busied herself in Mary's untidy kitchen.

"How many troubles and joys have you and I shared over a cup of tea?" Mary said reflectively.

"Too many to count," Anna agreed.

Mary's eyes bore into Anna's with a hint of insecurity. "You'll come have tea with me on Willow Street, won't you, Anna?"

"You know I will, my dear, dear Mary. I'll even help you pack and unpack." Anna reached for an empty box, wondering what their respective futures would bring.

———

Friday approached, and although it had been a long workweek, Anna was restless thinking about the weekend. Mary had been thankful for her help packing throughout the week, and her children were arriving to complete the finishing touches, leaving Anna to wonder where she fit.

She looked at the schedule of patients posted on the door. As she scrolled the names, the first patient popped off the page. It read: 8:00 a.m. emergency patient: Steve Henderson. Her heart fluttered in her chest. Anna smiled inwardly at the thought of seeing her rescued stranger again. She looked at the clock; it was 7:45. Hurrying to the bathroom, she gazed in the mirror, adjusted her ponytail, and pinched her cheeks to encourage a blush. She giggled to herself for being silly and then walked into the waiting room to see if her patient had arrived. Steve was filling out paperwork and looked up as she entered.

"Good morning, Mr. Henderson. I can seat you now." She smiled warmly.

He handed over the clipboard and followed her to the dental chair. As she shook the napkin and secured it around his neck with a chain, she noted the familiar hint of musk cologne. She looked into his golden eyes and back onto the clipboard.

"It says here you have a toothache? Dr. Miller will want me to take an x-ray for a better look," she said as she adjusted the x-ray machine around him.

"Ah, yep," he answered hesitantly as he folded the sleeves on his plaid shirt.

"Which tooth is bothering you?"

He opened his mouth and pointed to a molar in the back. "I think it's that one."

She gently laid a lead apron over him, placed the film carefully in his mouth, asking him to bite down, and adjusted the x-ray machine. She then stepped out of the room until the machine beeped.

Steve spit the film into his hand. He wiped his mouth with the back of his sleeve. "How are you? Rescue any more boaters lately?" His eyes twinkled.

"I'm fine. No, actually, it's been pretty quiet," she said shyly. "I'm going to develop this x-ray. Can I get you anything while you wait. A magazine perhaps?"

"No. I'm good. I'll say my prayers while I wait." He closed his eyes and leaned back in the dental chair.

Anna looked at her peaceful patient before exiting. He appeared relaxed and boyish as he sat with his eyes closed. Her hands trembled as she put the x-ray through the developer. She tapped her hand upon the machine nervously as she waited for it to be developed. A warm flush washed over her. *Whew! What's come over me?*

Entering the room, she placed the developed film onto the view box and turned on the florescent light. She studied the film for a few minutes before Steve interrupted.

"I have a confession to make," he whispered to get her attention.

"A confession?" She turned to meet his gaze.

"I don't have a toothache, Anna. I just wanted to see you again."

Anna's face flushed as Dr. Miller entered the room.

"Good morning, I hear you have a toothache," he said to his patient as he reached for a fresh pair of gloves.

Steve looked at Anna and then at the dentist and smiled. "Yes, I have a bit of an ache," he fibbed.

Flustered, Anna sat in her chair alongside the new patient. "I didn't find anything abnormal on the x-ray, Dr. Miller." She stammered as she tried to recover.

Dr. Miller positioned the dental chair back and asked Steve to open his mouth. "Let's take a look here." He studied the x-ray and looked perplexed. He tapped the tooth with the back of his instrument. "Does this hurt?"

Steve waited for the instrument to be removed from his mouth. "Nope."

Dr. Miller shook his head. "I don't see a problem." The dentist rolled away in his chair. "Any sensitivity to hot or cold?"

"Nope," Steve answered nonchalantly.

"Well, I'm baffled." He removed his gloves, washed his hands, and stared again at the x-ray.

Steve smiled at Anna, and she returned a glare before the dentist turned. "Is it hurting right now?"

"Nope, seems to be all healed. Maybe I just bit down too hard on something last night. Sorry to waste your time, Doc," he apologized.

"Well, okay then. If you have any other problems, be sure to give me a call. But it looks like today you're off the hook." The dentist shook Steve's hand. "Good to see you."

"Good to see you too, Doc. And thanks for seeing me on short notice. I really do appreciate it." Steve smiled. "How's your father these days? Hangin' in I hope?"

"Yes, he's doing all right. Thanks for asking. I know he misses your folks quite a bit, always reminds me how they were salt of the earth. If you ever get some free time I know Dad would love to see you. Stop by on the boat sometime. I know he'd appreciate that. Take care, Steve."

The dentist walked out of the room, and Anna removed the napkin from Steve's neck. He grabbed her arm before she could walk away. "Anna, please can I see you again?"

She looked into his pleading eyes. "What makes you think I'm not married?" she asked.

"Come on, you don't own a spark plug or a toolbox? Dead giveaway." He smiled.

"I can't believe you came in here faking a toothache! We have patients with real issues waiting." She pulled away to throw out his bib.

"I have an issue too. I can't get you off my mind," he said softly. "Let me make you dinner. How about tonight? You can trust me—ask the doc." He nodded his head toward the door. "We've lived in the same neighborhood for years."

Anna encouraged him to leave the dental chair.

He held his fingers in his ears like a spoiled child. "I'm not leaving until you give me the answer I'm looking for."

"Oh all right," she agreed. "I need to get you out of here so I can get back to work."

"Seven o'clock? You remember how to get to my place?" he said eagerly.

Anna nodded as she ushered him toward the waiting room. After their good-bye, she walked back into the empty operatory shaking her head and smiling. Remnants of his cologne teased her as she cleaned the room for the next patient. A chill of excitement travelled down her spine. *I have plans for tonight*, she thought as she mentally pondered just what she'd wear to this dinner.

CHAPTER 31

The evening was cool. With clothes strewn across the bed, Anna finally decided on jeans and a light sweater. The soft blue fabric along with pale shadow accentuated her eyes. She combed her hair and curled it, leaving soft golden tendrils along her face. Finishing with a dab of sweet perfume behind each ear, she looked in the mirror for final approval. Anna was happy to have plans for the evening. She had checked the answering machine when she came home from work. No message from Justin. The thought of spending the evening waiting by the phone for him to call depressed her and she was thankful for the distraction. It had been a long time since she had a date, and she was feeling slightly insecure. Wiping sweaty palms along her jeans, she forced herself out the door.

Anna arrived at the massive cabin among the pines. The pitched roof and recently treated logs shone in the evening sun. Anna gaped at the glistening palladium window located within the pitch. The first and second floors were adorned with multiple side by side mullioned panes overlooking the south side of Eagle Lake. Anna stepped in front of the two tall, wide wooden doors and rang the bell. While she waited nervously, she turned to look at the lake view and noted a screened gazebo nestled in a copse of trees. Enraptured by the scene of beauty, she was unaware of Steve.

"You like my cabin?" Steve smiled, seeing her mouth agape.

"It's really impressive. I don't think I've ever seen a log cabin quite so large," she answered, peeking over his shoulder for a view of the inside.

"I wish I could take credit for the building of it, but alas, this was my father's dream," he said. "It has his handprints all over it," Steve said fondly.

He opened the heavy door, and they stepped into a grand foyer. A round table stood midcenter holding fresh wild flowers that spilled from a shapely pottery vase. The aroma of the flowers mixed with the pungent scent of cedar tantalized Anna's nose. Steve motioned her to a book-lined library, deep and dark with red upholstered furniture along with well-worn leather chairs.

"This is one of my favorite rooms," he said. "I spend a lot of time here when I'm home. Take a seat," he offered as he stretched out in one of the soft chairs. The leather made a groaning sound as he made himself comfortable. Anna was drawn to marshmallow comfort as well in another chair. "Would you like lemonade?" He handed her a glass from a side table tray. "I'll take you for a tour of the house after our drink if you'd like?"

"Yes, I'd love to see the rest of your house," Anna said as her eyes surveyed her surroundings. "It's fascinating."

High ceilings with dark wood criss-crossed beams highlighted the main floor living room, dining room, and den in an open concept design. A well-appointed kitchen opened into the living area. In contrast to the dark wood finish in the other rooms, the kitchen featured ivory cabinets with glass doors along with open shelving. A five-foot-long island held a cook top and a sink. The speckled black granite top matched the spacious countertops. Gleaming copper-bottom pots and pans hung from a ceiling hook while recessed lighting cast a warm glow.

Steve stepped in front of a simmering pan. As he lifted the cover, the aroma sent a hunger through the space. "Did I say the library was my favorite room?" Steve laughed. "It's actually a toss-up. After cooking in this kitchen, I've taken a liking to playing with food." He spooned seasoned vegetables and handed it to Anna to taste.

She savored the pea pod soaked in juicy seasonings and nodded her head. "That's really good," she said, surprised.

"Hey, I'm a man of many talents." He laughed as he covered the pan. "I'll show you the rest of the house. I think this can simmer a bit longer," he said as he lowered the burner.

Anna took in the massive cabin. Rustic furniture and well-spaced gossip areas gave the rooms a cozy feel. A full wall unlighted fireplace waited patiently for end of summer chill. Anna was drawn to a photograph on the mantel of a woman in sport attire crossing a finish line.

Steve stood beside her. "That's my wife, Shelby. She died a few years ago. Who would have thought, a marathon runner…" He trailed off.

"I'm sorry, Steve. I didn't know."

Steve rested his hand on the mantel and inhaled deeply, "I'm okay. It's been a process, that's for sure." He shook his head. "I've grown a lot in my faith since then. I wouldn't wish it on anyone, but I certainly learned a lot about myself and what's important." He hesitated. "For a long time, I stopped living, I died too—I felt so guilty. Then I realized God has kept me here for a reason and a purpose. You can feel peace again after tragedy. It takes time that's for sure, but I'm living proof." He shrugged.

"What caused you to feel guilty, Steve?" Anna questioned as she looked at him and back at the photograph.

He took in a deep breath before responding. "It was St. Patrick's Day. Shelby wanted to go for a run. Normally I rode my bike alongside her as she ran, being the protective husband that I was. This particular day I was wiped out. I had worked all day with my dad, and I wanted to sit on the couch and veg. She begged me to go, but I was adamant." He lowered his eyes. "Shelby was hit by a drunk driver from behind. Had I been with her, it would have been me that would have taken the hit." Steve wiped his brow before continuing. "It took me a long time to realize that I couldn't have saved her. God wanted to take Shelby home."

Anna was quiet as she absorbed Steve's heartbreaking story.

Steve pulled himself together and moved toward the stairs. "I don't want to scare you off with morbid talk. I'll save that for after dinner." He winked. "Let me show you the rest of the house."

Anna nodded assent and followed him.

They toured the lower level, which held a sporting room, bar, and professional media room complete with royal blue velvet seating.

"Wow!" Anna exclaimed, taking it all in.

"You haven't seen the top floor yet," Steve said with a chuckle.

The third floor did not disappoint. Log bedrooms lined both sides of a long hallway interrupted by a large wrought iron chandelier holding numerous candle lights and at the end of the hall the palladium window hung. Anna was immediately drawn to its splendor. Aquamarine water glazed in the late evening sun. Speed boats raced leaving white foam in their wake while sail boats bobbed like toys, their colored sails contrasting with the water.

The beauty so astounded Anna, she mumbled, "This view is absolutely breathtaking."

"Yes. My father is an amazing architect. Have you heard of Henderson Logging?"

"You mean *the* Henderson Logging?" Anna's eyes popped at the realization.

"Yep. That's my dad," he answered proudly as he took her elbow and led her down the wide staircase to the kitchen.

Steve moved a stool to the kitchen island for Anna to relax while he finished making dinner. He stirred the chicken and vegetables and put together minute rice. Taking the rice and covering it with the seasoned mix, he handed a plate to Anna. He smiled as he encouraged her to taste his masterpiece.

"Well? What do you think?" he asked with expectancy.

"I think you are a very surprising man, Mr. Steve. What other talents do you have?" Anna's eyes twinkled.

Steve chuckled as he forked food from the pan. "Well, let's see… I don't know if it's a talent, but I love photography. I love being outdoors. I love to fish; ya know guy stuff," he answered. "What about you, Miss Anna? What do you like to do?"

Anna's eyes fell to her plate. She shrugged her shoulders absently. "I don't know, Steve. I don't know."

"What's wrong, Anna? Something is haunting you. I had a feeling when we talked about Shelby. I can tell something is on your mind. Go ahead, you can trust me," he said gently.

Anna moved her food around the plate before she answered. Her eyes met Steve's as he waited patiently for a response.

"I guess I don't have any hobbies. My hobby was my son." A single tear fell from her eye, and she wiped it quickly away. "I'm sorry." She took a napkin and dabbed the wetness. Anna inhaled a deep breath before continuing, "My son, Justin, left and joined the army. He didn't say good-bye. He bolted from my life. I guess I don't know who I am without him, and it scares me."

"I'm sorry to hear about your son." Steve paused. "I didn't realize." He let the words hang. "I can't imagine what you are going through, but I can sympathize with separation."

"How did you go on…" Anna hesitated, "…after Shelby?"

Steve averted his eyes to the ceiling. "A lot of prayer. One day at a time I guess. The best advice I can give is try to find things that you like to do, things that bring you peace. Learning new hobbies has helped me. Baby steps, Anna."

"Well, I do like to garden," she answered. "Flowers mostly. I cover my deck with potted plants in the summer. I love to be outside in nature. We have such a short growing season here in Minnesota," she said as she took another bite of stir-fry.

"There you go! I love to be out as much as possible in the summer too. Hey, why don't you go fishing with me tomorrow? The weather is expected to be beautiful." He left the stool and rinsed off his plate.

"Sure," Anna agreed. "It will be my first step to moving forward." She smiled as she handed him her plate. "By the way, that was the

best meal I've had in a long time. I'm done with take-out for a while."
She chuckled. "You've made me want to cook at home again."

"In that case, Miss Anna, I've done my good deed for the day,"
he teased.

The evening could not have been better. Steve's friendly, calm
demeanor brought Anna a welcomed peace. He showed her the outside of the property before their date ended. A fishing boat along
with a pontoon sat idly at the end of his pier. The sun had set and
the moon reflected a path of silver light across the water.

"Thank you, Steve. I had a lovely evening."

"I'm glad you came," he answered softly. "And I look forward to
tomorrow," he reminded, as he walked her to her car.

"Good night, Steve," she said as he held her door.

He kissed her softly on her cheek. Anna blushed.

"Night. See ya at eleven a.m. sharp." He smiled and waved as she
pulled out of sight.

CHAPTER 32

Anna packed chicken sandwiches, cheese cubes, fruit, and water bottles into a cooler in preparation for her fishing trip. She wished Justin would call. *He'll call soon. It's only a matter of time.* Taking a windbreaker from the closet, she strolled down to the pier to wait for Steve. The sun gleamed on the lake and anchored boats bobbed gently on the waves. A wonderful tingling sensation seared through her body as Steve cut the engine and slowly approached.

"Ahoy, mate!" He waved as he leaned in to grab the dock. "Ready to catch the big one?"

Anna handed him the cooler. "Yes, and I'm prepared if you forgot an extra spark plug. I brought extra food so we won't go hungry," she teased as she jumped aboard.

"Aren't you the comedian?" He retorted as he took an extra plug from his tackle box and held it up. "You're not the only one prepared." He laughed.

Steve handed her a lifejacket, and Anna sat beside him as they slowly pulled away from the dock. She watched as he looked for an old milk jug that marked his fishing spot. "We're not going far from your cabin, best fishing is right here." He pointed his finger to the floating jug.

Steve expertly cut the engine after setting the anchor. He took two poles and prepared them to cast. He put a worm on a hook and handed the fishing pole to Anna. "Oops, did you want to bate your own?"

"No, I fish, but I don't bate, and I don't take the fish off when I catch it either." She smirked.

"What? How do you fish alone then?" He chuckled.

"I don't. I fished with my dad. That's about it. I'm a master caster though," Anna proudly displayed her expertise as she stood on the boat and cast her line out with ease.

"Wow. You do know how to cast. Impressive," he said as he sent his own line out.

The two sat quietly as they watched their bobbers float along the water. It was peaceful communing with Steve and nature, to feel the soft wind tease her hair and the warm sun upon her shoulders. Contentedly, she watched him doing what he loved, pulling on his line every once in awhile to stir the action.

"What are you thinking about?" Anna spoke quietly.

Steve's face softened, and he smiled showing his dimples. "How nice it is to be here with a woman. I've never fished with a woman before," he confided. "It's different."

"How is it different?" She laughed.

"Less competitive, I guess. Instead of trying to one up you, I want you to catch a fish so you'll come with me again."

"Didn't you ever go fishing with Shelby?" Anna gently questioned.

"Nah, she wasn't into it. She couldn't sit still long enough."

Anna observed her orange bobber bounce in the water. Unsure if it was an actual fish or the wind, she jerked her pole back. Excitedly, she reeled as the fish pulled and tugged. Steve quickly stood, leaned over the side of the boat holding a net in anticipation. Anna held her breath, hoping she wouldn't lose the fighting fish. The pole bent, and she had to hold it between her legs to keep it from slipping.

"Have you got it? … You got it!" Steve urged her on.

Finally the small mouth bass was netted, and Steve brought it aboard to remove the hook.

"Wow, Anna! This is a keeper!" he said animatedly. "You won't like it, but you are going to have to hold this one up for a photo." He looked around the boat for his camera bag.

"Oh, no, no, no!" Anna shook her head. "I'll take the photo. You hold it," she said with a contorted face.

"Please, Anna. For me?" He looked at her with puppy dog eyes.

She couldn't refuse, and so for the first time in her life, she put her fingers into a slimy fish's mouth and posed for a photo. Steve took the bass from her and put it in the live well inside the boat.

"Nice work, my little spark plug," he said as he gave her a high five.

He set her pole again, and Anna cast it expertly back into the water. They sat together and waited with great expectation after getting their first fish. After several minutes, Steve reeled in a large perch. Anna took his photo before he added it to swim with her catch in the live well.

"Would you like a snack before putting your line out again?" she asked as she pulled the cooler toward her.

"Sure! What did you bring?" He peered into the cooler, dug his hand inside, and pulled out some cheese. "Thanks, Anna, this looks good. See? One more bonus to fishing with a woman," he teased.

They ate their lunch and enjoyed their time on the water. It was easy to be around Steve. He was fun and liked to tease, Anna noted; but he also was patient and gentle, and she sensed his tender heart. Being in his presence brought her a sense of peace. She couldn't think of anywhere else she would rather be than with him, and she couldn't remember a friendship bringing her such contentment. The weekend had flown by, and with that came regret for the new workweek ahead.

———⋙•⋘———

Walking into the cabin, Anna headed straight for the answering machine. She threw up her hands. No message from Justin and no supper. Thankfully, Steve had left her a message and asked if she had a nice day, which put a smile on her lips.

"Dear God, watch over my son. Please, if it be your will, let me hear from him soon. Help me not to worry and to trust in your plan for his life. I'm having a hard time letting go. Amen."

CHAPTER 33

The following Saturday morning dawned warm and sunny. Anna splashed through the shallow water, dragging her kayak. Balancing herself with one hand on her new toy and the other on the pier, she eased herself in, adjusted herself in the seat, and then tightened her lifejacket and began to tug on the oars as she hugged the shore of the placid lake. The water was like glass, not a ripple to be found. It took a few minutes to find a rhythm. Slowly the craft and the water became one. She glided along picking up speed and peered amid trees, waved to bystanders on the shore, and breathed in the serene quiet. Anna had not heard from Steve in a few days. She wondered why after spending so much time together he was suddenly silent.

"I'll go pay him a visit and show him my new kayak," she said aloud, pleased with her new toy. It was a hike to the south side of the lake, but because it was such a beautiful morning she didn't worry about how much time it would take her.

Taking water bottle breaks along the way and lifting her oars to glide every now and again, she was surprised and proud when she arrived. She turned her kayak so she could see his house as she approached.

A shocking scene played out before her. Steve stood with his back to her; his arm lazily draped over a woman's shoulders. Her long brown hair clung to his arm. He pointed to an eagle in the tree and leaned in to whisper something in her ear. Anna tried to quietly turn her kayak around. In doing so, she disrupted a family of ducks who flapped their wings making a ruckus as they splashed across the water. Steve turned to see the commotion.

"Anna? Anna!"

Anna rowed as quickly as she could away from Steve. Angrily, she pushed through the water with vigor. She watched as he raced to the end of the pier waving her to come back. Ignoring him, she rowed as hard as she could until she could no longer see him. Fuming, she got halfway home, and she could go no further. Her arms shook from the exertion she was unprepared for. She took a sip from her water bottle as the scene rewound in her mind.

"Now I know why he hasn't called. Stupid, Anna!" she chastised herself. "What was I thinking? Just because he spent some time with me doesn't mean I'm the *only* one he spends time with. Why is this bothering me so much?"

A bird flew overhead, and she watched it soar across the sky. *Wish I had wings.*

Her arms ached as she slowly made her way back home. Pulling up to the pier in front of her cabin, she saw Steve sitting on the bench, arms folded across his chest. He didn't move until she pulled her kayak up beside him.

"What are you doing here?" she asked pointedly.

"Trying to figure out why you took off so fast," he answered as he took the kayak and pulled it up on the pier.

"You seemed busy with your companion. I didn't want to interrupt," she quipped.

"Well, I wish you had. You could have met my sister," he defended.

"Your sister?"

"Yes. My sister Katie came by to see me after visiting our dad. She was pretty upset."

"Oh," Anna answered sheepishly.

"I've missed you the last few days, Anna," he whispered as he leaned in and kissed her softly on the lips. A jolt of electricity traveled through her leaving her breathless. "I'm sorry I haven't called." He sighed. "My father is in a nursing home. Katie and I had some problems with Dad this week. He walked into the woods and the staff couldn't find him. Unfortunately he is suffering with Alzheimer's. He didn't recognize Katie, and she was pretty upset."

Still trying to recover from the kiss, Anna laid her hand on his shoulder to steady herself. Steve brought her in and held her on the pier. His solid arms gave Anna the feeling of armor around her. She melted into his embrace and whispered in his ear. "I'm sorry I acted like a silly school girl. I'm sorry I didn't stop by to meet your sister but most of all I'm sorry to hear about your dad."

He kissed her gently. "When I saw you take off like a scolded dog, I was convinced you have feelings for me," he acknowledged. "You don't know how badly I've wanted to kiss you."

Anna looked down at her feet as she leaned her head on his shoulder. "I actually came by to show you my new kayak. I took your advice to try something new, and I must say, I really enjoyed my trip until, well, I think I overexerted my arms." She grimaced.

"What am I going to do with you, my little spark plug?" He laughed heartily. "It's a nice kayak, you'll have to take me out to give it a try sometime, but not now I'm starved. Do you have anything in the line of breakfast in there?" He gestured to the cabin. "I was supposed to take Katie to breakfast, but she begged off when she witnessed the misunderstanding."

Anna's face flushed. "I'm so embarrassed! I acted like a complete fool." She put her hands on her burning cheeks.

"Katie sure got a kick out of it," he teased. "I think she was happy for me when she saw me run after you. My sister wants me to be happy. She's constantly encouraging me to date. Now I've found you, and, Anna, you make me happy. I don't know what it is about you, but I feel I've known you forever. I must say, you're adorable when you're mad," he added with a chuckle.

Anna took Steve by the hand and led him into the cabin. "Take a seat. My turn to cook." She winked. With bacon and eggs frying in the pan, the kitchen quickly smelled of hot breakfast. Steve looked around the cabin and strolled to see a photo of Justin hanging on the wall.

"This is him?" he questioned.

"Yeah, it was his first wakeboard experience. I had it blown up to an eight-by-ten. That photo was taken years ago," she answered wistfully.

"Handsome guy…takes after his mother." He smiled at her as he returned to the kitchen table. "That's a great action shot, Anna. You have talent. It's hard to get the right focus on the camera for motion photos."

"I used my camera a lot more when my son was with me. Since he left…" She trailed off. She passed Steve a breakfast plate and a cup of coffee.

When she joined him at the table, she asked, "So tell me about your father."

"My dad has been stricken with that horrible disease, Alzheimer's. It's a strange disease. My mom died several years ago not long before Shelby. After she left us, it was like my father couldn't cope. In a strange way, the disease protected him from his grief. My parents were an amazing couple." He took a sip of his coffee. "I've had to come to terms with the fact that the father I knew is gone. The man I visit at the nursing home doesn't recognize me," he said sadly. "So I understand what you're going through with your son. Hold on to what you know, Anna. The good times you spent with him. I'm sure you are a good mother. The good news is that you'll see your son again; kids come around. I was a handful at that age, but the older I got, the more I understood how much my parents sacrificed for me. Letting go doesn't mean you'll never see him again."

Anna pondered Steve's wisdom. "You amaze me, you know that?" She smiled at him. "I'll tell you something that you may think is crazy," she confided. "It's been difficult not hearing from my son, but a long time ago, I had to let him go to his father's for the summer.

He was two years old, and I was really broken up about it. I railed at God and blamed him for the situation. Do you know what happened? For the first time in my life, I *heard* God speak to me audibly. It's an experience I will never forget," she whispered.

Steve dropped his fork on his plate and looked at her intently. "God spoke to you? What did he say?"

"*He's not yours; he's mine.*"

"Wow!" Steve said as he rubbed goose bumps on his arms. "That's powerful." He repeated the words reverently. "He's not yours; he's mine."

"Yeah, and thank you for reminding me. Sometimes when I get anxious about not hearing from Justin, I think about that day. I know God has him and will protect him, but it doesn't take away the ache in my heart."

"Anna, my sweet, I understand. It's normal to have those feelings, but when it cripples you from living, then it becomes a problem," he answered wisely.

Anna smiled at her new friend. He'd come into her life and changed it, bringing her slowly out of her shell and back into a life she'd forgotten how to live. She thanked God for sending him.

CHAPTER 34

Several days later, Anna tossed packing peanuts into a large clay pot and hummed softly as she added a layer of soil around a deep salmon-colored geranium. She then used a few white impatiens to fill in the edges and stood back to admire her flowers. "Mary will love this for her new apartment." She smiled, pleased with her creativity. She lifted the filled pot and placed it carefully in the trunk of her car and headed out to see her old neighbor.

As she approached, Anna noticed Mary talking with an elderly woman outside her apartment door.

"Anna!" Mary excused herself from the woman and took her in her arms.

"I'm sorry, I didn't mean to interrupt," she said as she watched the woman walk away with a hand wave.

"It's fine. I can see Marion anytime. She lives next door. Oh I've met so many nice folks, Anna!" Mary clasped her hands together in delight. "Come in, come in!"

Anna walked into the small space. Soft, warm paint color covered the walls and not a hint of packing boxes. "I came to help you unpack. You're finished already?" she said as she placed the flower pot on the kitchen counter.

"Oh dear, I have the sweetest neighbors. You would not believe it," she said with glee. "The movers did all the heavy stuff, but my new friends came over in the evenings and helped me to get settled. They're just wonderful," Mary said as she fanned herself with her hand. "You brought me flowers," she said appreciatively. Her face beamed.

"Just a little something to brighten your space."

"Aren't you the sweetest thing? Would you mind setting that down in front of my sliding door so it will get more sunlight?" She motioned her hand across the room to a large glass door.

Anna carried the pot and positioned it on the ceramic tile. "What a nice view you have." The apartment looked upon a courtyard with a water fountain and beyond it thick wooded pine.

"Yes," Mary agreed. "It's too warm today, but usually when you look out, you'll see lots of folks talking and laughing out there. It's so nice to be surrounded by people. If I get lonely, I just step out my door, and I'm greeted by many. I love it here—I really do." She bustled to the kitchen and poured some iced tea for Anna and passed it to her.

"Thanks, Mary." Anna took a sip from the glass and sat at the familiar kitchen table in the new space.

"How have you been, my dear? Any word from Justin?" She looked intently at Anna.

"No word yet, still waiting for his call." Her voice choked, and she cleared her throat. "I suppose he's so busy training he wouldn't be able to call even if he wanted to," she answered, making an excuse.

"I'm sorry, dear. I know how hard this has been for you. He'll come around, I just know it. But I have to say there is a new lightness about you? You're doing much better than I dared hope. I guess my prayers have been answered. You know I pray for you both day and night."

"Thank you for keeping me in your prayers, Mary. I hold you in mine as well. Seems to me you are getting settled in here just fine too." She patted her friend's hand. "I was concerned leaving the cabin and the lake would devastate you."

Mary stood with a hand on her hip. "I thought the same but decided it was all about attitude. I convinced myself I'm going to make the best of it and I did. See, it all worked out." She turned to the kitchenette. "Would you like to indulge with me? I found this moist, rich cake at the supermarket, and I just had to have it." She winked.

Anna took a forkful of the cake into her mouth. "I do have some news I'd like to share," she hinted.

"What's that, dear?" Mary licked the chocolate from her lips.

"I've met someone," Anna replied shyly.

"Oh! This is great news!" The older woman's eyes sparkled. "Tell me. Tell me. Your voice tells me you like this person a lot."

"Yes. I do. He's…well…he's…"

"Oh my, Anna, I think you're in love!" She clasped her hands to her chest.

Anna blushed.

"Who's the lucky guy?" Mary sat at the edge of her seat waiting for details.

"Steve Henderson." Anna floated his name into the room.

"Steve Henderson, from Henderson Logging?" Mary laid her hand on her cheek. "Oh you've got a winner there. He's a nice boy, comes from great stock." She nodded her head in accent.

"You *know* them?" Anna asked, shocked.

"Dear, don't be surprised. I've grown up around these parts—I know everyone. I haven't seen his father in years. Paul used to get together with him every now and again. Oh, I heard about Steve's wife, Shelby, a few years ago—tragic really. I'm so glad you found each other. I'm just tickled." She giggled.

"I can't believe you know the Hendersons!" Anna shook her head in disbelief.

"Well, like I said, I haven't seen Steve in years, since he was a lad really. Oh but they are a good family, a really good family. I couldn't have picked better for you had I picked him myself." She nodded. "Oh, and what a beautiful home he has. I heard he and his father built an amazing cabin on the south side of the lake. Paul told me about the plans. They were years in the making." She looked to the ceiling and pointed her finger. "I bet Paul had something to do with this." She chuckled. "I know you weren't given the gift to know my husband long, Anna, but he had a special place in his heart for you and that little nipper," she remembered affectionately.

"Funny enough, I think you may be right. Steve and I met because his boat engine croaked out beyond my pier." Anna chuckled.

Mary laughed heartily. "Oh yes, I do indeed think my Paul had something to do with this. He sent you quite a catch." She winked as she took the soiled dishes and laid them in the sink. "I hate to push you out the door, Anna, but I'm planning to go to bingo this afternoon at the community center."

Anna took the cue. "I should have called first, Mary. I will next time I decide to visit. I promise."

"Nonsense, dear, I'm so glad you came. Thank you for the flowers. I love them. Don't be a stranger. Maybe you could bring your new boyfriend for a visit sometime. I'd really like to meet the adult Steve Henderson," she said with a twinkle in her eye.

Anna hugged her friend good-bye. She was grateful that Mary had settled nicely in her new surroundings. It gave her hope. *Strange how life pushes you along, sometimes change is frightening, but it can be a very good thing,* she smiled as she stepped away from Mary's apartment, shading her eyes from the bright warm sun.

CHAPTER 35

Months had passed, and the cold Minnesota winter brought its wrath. Anna stepped away from the warmth of Steve's fireplace. Rubbing her hands together, she gazed at the photo of herself and Steve holding a large bass and chuckled. How far she had come she smiled to herself. Her heart had opened like a flower waiting to be picked. Steve came from behind her and handed her a warm parka, a mischievous smile lit his face.

"Hey, you said you were up for this. You're not going to chicken out now are ya?" he taunted playfully.

Anna smiled as she wrapped herself in the jacket. She looked at Steve who was fully dressed for the weather as he waited in anticipation. "I'm ready. Let's go snow shoeing," she said determinedly.

They stepped out into the frigid February day and slowly adjusted to their new feet as they trudged across his back yard and headed toward the woods. Steve had made a path between the large pines with a snow mobile. Anna noticed red rose petals scattered along the path.

"What's this?" She picked up a petal and held it to her nose.

"It's Valentine's Day, my love," he said as he took her gloved hand in his.

Although the temperature was cold outside, Anna felt warmth within her. She gazed at her sweetheart who was looking to the sky between the trees. Soft flakes tumbled down making it look as if they were standing in a snow globe.

"I wish I could capture this on film," Steve said wistfully. "It's almost as beautiful as you." He stopped on the path and held Anna too him. "I love you, Anna," he whispered.

There cold lips touched bringing instant heat. "I love you too, sweetheart."

He held her for a long time not wishing to let her go as they watched the frozen glitter fall around them. Steve led her to a tree where he took out a jack knife and carved a heart with their initials. Anna smiled as his frozen fingers attempted the art. His youthful personality made her feel alive and young again. They trudged through the woods enjoying the beauty until the cold forced them back to the warmth.

They came in from the deep freeze, and Steve laid a blanket in front of the fireplace. He rushed to the kitchen and brought a tray of hot coffee and a red velvet cake with creamy white frosting.

Anna clasped her hands. "That looks delicious and so pretty!"

"I made it myself," he proudly touted. He turned to a side table, cut a piece, and handed the plate to Anna.

Anna giggled as crumbs slipped from her lips and landed on her red sweater. She wiped her mouth with her napkin and then took another bite. As she did so a hint of sparkle caught her eye. She plucked a beautiful diamond from the frosting and held it in a trembling hand.

Steve took her face in his hands as he sat with her in front of the fire. "My sweet Anna, I love you with all my heart. You are the missing puzzle piece to my life. Please say you'll be my wife, my Valentine forever."

Anna looked into his tender eyes and found the reflection of her own there. Without hesitation, she answered. "Yes! Yes! I love you, Steve, and I am honored to spend the rest of my life with you."

He slipped the ring on her finger and slowly licked the frosting from the diamond. Raising his lips to hers, he kissed her passionately, sending electricity through her body. They held each other lovingly and watched the flames flicker in joyful anticipation of their future together.

CHAPTER 36

The couple decided to elope the following summer. With still no word from Justin, Anna thought it would be too difficult to have a family wedding without his presence. They planned an intimate gathering in Minnesota in the spring in order for the families to meet. Anna was anxious to introduce Holly, Chris, and her parents to her new love. She cleaned and scoured the cabin in anticipation of their arrival. She sent for a driver to retrieve them from the airport, thinking her car would not be large enough to handle all of the passengers along with their luggage. Waiting for them was like watching a pot of water boil, slow and tedious, until finally she heard the banging of a car door.

"Hi!" she called as she rushed to the van to greet her family.

They smothered each other with kisses and hugs. "Where's Chris?" Anna asked her sister.

"Sorry, Anna, he couldn't make it. He got called away on a work thing." She waved her hand in frustration. "He said to give you his best and congratulations!"

"That's too bad. Gee, I would have come to the airport had I known. I would have been able to pick all of you up," she said, defeated.

"That's okay. I waited for Mom and Dad to fly in, and we had a chance to catch up before getting here, so it worked out. No worries, sistah!" Holly wrapped her arm around her sister's shoulder.

"Anyone care to help me with the bags?" Donald said, growing increasingly impatient at the mounds of luggage coming out of the van.

"It's been a long flight, girls," Sara whispered to her daughters. "Your father is on the warpath," she warned.

The sisters giggled as they reached for bags and helped lug them into the cabin. Anna handed her father a cup of worms from the refrigerator along with a fishing pole. "Dad, why don't you take yourself down to the pier and relax for a few minutes?"

"Wow, have you changed, little girl! Keeping worms in the refrigerator, you really got the Minnesota in you now, huh?" He chuckled as he reached for the cup.

"Yeah, that and a bit of Steve." She laughed.

Donald willingly left the women gather around the kitchen table to gossip and hummed happily as he headed to the water.

"So where are you hiding him?" Holly's eyes searched the cabin. "I thought we'd get to meet this Steve right away. We've heard so much about him for months now," she teased, rolling her eyes.

"He's invited all of us to a party at his place tonight. You'd better be on your best behavior," she jabbed kiddingly.

Holly nudged her in the ribs with an elbow and shot her a mischievous grin.

"I'm happy for you, Anna. You deserve every bit of happiness." Sarah's eyes misted. "I wish Justin would contact you so you could tell him what's going on in your life. How will he even know that you've moved to Steve's place after you get married?" Her mother worried.

"I still have the same cell phone. He knows how to contact me. It's been months, and sometimes it feels like years since I've seen my son. I never would have dreamed that this awful thing would happen between us. Not in a million years would I have imagined it." She shook her head in defeat as tears threatened to well in her eyes.

"He'll come around," Holly encouraged. "For now, we are here to celebrate! And celebrate we shall! Because I have news too—I'm pregnant!" She blurted as she patted her tummy proudly. "After all the infertility procedures, Chris and I finally made a baby! I'm three months along!" She said as she lifted her sweater to show a mere bump.

Sarah and Anna looked at Holly in shock and then jumped from their chairs to cover her in hugs and kisses. "What a surprise, I can't believe you didn't tell us sooner!"

"I didn't want to say anything until I knew for sure this baby is okay. You know how hard this has been on Chris and me all these years," she said seriously. "I've got to go tell Dad the news so he won't feel left out." She stepped outside to meet her father at the lake.

Anna handed her mother a bottle of water. "Can I get you anything else?"

"No, thank you, honey. I think I'm still in shock that I'm going to be a grandma again." Sarah laid her hand on her cheek. "Please, God, watch over them and their baby," she whispered.

"I'm so happy for them, Mom. They've waited a long time. Strange how that is, Justin came into my life so easily, and Holly had to work so hard to get pregnant."

They stood at the window and witnessed Holly and her father embrace when Holly gave him the news. "I'm glad you're here, Mom."

"I'm glad I'm here too, love." Sarah threw her arm over Anna's shoulder and kissed her on the head before they joined the others at the lake.

CHAPTER 37

As they pulled into the driveway, Anna heard the gasps of her family members in awe of Steve's cabin. "Yep, this is going to be my new home after we marry," she said, still in disbelief herself.

Sarah stood outside the car and looked up at the large pines, while Donald peeked around them taking in the lake view. Holly held her tiny bump as she walked toward the house uttering, "Wow! Wow!"

Steve opened the door allowing the aroma of Italian food to greet them. "Welcome, all," he said with a wide grin.

Anna introduced her family to her fiancé. He took her parents on a tour of her soon-to-be new home while she and Holly checked on the dinner.

"Anna, he's cute!" Holly poked at her sister in the kitchen.

"He's amazing. I don't know what I did to deserve him. I really love him, Holly." She smiled as she stirred a pan of seasoned red sauce.

"I know. I can tell. You got that giddy girlie love thing going on," Holly teased. "I'm so happy for you, sis," she added seriously. The doorbell rang, interrupting them, and Anna rushed to greet her guests. A slender woman with long brown hair and Steve's eyes stood with open arms.

"Katie, it's so good to finally meet you," Anna welcomed.

The two women embraced. "You are so special to my brother. I'm happy you found each other." Katie looked over her shoulder for her husband. A tall, slender man with wispy brown hair approached and held out his hand. "Anna, this is my husband, Ben."

"So good to meet you, Ben." Anna held the door for them to enter.

Steve and her parents finished the tour and the families convened in the kitchen. Laughter and chatter filled the large cabin until way past dinner hour. Steve secretly took Donald aside to ask if he would like to see his boats, and the two set out to explore.

"This is quite a spot you have here. The log cabin set on the water—every man's dream," Donald expressed as they made their way to the lake.

"Yes. My father was an amazing architect. He had a vision. This was his dream. I only wish he had more time to enjoy it before he became ill," Steve said regretfully.

"Yeah, life does that to us sometimes," Donald added with a headshake.

The two stepped onto a large pontoon boat tied to the wooden pier. "I want you to know, sir, that she is my best friend. There is nothing in this world I wouldn't do for her. She is an answer to my prayers. I love her very much."

Donald put his hand on Steve's shoulder. "I know that, son. My daughter radiates happiness when she's around you. I can't tell you how happy that makes me. You know, I still worry about my girls even though they are grown women. Anna is very special. Treat her with love and respect, and you have my blessing. Hurt her, and I will come after you," he added as he laughed heartily in jest.

Hoping that Donald was kidding, Steve laughed along. To lighten the mood he asked, "Would you like to go fishing tomorrow? I think Anna mentioned that the girls are going shopping or something."

"Right up my alley, big guy," Donald agreed. "I don't want to get stuck shopping. I'd love to go fishing."

Anna joined the men at the lake. "You two aren't thinking of taking off fishing, now are you?"

"Tomorrow, little girl, don't worry. We'll wait until tomorrow." Donald laughed. "I'm going back to the cabin and leave you two love birds alone." He chuckled as he walked away leaving the couple to stand on the pier.

Steve and Anna embraced as they watched the sun set over the lake. "I'm so glad we brought our families together," she said softly. "It's making our pending wedding a reality."

"It is real, my little spark plug, and I can't wait until you move in with me and stay with me forever," Steve uttered, as he kissed her impatiently on the lips.

———•◦•———

Spring turned into summer, and Steve and Anna were married in an intimate ceremony as they'd they planned. On a sunbathed day, the couple exchanged their vows. Anna wore a simple white sundress; her hair fell loosely around her shoulders. She walked barefoot toward Steve as he waited in a pair of khaki shorts and crisp white polo. The sun shone bright as they wed in the gazebo on Steve's property. The pastor had come along with his wife to sign as a witness to their love. As they gazed into each other's eyes and committed themselves completely, Steve allowed a single tear to fall. "I do." As Anna spoke the words, her heart swelled. There was no question; their love was forever. They kissed, sealing their bond, and the two radiated jubilation as the pastor's wife sprinkled them with white rose petals.

———•◦•———

Anna could not believe the happiness Steve had brought to her life. He was her best friend, steady support, and always looked out for her best interest. She silently thanked God for answering her prayers and blessing her with his love. The boxes and furniture had been moved from the old cabin, and Anna was quickly getting accustomed to the larger space.

One day soon after they'd said their vows, Anna worked at transferring her clothes into Steve's closet.

"Whatcha doin'?" Steve asked as he came around Anna, wrapping her in his arms.

"Finishing up." She sighed happily as she nuzzled into him. "I'm going back to the cabin today to do one last clean up before I hand the keys over."

"I'll come with you," he offered as he turned her to face him.

"I'd like to do this myself, if you don't mind, Steve. I need to say good-bye to the place, so many memories…" She trailed off.

"I understand. I'll stay and get the boat gassed and ready for tonight. I have a surprise," he said with a twinkle in his eye.

"Really? What kind of surprise?" she asked eagerly.

He kissed her neck. "Not telling. You have to wait, my love," he teased as he kissed her good-bye.

———————

Anna walked into the empty cabin where she'd raised her son and peered around. It seemed so desolate and lonely. She strolled toward Justin's old room with a heavy heart. It didn't look like his room anymore with his posters removed and fresh paint on the walls. She sighed and closed the door and then ran the vacuum cleaner one last time. As she surveyed the space, a wave of nostalgia washed over her. She smiled recalling the many Christmases when Justin would run to his stuffed red stocking hanging on the fireplace as she ran her finger along the rusty nail from which it hung. Her lip quivered. She turned to the kitchen and recalled the many homework assignments, rushed dinners before soccer practice, and countless batches of chocolate chip cookies.

As she stepped to the sliding door, a picture of Steve bent over in his stalled boat flashed through her mind—their first meeting. The memory brought a smile to her lips and thankfulness for how far they had come. One last stroll to the lake and as she stepped on the pier, a school of minnows scattered in the calm water below. She chuckled as her mind recalled Justin and Scotty jumping and splashing in the cool refreshing lake to tease the tiny fish. Her eyes averted to the south side, toward the new home she'd come to love, thankful that she'd merely moved to the other side of the lake.

Anna straightened her shoulders as she turned back to the cabin.

"Well, this is it, Lord. Thank you for the fond memories and for allowing me to raise my son in this magical place," she prayed aloud. She locked the doors for the last time and smiled, content to spend the rest of her days with her new husband and hopeful that one day soon she would reconcile with her son.

That evening, when darkness had fallen, Steve asked his wife to dress in warm clothes. He led her to the pontoon boat that bobbed idly tied to the pier. It was dusk, the sun had long set, and he carried a blanket on his arm.

"You taking me for a moonlight cruise?" she asked as he held her hand to board.

Anna noticed the flashlight and picnic basket prepared and waiting in the boat.

"Yes, that's part of the surprise," he said playfully.

The two slowly motored out on the blackened water. A cool breeze blew in the summer night, and Anna was thankful that her husband had suggested a jacket. The moon was full, leaving a silver path on the lake. Steve cut the engine and set the anchor. He moved close to her on the seat and wrapped them both in the blanket.

"This is nice," Anna commented as she snuggled with her husband and wondered why they were sitting idly in the middle of the lake.

"Wait a moment and then look up." He pointed to the darkened sky.

Anna became more confused by the minute but did as he'd suggested. Suddenly fireworks burst forth in the sky, shooting spikes of glittering color. A wide smile etched her face as she looked at her husband. "Did you plan this?"

"I know people." He smiled as he leaned her head back on his shoulder.

The two sat through their own private fireworks show, and Anna's heart burst with pleasure.

"You are full of surprises! Thank you for this, you're also incredibly romantic, I might add." She kissed her new husband on the lips.

"That's not all," he said as he lit the flashlight and pulled a card from the basket. Steve handed Anna an envelope. Enclosed were two airline tickets to Maine dated for early September. "Since we didn't plan a honeymoon, I want to take you back home so you can show me where you grew up," he said excitedly.

Anna was overjoyed at the prospect of showing him her home state of Maine. "Have I told you how much I love you, Mr. Henderson?"

"Yes, Mrs. Henderson, and you can keep telling me for a lifetime."

CHAPTER 38

Anna stood and brushed her windblown golden curls away from her face. She climbed down the jagged rocks toward the beach. As she reached the bottom, a black Labrador trotted toward her. A young man shouted, "Sarge, get back here!" She reached down and patted his wet, matted fur. The large pup jumped and knocked her off balance. As she tumbled forward, her knees landed in the wet sand. The young man ran over and scolded the dog soundly.

"Sarge, stop! I'm sorry, ma'am! He's friendly but a bit overzealous. He means no harm."

Anna smiled. "I'm fine really. I lost my balance on the rock, that's all."

"You from around here?" he asked. "I haven't seen you in this hidden cove before. Most people don't know it exists."

"Ah, I used to come here to visit my aunt as a child. It's my peace place," she replied with a nostalgic sigh.

He nodded his head in agreement. "My name's Nate, and this here is Sarge," he said as he placed the leash on his pet's collar. "I'm here on leave, visiting my parents. It's where I come to center myself as well."

"My name is Anna. Pleasure to meet you. Did you say you were on leave?"

"Yeah, I just got back from a tour in Afghanistan. I'm in the US Army, ma'am."

Anna's heart leapt in her chest. She felt as if the wind had been knocked out of her. Nate must have noticed as he quickly asked, "You okay, ma'am?"

"Yes. I'm okay," she stammered. Her mind lingered on thoughts of her son, Justin. "I'm fine. I must have lost my breath when I fell," she recovered.

"Again, I apologize for my dog's behavior, looks like I need to spend more time in the training department." He extended his hand and reached for Anna's. "Nice to meet you, ma'am." Nate let the leash loose and watched as Sarge sniffed around the rocks. "I better get him out of here before he drinks the salt water again." The young man chuckled as he nodded his head to Anna and turned to lead his dog toward the beach.

"Nice to meet you too, Nate." Anna smiled warmly at the young man as he turned and began jogging out of sight.

She stretched her arms to the sky and deeply inhaled the sea air again. *It's like a soothing balm; there's nothing quite like it. If I could only bottle this up and take it home*, she thought. Anna took her shoes off and walked slowly through the sand that had been warmed by the late summer sun. She lazily drifted toward a bench. She leaned back, face to the sun, and dug her feet into the soft white powder. Her right foot touched something hard. She reached down and picked up a small pocket Bible. She dusted the sand off and looked at the outside cover. The book was army fatigue pattern and titled: Holy Bible New International Version. She opened the small Bible where scratched handwriting read:

> To Nate, Psalm 17:8 "Keep me the apple of your eye; hide me in the shadow of your wings from the wicked who assail me, from my mortal enemies who surround me."
> (God will protect you, Nate... Always, J.G.)

Anna's heart thundered. J.G.? Could it be? J.G. or Justin Gallo. She jumped from the bench and looked up and down the beach. Nate was nowhere to be seen. She sat down again and ruffled through the pages to the Psalm that had been quoted. It was bookmarked by a photograph. Two smiling young men in army fatigues stood together arm in arm in the desert sand. It was hard to recognize features because they were wearing helmets. Squinting her eyes, she attempted to read the name badges on their uniforms. GALLO. She could barely make out the name as the photo had been taken from a distance. She looked away and then back at the photograph. It was confirmed. The man in the middle of the photograph was her son, Justin Gallo. The tears welled in Anna's eyes as she held the photo to her heart.

"Oh, Heavenly Father," she prayed, "*help me* see my son again."

CHAPTER 39

Anna sat for a long time gazing out to sea. Her mind fixated on memories of Justin, and her body ached as if she were suffering from the flu. She ran her hands up and down her arms feeling the chill as the sun sank below the horizon. As she walked toward the trail that would lead her back to her husband at their seaside cottage, the glistening sea glass caught her eye. She bent and picked up the little green treasure from the beach. She remembered how Justin would bring her pieces of glass after visiting his father for the summer when he was a child. Anna fell to her knees and began to pound the soft sand with her fists. "Why, why, why, God, why?" Her grief and loneliness overcame her as she sobbed until she was spent.

"Anna? Anna?" a familiar voice entreated.

"Steve!" Anna jumped to her feet and wrapped her arms tightly around her husband's neck.

"Anna, my Anna! I've been worried sick about you! You told me you were going for a quick walk. I was concerned when you didn't return!" He pulled her gently toward him and brushed the matted curls from her eyes. "Why are you so upset, sweetness?"

Anna placed the pocket Bible in Steve's hand. "I found my Justin."

He looked at the Bible then at her with questioning eyes. She relayed the story. "I met someone on the beach…a young soldier." She showed him the photo as tears fell freely. Anna filled Steve in about the encounter with Nate and her hope of seeing him again.

"We'll find your son." Except for those encouraging words, the shock had left him speechless. Steve removed his zipped sweatshirt and wrapped it around her. He held her in a long embrace as they gazed out to sea. The tide pulled in and crashed along the rocks of the jetty, rolling rhythmically as if playing a song. He held his wife and after the sun had set he started to lead her toward the cottage. Steve held her close as they walked quietly home. By the time they arrived at the beach side retreat, Anna could not ignore the rumble in her stomach. She had hardly eaten anything most of the day, and the smell of something simmering in a crock pot enticed her.

"What have you been cooking, my darling husband?"

Steve looked at his wife with a mischievous grin. He rubbed his hand along his shaven beard. "I made soup. We can sit out on the deck and revel in the last of the summer breezes. I want to show you the star I picked out for you."

Anna looked up at her husband. He was still as sweet as the day she had met him. She remembered her immediate attraction. The softness in his hazel, almost golden eyes left her giddy. His shiny auburn hair was feathered back, and his smile revealed the dimples in his cheeks. She loved him more today than when they met and felt blessed that he had come into her life.

"That sounds wonderful. I'll serve it up, and meet you out on the deck, okay?" She placed her hand upon his cheek. "What did I do to deserve you?" she asked as their eyes met.

Steve raised his eyes to the ceiling. "God had a plan and a very good one. I love you, Anna." He kissed her cheek and strolled out to the deck, tossing a blanket over his shoulder as he went.

The couple sat in silence as they devoured the cups of steaming soup. The darkness of the night was illuminated by a gleaming full moon shining upon the open sea, which tossed sparkling flecks as the wind brought the waves into shore. A hurricane lamp sat on a side table, its flickering candle light danced in the breeze.

"Come sit with me," Steve beckoned.

Anna crawled onto her husband's lap, and he wrapped the fleece blanket around them. She felt so safe in his arms, so incredibly loved.

"How are you feeling?" he asked cautiously.

It was one of the traits she loved about Steve. He never pressed, never implied, and was always patient, allowing her to talk when she was ready.

"Shocked, I guess. I never would have thought I would meet someone who knows Justin. I have to find Nate again. He knows where Justin is!"

"I know how you've missed him, Anna. I know how haunting this has been for you. We will find him. I promise. I know we only planned to be on vacation a few more days, but we'll extend it if we have to. I don't think anyone is renting this place since summer's almost over." He glanced toward the cottage. "I'll call the agent tomorrow and see if we can extend our stay indefinitely. I'm sure she'll understand."

Anna rested her head on Steve's shoulder, warmed by his embrace. "Thank you, sweetheart. I want you to meet him, since you never had the chance. I want him to know that we got married." She sighed deeply. "I want to know where he's been and what has happened in his life. We've missed so much." She sighed sadly.

"What did you tell me a long time ago that brings you comfort when you think of Justin," he gently reminded her.

"Yes. I know God has him in his tender care."

CHAPTER 40

Anna lazily rolled over and looked at her husband who lay lifeless in the bed. It had been late when they'd come in from the deck the previous night. Although she was tired, she had tossed and turned while thoughts of her son tormented her. She was close to finding him—she could feel it. Meeting Nate on the beach gave her tremendous hope. The pocket Bible lay on the bedside table. Anna picked it up and pulled out the photograph. Steve woke to his wife staring at the picture and gently put his arm around her.

"We will find him, Anna. I promise." He stroked her arm to comfort her. "Did you get any sleep?"

She sighed. "No, I was restless all night. I want to find him," she said determinedly. Anna pushed the covers aside and threw on a pair of sweatpants and pulled a ponytail through a baseball cap.

"Where are you going? We haven't had coffee yet," Steve said, disgruntled.

"I'm going to walk the beach. Maybe Nate takes his dog out to walk in the morning," she said as she adjusted her ball cap.

"I'll come with you," Steve said, following her to the kitchen.

Anna paced anxiously as her husband waited for the coffee to percolate. *It's like watching paint dry*, she thought as images of Justin flooded her mind. She stepped outside and allowed the salt sea air to calm her. The morning sun had not fully arisen, so she zipped her sweatshirt to ward off the cool breeze. Slowing her breath, she allowed the ocean to cleanse her like a soothing balm. Steve joined her outside and handed her a cup of steaming brew. Anna placed the warm mug between her hands to warm them.

"Thank you, sweetheart. It's colder out here this morning than I expected," she said as she brought the steaming cup to her lips.

"My Anna baby, I love you so much it hurts me to see you sad," he said softly as he combed his bed head tousled hair with his fingers.

"I'm not sad. I'm anxious because I know we're close to finding Justin. The certainty that Nate knows of him excites me. He's been lost to me for too long. Maybe Justin is ready now to see me again. Maybe he's had enough time on his own."

"Try not to be anxious. We'll get answers. Let's get going." Taking the cue from her eagerness, he took their empty mugs and placed them on the outdoor table.

Hand in hand the couple stepped out on the cliff walk. The path opened up to a great expanse of sea and rock. Anna watched as the sun reflected off the water like tiny glitter specks. The path soon narrowed, and the two carefully navigated through beach rose thorns. They ambled single file. The small cove where she'd met Nate loomed ahead. Anna stopped in her tracks; and Steve, unaware, bumped her from behind.

"Ouch! You stepped on the back of my heel," she whined.

"Sorry, baby, I wasn't paying attention. What made you stop so suddenly?"

Anna pointed to the rocks. "I saw a dog, but it's not the one. Nate's dog is black," she said as she continued down the cliff walk.

They walked side by side as the path opened up to reveal the beach. It was a quiet morning. An elderly gentleman walked with purpose in his leisure suit while a golden retriever bounced after him. Except for the man and his dog, the beach was disserted. Anna felt deflated as her husband led her to sit with him on the bench.

"What do you want to do now?" Steve questioned. "We can't keep coming to the beach, hoping Nate will show up." He wrapped his arm around his wife as the two stared out to sea looking for answers.

Anna watched the golden retriever run in front of his owner. "Wait a minute! I have an idea," she said animatedly as she snapped her fingers. "We can call the veterinarians in the area to see if they care for a dog named Sarge. How many black labs have the name Sarge? Then we'll find Nate!" Anna pleased with herself, jumped from the bench, and ran back toward the cliff walk.

Steve jogged behind his wife and watched as she dodged the rose thorns until out of breath they made it back to the cottage.

"Anna, you're going to have to settle down, or you'll kill me!" he said as he handed her a phone book and flopped over with his hands on his legs.

Anna flipped the pages of the yellow-stained book. She chided herself for not allowing her husband to bring his laptop on their vacation. She'd been concerned he would be tempted to work and not relish in their retreat. The computer would have come in handy now, and she was angry at herself for making such a big deal about it. Finding a list of vets in the area, she began to make calls. Frustrated, she tossed the book aside. No one had heard of a dog named Sarge or a man called Nate.

"How can that be? Doesn't everyone take their dog to the vet?" she quipped in frustration.

"It was a good thought, Anna. Let's put our heads together and brainstorm. What about gyms in the area? If he's in the army, he probably works out." Steve stroked his beard thoughtfully.

"I don't know, Steve. This is crazy. Someone has to know this guy." Anna rubbed her hand along her rumbling abdomen. "I'm starved. Maybe we should take a break and go grab some lunch."

"I'd love a lobster roll, if you're up for it," he suggested.

After a quick shower, they strolled hand in hand to the Crab Shack. The smell of fish and chips wafted through the air. The small café held several tables with red-checkered cloths and a luncheon bar. Steve held the chair for Anna as they seated themselves. The waitress handed them menus.

"Can I get you two a drink?" the older woman questioned as she snapped a wad of gum.

"Bottled water is fine for me," Anna answered.

"Same for me." Steve nodded as he reached across the table and touched his wife's hand. He stroked it and looked lovingly into her eyes.

"Do you want to go visit the seaport museum today and see the tall ships? You told me you wanted to go there," Steve offered.

Anna thought for a moment. "Maybe." She shrugged her shoulders. "If you want." Her eyes drifted across the menu.

The waitress came with their drinks, pulled a pad out of her pocket, and a pencil out of the bun in her auburn streaked hair. "Are you ready to order?"

"I'll take a lobster roll, with French fries please. Anna, what will you have?"

"I'll take the fish and chips please, thanks."

The woman quickly wrote the order on the pad. "That will be right up." She smiled as she turned on her heel to the kitchen.

Anna pulled the pocket Bible from her purse. She glanced at the picture she had of her son. It saddened her to think of what she had missed. She placed the photo on the table against the salt and pepper shakers.

"You don't mind if Justin dines with us, do you?" Anna smiled as she glanced back at the picture.

"No, I don't mind. This is going to work out, Anna. I know it's driving you crazy. Maybe we should go to the museum so we can brain rest for a few hours today. I'm afraid you're going to let your anxiety get the best of you otherwise. Leave it in God's hands, Anna. Will you try to trust?" He stroked her hand.

"I'm sorry, Steve, but I hate it when you're right." She winked at her husband adoringly.

The waitress came and placed their food in front of them and glanced at the photo on the table. Curiously she asked, "Is that a family photo?"

Anna smiled and handed it to her. Before she had a chance to explain, the waitress commented, "Well, for heaven's sake, how do you know Nate?"

Anna looked from the waitress to Steve and back again as her heart quickened in her chest. "You know Nate?"

"Sure, darlin', he's my nephew. How do you know him?" She snapped her gum rhythmically.

"My son is in that photo, and I'm trying to reach him. I found Nate's Bible on the beach along with the photograph. I need to return it to him and ask how I can get in touch with my son. Can you please help me?" Anna asked desperately.

"Why don't you give me a number where he can reach you, and I'll have him get in touch with you? I don't want to give his number out. He just got back from Afghanistan and he's had a hard transition. Please understand." She handed Anna her order pad.

"Oh, certainly." Anna wrote her cell phone number and handed it back. "Please ask him to call me. I'll be waiting anxiously."

"Fair enough," she said as she stuck the note in her pocket. "Enjoy your lunch." She turned away to wipe a nearby table.

Anna grasped Steve's hands tightly across the table and squealed with delight.

"If you only would listen to your husband," he joked. "Now can we please go see the tall ships while we wait for him to call?"

"Yes, honey, anything you want...*anything!*" she said breathlessly.

"Anything?" He mischievously raised an eyebrow as he popped a French fry into his mouth.

CHAPTER 41

Anna and Steve finished their lunch at the Crab Shack café. Anna waved good-bye to the waitress as they left. She hoped Nate's aunt would give him the message soon. The belief that she was finally going to find Justin was surreal. Oh, how she had prayed for this moment, and now it was closer than ever before. She smiled as she and Steve walked hand in hand along the sidewalk. Life could not be better with her supportive husband by her side and pending answers to her fervent prayers.

Their next stop was the maritime museum. A massive ship was docked in the harbor. Its tall, white-massed sails flapped in the breeze. Steve, an avid photographer, had taken his camera from the car. He leaned back adjusting the lens for the perfect shot and reviewed the picture on his digital camera before leading Anna toward the vessel. A sign read, *Bluenose II.* They learned the ship's home port was Lunenburg, Nova Scotia. It was one of the world's most famous fishing schooners, with undefeated races according to history and legends. Known to have the largest working mainsail in the world, its impressive sail made Anna feel like an ant against its majesty as she craned her neck to view.

As they boarded, an offer was made to purchase a Canadian dime, which boasted the image of the original *Bluenose.* Steve bought one and popped it into his pocket. Distracted, Anna reached in her purse and checked her cell phone, begging for it to ring. She put it into her pocket for assurance that she would feel it if it vibrated. This was one call she did not want to miss. A pungent scent of kelp surrounded them as they walked the mahogany boards of the ship. Anna slid her hand against the polished wooden boom; it was cool and smooth to her touch.

She stood and smiled for a photo in front of the large brass wheel at the stern of the ship while pulling her hair behind her ear as the breeze fought to rustle it.

Steve hugged his wife and smoothed the hair from her face. "You're beautiful. You know that?" he said as he held her protectively from the wind. They walked single file to the bow of the vessel which proudly waved the Canadian flag.

"Can you imagine sailing this thing? It must be exciting," Anna commented. They had learned the sailors stayed on the ship for six months at a time. The thought of being out on the open ocean aboard this expansive vessel sent a shiver down her spine. She wasn't sure if the goose bumps that began to form were from the excitement or the cool wind that was picking up. Steve rubbed his hands up and down her arms.

"Let's get you inside the museum and out of this cold," he said while throwing an arm around her shoulder.

Anna agreed and the two set out to peruse the artifacts inside the museum. They stepped into the dimly lit stone building. Treasures lined the walls highlighted by spot lights. Glass cases enclosed replicas of old war ships stood humbly in the center of the room. The finally detailed replicas obviously took years of patient labor. They studied a case holding various intricate sailors' knots. An old copper bell sat atop the case. Anna reached into her pocket, flipped open her cell phone, and searched for a possible missed call. Nothing. Steve reached for her hand and led her away to look at uniforms worn by sailors of a distant time in an attempt to divert her from the cell phone.

Distracted, Anna tried hard to focus on her surroundings. She couldn't contain the excitement building in the pit of her stomach. Reading the framed signs posted to the wall did not help. She found herself reading the words over and over again. She looked at her husband who intently reveled in the whole experience. *God, please help me to enjoy this moment with my husband. I'm having a really hard time being patient.* She smiled at Steve who pointed to a sign offering drinks, and they followed it outside to another building which led to a coffee house.

"Want a cup to ward off the chill?" he offered.

"Sounds wonderful to me," Anna agreed.

They ordered two coffees to go and decided to return to the beach before going back to the seaside cottage. As they drove by the sea, Anna felt a tug in her heart. She missed the ocean even after all these years. Life at the lake in Minnesota had been good to her, but as they drove a wave of memories from childhood engulfed her.

"What's on your mind?" Steve asked as he reached to touch his wife's cheek.

"Sometimes coming here really makes me miss home, where I grew up and was raised. Mom, Dad, and Holly are so far away from my life in Minnesota. Being here makes me feel like they are with me, brings back a lot of fond memories," she said pensively. "To you the smell of pines and cedar brings you home. To me the smell of the sea is home." Anna rolled down the window to take it in and breathed deeply of the salty fragrance.

"Are you sorry you moved to Minnesota and away from this?" He motioned his hand to the ocean.

"No, darling, if I hadn't, I never would have met you. I grew up with Justin in Minnesota. It's my home now. I'm just reminiscing, that's all." She laid her hand upon his thigh, and he took hers gently in his.

They rode in silence until the beach loomed ahead. Anna's heart fluttered as they approached. Her eyes darted around looking for Nate or his dog. Steve reached for sweatshirts in the backseat and handed Anna one.

"Better put this on. Sun's almost down."

Anna pulled it over her head and snuggled her hair into the hood. She pulled the string tight as a shield to cover her from the wind.

The sun was setting over the horizon; a yellow ball surrounded by deep orange and red against the dark velvet water. Anna looked at Steve who ran for his camera. *Click, click, click.* She watched as he bent on one knee and adjusted his camera to take multiple shots.

"Wow, this is amazing!" He looked at his wife with a radiant smile. "One of these shots will go on our living room wall when we get home. I can envision it!"

Steve's enthusiasm was so contagious she almost forgot the reason they'd stopped at the beach. "I'm thinking maybe it would look good on the wall behind our bed. As the sun goes down…so do we? What do you think?"

"Now you're talking." He backed away from his camera and winked.

Anna scanned the darkening beach looking for the familiar face. He wasn't there. She was just going to have to wait… And waiting for news she had been waiting so long for, made her anxious.

"I think I got enough shots." Steve put the camera back into the safety of the case. "Do you want to walk for a bit?"

"I don't think so. It's getting pretty cold. Maybe we should go and grill something to eat," she suggested.

"I'm famished! I like the sound of that," he agreed.

Anna took a long, hot shower while Steve prepared and grilled hamburgers. She threw on warm sweats and a fleece and joined her husband on the couch in front of TV trays.

"This is delicious," she said, as she savored every bite.

"Glad you like it." He took the remote and clicked on the TV while they ate their supper.

Anna cleaned the supper dishes while Steve curled on the couch to watch a movie. After she'd finished she paced the floor unable to calm her busy mind. "Want to go dancing?"

Steve answered her by pulling a blanket from the top of the couch and curling it around himself. "Anna, really? I'm so comfortable. Besides, you know I have two left feet. Why don't you read your book?"

"I guess." She pouted as she sat in a chair and attempted to read. Her eyes glanced from her cell phone to the clock on the wall until she realized it was probably too late for a call from Nate.

Anna awoke with a start. Her book lay on her chest, and she was kicked back in the chair. Steve was still asleep on the couch, and the TV had been turned off. Peering out the large picture window, she noticed sea gulls swarming on the rocks. The thick morning fog had not lifted and dense clouds covered the water. She raised her cramped body from the chair, rolled her head to ease the kinks then stretched her arms up and stifled a yawn. Tripping her way to the coffee pot, she gazed at the clock: 8:42 a.m. The smell of the percolating brew stirred her husband.

"Morning!" Steve stretched out on the couch. "I guess we never made it to bed last night. I didn't even see the ending to my movie. I was wiped out. It must be the sea air that makes me so tired."

"It's later than I thought too. The fog makes it so dark, it feels like it's earlier than almost nine. I'm not sure we're going to see the sun today." Anna handed her husband a cup of hot coffee.

"Bummer, I was hoping to visit a light house to get some more photos," he said dejectedly.

The sound of a cell phone jarred them both. Anna's eyes widened as she looked at her husband before running to pick up the phone.

"Hello?" She felt her heart quicken.

"Hi. I'm looking for Anna."

"This is she. Nate?" she questioned.

"Yeah, sorry. Did I wake you?"

"No, no. I'm up. I'm so glad you called. Um, I think I found something of yours. Did you lose a Bible? I found it on the beach. I was hoping to return it to you. I think my son is in the photograph that was tucked inside. I was hoping maybe you can help me locate him." Anna paced back and forth as she waited for news.

"Wow! I was wondering where that went. I can't really talk right now. I'm out of town, but I'll be back late tonight. Can we meet tomorrow morning at the beach? Say around ten?"

"Sounds perfect. Thanks."

"See ya then." He abruptly hung up the phone.

Anna's hands trembled as she stared at the silent cell phone.

Steve questioned her with a furrowed brow.

"Well?"

"I guess I was hoping to get more information, but he hung up so quickly. We're meeting tomorrow on the beach." Anna held a shaking hand to her heart. "How am I going to wait a whole other day?"

Steve went to his wife and held her. "Patience, my love, patience."

CHAPTER 42

Anna and Steve sat on the seaside cottage deck, sipping coffee as they watched a weak sun struggle in the morning sky. The cumulonimbus clouds gathered, leaving a hint of a stormy day. Waves crashed in the distance, blowing sprays of white foam in their wake.

"Looks like it may storm later." Steve pointed to the sky. "It's a good thing we're meeting Nate soon. It doesn't look like a great beach day; that's for sure." He ran his hand along his smooth beard.

"Any storm won't be as bad as the one in my stomach," Anna said excitedly. She smiled at her husband. "I can't wait to find Justin. I know he'll be shocked at how much my life has changed."

"Do you think he'll like me?" Steve asked with a hint of insecurity.

"My love, who wouldn't love you? Certainly he will," Anna answered with conviction.

Steve rose from the chair and stretched. "Yeah, I'm quite a catch." He winked, picking up her empty coffee cup. "I think we can start out to the beach if you're ready. I'll take these mugs in and grab jackets for us."

Anna watched the raucous gulls feeding on the rocks below. A large wave crashed and sprayed the jagged boulders, carrying a cool mist on the wind. Steve returned and handed his wife a windbreaker along with Nate's Bible before they set out on the cliff walk. The walk to the beach calmed Anna's nerves, but the anticipation of talking with someone who was so close to her son made her tingle inside. Each stride forced her to inhale deep breaths of salty sea air. In her haste, they were at the beach with no sign of Nate. Steve beckoned Anna to sit on the bench to wait as her eyes scanned the entire beach in search of Sarge or his owner. He took the Bible she held in her hand and flipped to a familiar verse:

To calm his wife, he began to read aloud: "Where can I go from your Spirit? Where can I flee from your presence? If I go up to the heavens you are there; if I make my bed in the depths you are there. If I rise on the wings of the dawn, if I settle on the far side of the sea even there your hand will guide me, your right hand will hold me fast" (Psalm 139:7-10).

Anna placed her hand on Steve's arm to quiet him. She pointed to Sarge who trotted across the beach and down to the water. Anxiously she jumped to her feet and grabbed her husband by the hand. They walked toward the young man who stepped onto the sand and tossed a stick into the ocean. Sarge bolted into the water, retrieved the stick, and with head held proudly brought it back to his master.

Nate, Anna, and Steve eased toward each other. Nate welcomed Anna with a tenderness she hadn't known could exist between two strangers.

"I can't believe this is happening; I can't believe you're Justin's mother." He gestured Anna and Steve to sit in the cool sand beside him. Sarge put his wet head on Nate's leg and closed his eyes.

As Anna handed him the missing Bible, she asked, "Have you seen him? Have you seen my son?" Anna searched the soldier for answers.

Nate's baseball cap covered most of his face as he looked down at Sarge.

He cleared his throat. "I have something for you."

Nate reached into his jacket pocket with one hand and reached for Anna's hand with the other. In her hand he placed a Purple Heart. He looked at her as the words choked in his throat.

"Your son saved my life. He died saving me." Nate's eyes watered, and he rubbed his nose with his arm.

The blow overwhelmed Anna. She felt a dark, wretched wail come from her center and out through her mouth like a bolt of lightning—the sound was horrific. She clutched the Purple Heart to her breast. The shock hit like an enormous tidal wave.

God, noooo! This can't be!

Steve tenderly wrapped his arm around her shoulder as she shook and wept. Nate allowed her to grieve and sat quietly with his head down looking at his cracked overworked hands.

After the sobs subsided and her shallow breath returned, Nate looked at Anna and mouthed, "I'm sorry."

Anna met the hazel eyes of the stranger and was eager to probe for answers. She noticed, however, the lines around his eyes and the dark shadow beneath them, the wrinkles in his forehead, and the protruding vein in his temple. Her compassion for the haunted young man tugged at her heart.

"Please, can you tell me…tell me everything about Justin."

Nate put his head in his hands. "I don't know where to begin…" He trailed off.

She wanted to know everything right away but realizing Nate's emotional state she knew she must be patient. The quiet as she waited was deafening.

He inhaled deeply, and then began. "Justin was like my brother. Back at the platoon, we all called him Just-In, as in Just-In-Time." Nate smiled weakly. "He always seemed to be at the right place at the right time. He said it was 'God's timing,' and we poked fun at him about that. He told me it was something his mother taught him—that God's timing is perfect." He looked searchingly at Anna.

She smiled weakly through her tears.

"He was in my platoon after basic. We trained and lived together and were both sent overseas eight months ago to Afghanistan."

"Can you tell me how he received the Purple Heart?" Anna whispered.

Nate cleared his throat. "Well, it was just a few weeks ago. It was a very hot day. There were four of us riding in the Humvee. Justin was in the passenger seat, and I was in the back behind him. The guy that was driving—his name was Mark—had received a care package from home loaded with Gatorade. We were all sucking it down like mad and laughing because we knew if we didn't finish it in the truck, the other guys in the platoon would steal it when we got back to camp. Pardon my saying...but Mark had to take a wiz. So he pulled over on the side of the road, and we all got out to lookout...ya know...for unfriendly fire. That's when it happened..." Nate closed his fists together until the knuckles whitened. His lips clamped together in a grim line.

Anna waited what seemed an eternity and then asked cautiously "Please, I need to know more. What happened...to my son?" "Yeah..." He shook his head and took in a large gulp of air and went on. "It happened so fast...the enemy surprised us from behind an old, broken-down building... Shots were fired... Justin jumped on top of me and covered me with his body. He...he...he...died instantly. They must have thought I was dead too...but Justin...well, he...covered me..." Tears rolled from the young man's eyes. "I was the only survivor...and to this day I can't look at Gatorade. It makes me puke," he said angrily.

Silence prevailed for several moments. Anna looked at the medal of honor that sat in her sweaty palm. The salt from the sea spray along with her tears made her eyes burn. She wiped them with the back of her hand.

"Thank you for telling me. I know this must be difficult for you to relive."

He choked. "I should be the one comforting you."

"Justin was right." Anna placed her hand on the soldier's.

"About what?"

"God's timing is perfect. I'm so grateful we met."

"Yeah." Nate sighed. "I learned a lot from your son...things I'm still trying to sort out. In fact I have to run along shortly...I hate to leave you like this, but I have an appointment at the VA hospital for another eval. They're doing a lot of psych work on me to see when I'm ready to return to combat. I think meeting you here, although difficult, has been the best thing that has happened to me since… well, since…"

"It's okay, Nate, you've told me enough. I understand," Anna replied. "I'd like to see you again. Maybe you could tell me more. Can we keep in touch? How long are you home?"

"Not sure how long I'm home, depends on my progress with the psych eval. Physically I'm okay… But mentally…well, as I said, I can't even watch a Gatorade commercial on TV, so what does that tell ya?" Sarge yawned and got to his feet. "There's a good dog," Nate said as he stroked the black lab's head.

"One more thing…" Nate reached into his pocket and handed Anna a crumpled envelope. "This is the only other thing I have of Justin's. I'll give the first sergeant your number though. He'll send you the rest of his stuff. The military tried to locate you. I took this letter in hopes to find you myself and here you are," he said in awe as tears fell down his cheeks, and he wiped them quickly for fear of showing weakness.

Anna looked at the envelope. It was a letter addressed to her and postmarked to her old address. The words *return to sender* stood out in red letters. She took the sealed envelope and placed it into her pocket.

Sarge gently nudged his master as he stood to brush the sand from his jeans. He gave a hand to help Anna up and held her in a quick embrace.

"Thank you," she whispered.

The three walked toward where Nate held up a hand gesturing the way he was headed.

He nodded one last time to her and Steve and then turned toward the road where he began to run. She watched the young man, no longer a stranger, sprint faster and farther from them.

As his image faded, she felt all of her hopes and dreams, her Justin, slip further and further away. She wanted to chase him. She wanted to scream: *No, this was a mistake! Surely this was a mistake?*

Steve took his wife's hand and turned her to walk toward the water's edge. Anna buckled to her knees along the shoreline. Her hands grasped the wet sand in tight fists as she sobbed. Steve surrounded her from behind and allowed her a few minutes. As the tide pulled in close, he picked her up to stand and wiped the wet sand from her best he could. He held her in a long embrace and wiped her matted hair from her face. Steve led his wife back to where they were sitting with Nate, his impression from sitting in the sand still evident.

Anna collapsed on the cool sand aside her husband. The dark clouds were menacing overhead. "You all right, Anna?" Steve asked cautiously.

She shivered from cold and shock. "I think somewhere deep inside, I knew," she said hauntingly. "Steve?"

"What, sweetheart?"

"I need to sit on that rock and be alone for a few minutes, all right?" She motioned to her favorite spot, the one she could escape to.

"Baby, I understand. I'll wait here for you. It looks like the storm will break soon though. I love you, Anna," he said, as he watched her walk away.

Anna climbed the rough jagged rock on the coast of Maine and sat with a heavy heart as her tears fell unabated on the ragged envelope. Angry waves crashed along the rock sending sounds of thunder. Anna didn't feel the cold. She didn't feel anything. Her hands trembled as she tore open the envelope. The words in Justin's handwriting read:

Dear Mama,

I'm writing to tell you I'm sorry. I know that when I left home I didn't say good-bye. I know you don't want to hear this, Ma, but I had to get away. I couldn't be a mama's boy anymore. I didn't want you to protect me... I wanted to protect you. Guess what. I'm a man now, Mama! I know I said that you didn't teach me anything. But you've taught me so much, and I want to thank you. My faith in God has sustained me through my training, and out here on hot brutal days, God is my strength. You gave that to me, Mama. You showed me the truth. I've met so many great guys here, some needing me to pass on our faith. I've seen many a strong man weep in the presence of us reading our Bibles and praying together. Sometimes I feel like an unequipped missionary, and then I smile and think of you. I know this is not what you want for me... out here in the dry sandy desert. But God brought me here, Mama, so keep the faith and know, the next time I'm on leave I'm coming home to see you. I love you, Mama, and I'm sorry I hurt you.

Your son,
Justin

Anna folded the tear-stained letter and expelled a groan of agony. She sobbed uncontrollably as her body shook in distress. As she wiped her eyes with the sleeve of her jacket, she was blinded by brilliant rays that emerged from the thunder clouds. Brilliant white light streaked from the sky and touched her shoulders. She looked to the light, raised her hands to God, and whispered,

He's not mine; he's yours.